THE TRANSFORMATION OF CHASTITY JAMES

KATHLEEN MORRIS

Dunraven Press

First print edition Five Star Publishing, a part of Gale, a Cengage company. March 2021

Ebook Edition ISBN 978-1-7379866-0-7

Paperback Edition ISBN 978-1-7379866-1-4

Dunraven Press, October 2021

Cover Art and Design by Tabulanis

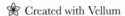 Created with Vellum

For Christiaan, who pushed.

PROLOGUE

*I*t would seem I have a knack for killing.

My father had said so when, at the age of ten, I shot my first deer under his tutelage. How was that deer different from the man whose blood was now pooling around my boots? I felt a fleeting regret about the deer but only a righteous fury about the man. I remember watching the light dim in the deer's beautiful, brown eyes. The man's small, bloodshot eyes simply stared up at the ceiling like dull marbles, seeking a redemption he'd never receive and didn't deserve.

The Bowie knife was very sharp. I wiped it clean on his trousers and dropped it in my bag. No point in leaving a nice knife like that for someone else. I debated for a minute about the Colt .45 and the gun belt, only because I'd have to get it off him, but some scarcely discernible sense of future need prevailed, and I managed to roll him back and forth enough to accomplish the task. Maybe they'd figure a man wouldn't go courting with a loaded gun.

The sweet, coppery reek of fresh blood seemed to take up all the air in the room. I needed to get outside and leave him to his rest, a thing I hoped he'd never really have. Let his soul mire in the howling dark with the rest of his kind.

PART I

The road to hell is paved with good intentions.
--St. Bernard of Clarveaux

CHAPTER 1

*H*arrowhill Farm
Lexington, Massachusetts
August 1878

"No DAUGHTER of mine is traipsing off to the frontier full of outlaws and savages, and that's the end of it."

I sipped my tea, placing the porcelain cup carefully back in the saucer. I took a bite of watercress sandwich and nodded approval at Lizzie, who stood in the back of the parlor, hands folded over her white apron. Late afternoon tea was a ritual at Harrowhill going back more than fifty years. *And it doesn't matter that we aren't what society deems to be appropriately dressed for it,* I thought, looking down at my trousers and dusty riding boots.

"I wouldn't term it 'traipsing,' since I will be gainfully employed, not to mention traveling on the train."

Leland James snorted and swirled the brandy in his snifter, his large hands practically engulfing the thin crystal globe. "A moot point, my dear Chastity."

I popped the last of the sandwich into my mouth and saw little purpose in arguing. I was going, and that was the end of

5

it. Leland would have to accept it. He couldn't stop me. I was twenty-two, after all. He could threaten to disinherit me, but I knew he never would. I had every intention of running Harrowhill when he was unable to do so, and he had groomed me for it since I was ten.

"What's a moot point?"

Matthias stood in the archway, arms crossed over his chest and a sardonic smile on his bronzed face. He sauntered over and sat next to me on the couch, and Lizzie, prepared as always, placed another brandy on the table. Matthias nodded his thanks and took a sip. "Family disagreement?"

Leland rolled his eyes in anguish and ran his hand through his shoulder-length golden-brown hair. "As if you didn't know. She's told you everything on her mind since she was four. Would you please talk some sense into her? This entire idea is ridiculous, not to mention dangerous."

He turned back to me. "Why in God's name do you think you need to play schoolteacher to a pack of grubby children in some cattle town? Vassar certainly didn't groom you for that."

"Actually, it did," I said. "In my mind, the true purpose of getting a good education is to use it to teach and enrich the lives of others."

Leland groaned dramatically. "My God, what have I wrought? I must've been out of my mind to send you there. Your life has already been enriched, learning how to run this place after I'm gone." He motioned for another brandy. "So after you change the lives of some sod-dwelling snivelers, then you'll be fulfilled and return to us, hopefully before I'm on my deathbed? Burning to quote John Donne to the mares in season to enrich their lives, too?"

Matthias laughed. "You could trod the boards yourself at the rate you're expounding, Leland. If Chastity wants to explore the world beyond New England, I see no fault with that, and she's got a purpose she's willing to work for. She's not some hothouse flower who wants to spend afternoons in

Worth's Paris salon. Hell, young men from families like ours take a year or two abroad all the time. After Harvard, you and I spent two years in Italy, if you recall. What's so different?"

Bless you, Matthias, I thought. Having a Mohawk Indian as an uncle was possibly the best thing that had ever happened to me, along with having the world's most wonderful father, even if he was being obstinate. My mother, Fawn, Matthias's half-sister, had died when I was three, and I remembered next to nothing about her except the scent of lilacs and cedar, a gentle touch, and a curl of blonde hair the same color as mine that I had preserved in a locket. I'd been raised by the two gentlemen in this room and was glad of it. They'd given me boundless love, protection, and the freedom to believe I could do anything. I was raised pretty much the way a son would have been: taught to ride, hunt, defend my own opinions, and, yes, even fight if I had to. Leland was reaping the consequences of that upbringing now, and I wasn't going to back down.

"Christ Jesus," he muttered. "Two against one. I'm doomed. 'Sharper than a serpent's tooth …' "

Now I laughed. "It's only a year's contract, Lear. I'll be back next summer, well-traveled and likely much wiser to the ways of the world, a good thing."

"Insanity." Leland swallowed the last of his brandy and stomped out of the room. He called from the hallway. "Don't forget, the Mastersons and the Carters are coming for dinner. I'm sure they'll enjoy hearing about your career."

Crap, I thought. Matthias gave a nearly imperceptible sigh.

* * *

HARROWHILL HAD BEEN in the James family since the Revolutionary War. A five-hundred-acre horse breeding facility and farm that raised all its own feed and food, we provided a living for over fifty people besides ourselves. Our horses were renowned, and every spring the buyers arrived at Harrowhill to bid on the animals we put up for sale. To say we did well was an understatement. Harrowhill horses brought premium prices because they were, simply put, the best. My great-grandfather, Benjamin James, had originally brought horses from Ireland and England, and those unparalleled breeding lines had only improved with time. I was justly proud to be a part of it.

We were close to Boston, and often went into the city for entertainment and cultural opportunities, but generally spent social occasions with the neighboring families. Most of the matrons in the county considered me scandalous and over-indulged. Nevertheless, they were undaunted in their attempts to push forward their sons as marriage candidates. Leland, Matthias, and I laughed about it a lot, but in the last year, since I'd returned from Vassar, there had been a gleam of interest in Leland's eye, and I knew he was thinking about my prospects for furthering Harrowhill's line of humans as well as horses.

As far as I was concerned, prospects around the area were dim, but that didn't stop them from coming. Many a morning I'd found a likely contender presenting himself for a ride or inviting me to this ball or that dinner party. This evening would offer more of the same. Both the Mastersons and the Carters had what they thought were eligible sons.

We'd dressed for the occasion, something we didn't normally do on a family dinner night, but here we were: Matthias and Leland, both with waistcoats, shined boots, and hair tied back; and me, in a summery sprigged muslin with a coronet of braids, thanks to Annie, my maid. The Master-sons—Emily, Robert, and son Harold—had arrived early and taken sherry in the parlor with us. Emily Masterson was a plump woman who ruled her husband and son with undis-guised glee, while Robert and Harold resembled rabbits, both in teeth and demeanor. I found them tedious, but

Leland had always cultivated the well-to-do families in the county in the interest of business, and Robert was a banker. Matthias, as usual, was mostly silent, doing his inscrutable Indian act.

"So, Chastity, what have you been doing with yourself since you've been back from college?" Emily Masterson asked, giving "college" an emphasis that signaled her distaste.

"Thank you for asking, Mrs. Masterson," I replied, shooting Matthias a warning glance. He had a tendency to make faces, and I had a tendency to laugh when he did. "I've been busy around the farm, working with the horses."

"Ah," said the matron. "You certainly are an ... unusual young woman."

Harold chimed in, giving me a toothy smile. "On the way here, I was just telling Mother how hard you work, Chastity. You must make time for some other pursuits, like dancing, or a picnic, now that the weather is so nice. I'd be delighted to escort you."

I smiled. "Thank you, Harold, how lovely. Perhaps." *Not in a thousand years.*

The Carters arrived, towing their son, Thomas. They were a burly bunch, John Carter red-faced and hearty, Anne nearly his match, and Thomas a perfect copy of both his parents. All towheaded, they seemed to match their livelihood as the largest corn producers in Massachusetts. They had no pretensions, which made me like them better than the Mastersons, but not much. They were staunch Methodists and never let an opportunity to mouth a platitude pass by.

We managed to get through the main course before Leland threw me to the wolves when dessert—Hilda's famed peach pie with fresh-churned ice cream—was served.

"Chastity's anxious to spread education to those less fortunate," Leland said with a sly look at me. I could've cheerfully stabbed him with my dessert fork. "I know you'll appreciate the Christian selflessness of her idea, Anne."

"Oh my. What are you taking on, Chastity?" Anne asked. Everyone at the table gazed at me curiously, too.

You asked for it, I thought, and took a deep breath. "I'm going to Dodge City, Kansas, to teach in their new Boot Hill school. It's a marvelous opportunity, and I'm very excited about it."

Forks clattered and mouths opened, not for the wonders of peach pie, but in astonishment at this announcement.

Leland hid his smirk and managed to look forlorn, the sneak. "I'm so proud of her but devastated, as I'm sure you can understand. It's such a dangerous and unknown place and to think of my little girl in that melee, well …"

Emily Masterson was the first to recover. "Oh, Chastity, I respect your desire to bring enlightenment to the frontier, but this is just not something a young woman of your breeding could possibly undertake. Have you thought about your safety?"

"There's wild Indians out there, scalping people," Thomas blurted, and everyone's eyes went to Matthias in embarrassment. "I mean, it's a lawless place, I hear."

Robert Carter put up a hand. "If God calls, we must answer, but I entreat you, young lady, to rethink this decision."

Harold had gone pale. "Miss Chastity, how could you even think of such a thing?"

This had gone far enough. "Please, all of you. It's not a wilderness. The town council of Dodge City advertised for teachers, and I responded. They sound like decent, civilized people, and they need my help, or at least someone educated, to teach their children. It's an opportunity that I wish to undertake. And,"—I looked pointedly at Leland—"it's only for a year. I have a contract."

Silence fell over the table. Leland sighed. "That's true. Although for me, it will be a very long year, concerned about my daughter's welfare. Did you mention how much they will be paying you, my dear?"

I clenched my teeth. "No, I don't believe I did. It's forty dollars a month, Father, as well as room and board. I will have my own quarters in the schoolhouse itself."

"Well, they aren't a wealthy town, are they?" Leland said. "That will scarcely keep you in hair ribbons."

"Then it's a good thing I have plenty of those, isn't it?" I said sweetly. "So that's one less thing for you to worry about."

Everyone left shortly thereafter, no lingering over port or cigars after that shocking pronouncement, while the three of us sat in the parlor as the moon rose over the green fields of Harrowhill.

"Feel better?" I said.

"Not really," Leland said. "I was hoping you might come to your senses. I see that hasn't happened yet."

Matthias lit a cigar and wandered over to the open French doors, the smoke wafting through the room and mingling with the scent of new-mown grass from the lawns. "Chastity, tell us why you're so determined on this course. Ever since you confided this to me, I've been concerned and, frankly, baffled, as has your father."

I felt awful. I hadn't really thought about how this could affect them, and that was shortsighted and foolish of me.

"I'm sorry. Truly I am." I paced around the room, my muslin skirts swirling around my legs. I stopped and looked at the two people I loved more than anything in the entire world. "You've both given me so much. I've had so much more than anyone else, and will have in the future, with no real effort on my part."

They both opened their mouths to protest, but I stopped them. "No, it's true. I've worked hard; learned about the farm, the horses, and the business; and I love it. But at school I discovered something else. Giving back, helping others see a world they might never be aware of except for me telling them about it, inspiring them so they might have the opportunity of a future like mine—that's something I want to do."

"My dear, there's many avenues to accomplishing idealism besides going hundreds of miles away to very uncertain circumstances," Leland said. "You don't need to do that."

"Yes," I said, "I do."

Matthias, silhouetted against the window, turned to me. "Tell us."

I hesitated for a second, but there it was. "I want to be completely on my own for a time. Not coddled by all of this or even the strictures of a college staff. I've never been anywhere besides those two environments, not really. I want to prove to myself that I can make all my decisions, and good ones, if only for a year."

I gazed at them both, and the love in their eyes almost stopped my heart. "You raised me to be independent; you know that. So I want to find out what that's really like, and the only way to do that is exactly what I've chosen. Yes, I'm afraid. But I'll come back a more complete person, the way you've always hoped I'd be. I love you more than life and will miss you both like it's a hole in my heart, but I want to do this."

For a long time, there was no sound in the room except for the call of the night birds in the trees outside. I scarcely breathed.

Behind me, very softly, Leland said, "Godspeed, my darling."

CHAPTER 2

*D*odge City, Kansas

ENDLESS. Endless sky, endless empty plains, endless journey. I shifted on the seat from one hip to another, but it didn't help. Dodge City was on the horizon, or so the conductor said. It couldn't come soon enough.

Sweat rolled down my back under my brown serge suit jacket as I stood on the platform, surrounded by my two trunks and a box of books, waiting for someone from the school board to arrive. All the other disembarking passengers had left. When no one appeared to greet me, I asked the stationmaster to send a message to Mr. Zimmerman, the head of the school board, who had sent my contract. I sincerely hoped it wouldn't be much longer, because, besides the heat and dust, a horrible stench had nearly knocked me to my knees.

"Miss James," called the portly, bearded man who stepped onto the platform. "I deeply apologize for my tardiness. I thought you'd not arrive until tomorrow." He was sweating, too, whether from the heat or anxiety I couldn't tell.

"Frederick Zimmerman," he announced. He held out his hand, which I shook firmly, surprising him a bit. "Welcome to Dodge."

"Mr. Zimmerman," I said. "Thank you. It's very warm, shall we …

"Of course." He stared at me. "Oh my, you're very attractive, Miss James," he stammered. "Excuse me, I mean, well, one never knows what to expect."

"I beg your pardon?"

Mr. Zimmerman coughed, clearly embarrassed. "It's a long distance, mail and all, and even though …" He trailed off and turned to the teenage boy who'd followed him. "Jonah, please load Miss James's baggage into the wagon." He took my arm and guided me through the small station and onto a seat in an open buckboard. Zimmerman took a seat beside me while the boy struggled alone, loading the trunks and box into the open bed.

We were on what was obviously the main street, and we joined the melee of wagons, horses, and people—the clouds of dust a miasma of brown grit. I coughed and covered my mouth. Wooden buildings, some two story, crowded together like teeth in a mouth too small, a mash of retail emporiums, saloons, restaurants, and hotels.

Zimmerman, clearly proud of his town, expounded as we joined the traffic. "This is Front Street, a busy place, as you can see." He gestured at a building as we passed. "That's my establishment right there, Zimmerman Mercantile and Gunsmith."

It was a two-story building with a dozen or more men standing on the wooden sidewalk in front. I murmured some assurance that I'd seen it, and Zimmerman continued.

"The railroad tracks and Front are the dividing line for Dodge City, Miss James. South is the cattleyards and a little rougher part of town. On the north side, things are more gentrified, and, of course, that's where we're headed."

I'd read several newspaper articles and already knew this but saw little point in mentioning it. "Mr. Zimmerman, what is that *smell*, if you don't mind my asking?"

"What smell?"

My heart sank, just a bit, but *in for a penny*, I thought. "Well, it's a bit like decay mixed with barnyard; can you not smell it as well?"

Zimmerman laughed. "That's the smell of money, Miss James. Buffalo skins and cattle pens. We're so used to it, especially when the wind's blowing out of the southwest, I just don't even register it anymore." He turned to me, slapping the reins on the two horses. "After a few days, you won't notice it either. No one does."

A few minutes later, we'd turned off Front Street and traveled north down another dirt street, this one bordered by clapboard houses, some of them two story with small lawns and vegetable patches growing in front. I could see laundry hanging from clotheslines in areas behind the houses. This part of town was much quieter, the air fresher, and I took a deep breath.

"I arranged for you to board for now with the Sampsons, Miss James. All our teachers have stayed with families, and I think you'll find them good, God-fearing people."

"Thank you. I'm sure I will." I smiled at him. "Tell me, how far is the school from here?"

"Well, the current one is just around the corner," Zimmerman said. "But the new Boot Hill school will be ready in another month. It's much bigger, and I'm sure you'll find it quite modern and more suitable." He pulled up in front of a two-story brown house. "One of the reasons we hired someone like you from back East. New school, new teacher, and all that. A modern, fresh start for the youngsters of Dodge City. We're forging into the future."

Well. I didn't have any idea I was to be a pioneer in the educational future of Dodge City, but I was more than willing to accept that mantle. "Boot Hill?"

He grimaced and then laughed. "I realize that's colorful. Used to be the cemetery for those that … well, had nowhere else to go, or found themselves on the wrong side of the law." He gestured towards the hill west of us, and, indeed, there was a structure atop it, and I could see workmen bustling around. "We've moved the former residents and cleared all that away, Miss James; don't you worry." He held out a hand and helped me down from the wagon. "Surely you're not the superstitious type, a college-educated young lady?"

"Of course not, Mr. Zimmerman," I said crisply. I didn't believe in ghosts, but it was disquieting to think I'd be teaching atop the former graves of outlaws, although I certainly wasn't going to say so. *Welcome to Dodge, Chastity.* I wondered what other little surprises were in store, but it didn't take long to find out.

Maude Sampson's hair was pulled into a bun so tight her smile was a rictus, quickly fashioned in her pale, plain face and just as quickly gone after a terse, "Welcome to our home, Miss James."

Jonah brought in my luggage and deposited it in the nether regions of the house at Maude's direction as Zimmerman patted me on the shoulder and wasted no time departing after reminding me school would commence in a week, thus allowing me time to get to know the community.

The buckboard rattled away, and Maude and I stood in the front room amid dust motes floating in the sultry afternoon air. A horsehair sofa was placed under the front window, with two equally uncomfortable-looking chairs flanking it. A kerosene lamp sat on a three-legged table covered with a lace doily, and an upright piano completed the furnishings, a large Bible on top of it, the only book in the room.

"A piano," I said, smiling at Maude. "How lovely. Do you play?"

She nodded. "The works of the Lord, Miss James."

Would "Ode to Joy" fit in there, I wondered, or would Beethoven be too worldly? I banished that thought and instead asked, "Could I perhaps play it sometime?"

Maude pursed her lips. "Perhaps. Let me show you your room."

I thought we'd be ascending the stairs to the second floor, but I dutifully followed her into the dining room, where a table and six chairs took up most of the space, and into the kitchen at the back of the house. It was a bit larger, housing a behemoth of an iron stove on the back wall, along with a sink and counter, and two walls of wooden cupboards curtained with plaid calico. Sunshine brightened the room and the small table and chairs underneath the window. Looking outside, I spied a chicken coop and the outhouse, set back thirty yards or so from the back door. I'd been expecting that but actually seeing it brought home to me how far from Harrowhill I really was. Leland had installed indoor plumbing before I was born, and, although I'd certainly used privies at other places, I'd not relished the experience.

A pantry and another door opened to the right of the kitchen, and Maude Sampson stood before it, gesturing me to enter. My trunks and the box of books took up most of the space in the little room, while a narrow iron bedstead nestled against the far wall, covered with a faded quilt. A small table with a candleholder stood beside it, and a narrow cupboard with a washbasin and ewer filled the remaining space. I stepped in two paces and my knees rested against the bed. There was no window.

"I hope you'll be comfortable here, Miss James," Maude said and shut the door.

Well. I sat on the bed, which was hard as a rock. "Comfortable" seemed out of the question in this cell, and I wondered if novitiates in a nunnery at least had a window. Likely they did. I took off my hat and washed my hands and face in the tepid water from the basin, smoothing back tendrils of hair that had escaped my braids. *You're a schoolteacher now,* I reminded myself, *not the privileged daughter of Leland James. You wanted this, so accept the consequences.* That thought would come back to me often in the next few weeks.

I unpacked what articles of clothing would fit in the small cupboard, a few books, and some toiletries and sat down on the bed. My stomach growled, and I looked at my watch to see it was only one o'clock. I'd always had a healthy appetite, but Maude had made no mention of lunch, or dinner as they called it here, and supper loomed in the far distance. I opened the door, closing it behind me.

Maude sat at the kitchen table, shelling peas. I pulled out another chair and sat down beside her.

"May I help?"

She didn't look up. "If you like."

"So," I said, breaking the silence as we worked. "How long have you lived here? Any little Sampsons?"

"Hiram and I have two children," she said, "Mary and Samuel. They'll be students of yours, Miss James."

"Oh, how nice," I chirped. "Where are they?"

"Helping their father at the freight yard," Maude said. "Idle hands are the devil's playground, and he needs all the help he can get." She looked at me somewhat resentfully. "When school starts, it'll be harder for him. But they tell us it's for the best."

The peas were done. I stood up, brushing off my hands. "I'm looking forward to meeting Mr. Sampson and the children. I thought I might take a walk and get to know the town a bit. What time are you planning on supper?"

She took the bowls of peas and pods to the counter and turned around, hands on her hips. "Miss James, I guess Mr. Zimmerman didn't explain things proper. We will supply breakfast and supper, at six o'clock a.m. and five o'clock p.m. sharp. Any other food you require, or lunches, are your look-out." She took a breath. "We have Bible reading after supper, which we hope you will attend. On Sundays we attend the Methodist church in the mornings and have Sunday supper at three o'clock. If you want candles, you must supply them. And the water pump is outside, near the privy, for your needs. If you wish to bathe, there is a tin tub, but also there is a bathing facility on Front Street you may use. Of course, no gentlemen callers are allowed, and we aren't much for visitors—time is valuable."

I stared at her. Hostility rose from her in waves, and I wasn't sure why, as I'd been in her domicile less than an hour. Maybe the school board didn't pay them enough, or maybe it was something else. Whatever the problem, I needed to address it. I stepped towards her and took her hand in mine.

"Maude," I said. "I apologize if somehow we've gotten off on the wrong foot. I'm very grateful for your hospitality"—she tried to pull her hand from mine, but I hung on firmly—"and I wish you to know that I will strive to be a welcome addition to your home and not a burden in any way."

She wrenched her hand away and turned her back on me. Her thin shoulders trembled, whether in anger or anguish I couldn't tell.

"Please," I said.

She turned around, and, while a tear coursed down her pale cheek, her mouth was twisted in fury. "You're all the same, you women, but you're the worst so far. Coming in here, thinking you know everything, showing up people like me, like you're better." She plucked the peplum of my suit jacket, turning it over in her fingers. "This getup you're wearing, that's just the outside costume, and inside, who knows what you are?"

Good Christ, I thought, echoing Leland. *The woman was addled.* Somehow I had to fix this if I was going to last even a night in this house. Without thinking, I put my arms around her. She stiffened, but after a few seconds she began to sob while I held her, patting her back, the only comfort I knew. Hysterical women and I hadn't crossed paths often. After a few minutes, she pulled back, and I led her to the chair at the table and sat beside her as we had before. She allowed it, and I handed her my handkerchief. She blew her nose, not meeting my eyes.

"I know it must be difficult to have people you don't know invade your privacy, Maude. I promise not to be intrusive, as much as I can."

"Oh, Miss James, I feel awful. You must think I'm having a fit."

"No, no, not at all," I said, although it wasn't necessarily true. "Has something happened before that brought this on?"

She wrung the handkerchief in her hands and looked up at me. "The last teacher we had board with us, she … she … went after Hiram." This admission nearly brought on a fresh spate of tears, but she swallowed and went on. "She ended up marrying a rancher and left, thank goodness. I don't know what I would have done."

"Oh. Well, that's terrible, Maude. You need have no fear of that with me. I have a fiancé back East, and we plan to be married as soon as he finishes medical school in three years." I leaned closer and nearly whispered in her ear. "Please don't mention this to the school board, of course, in case they think I'll be here forever." I couldn't help but wonder just how terrible life could be for a woman with no means of support when her man left her, not just in Dodge but anywhere. It wasn't a thought I'd ever had before.

Now that we'd shared secrets, mine imaginary, but still, Maude quieted and even gave me a tentative smile, smoothing her calico skirts and straightening her hair.

"Tell me about yourself, Maude," I said. "How did you come to Dodge City?"

"That's not much of a story," she said. "I was born twenty miles from here. I came to town with my daddy one day and saw Hiram working with some horses. He took a fancy to me, and within the month we was married. I was fifteen."

That sounded god-awful to me, but I smiled and nodded. "How old are the children?"

"Samuel's ten and Mary eight," she said. "The births was hard. Doc Randall says I'm not like to have another. The Lord's will, I guess."

This woman was twenty-five, only two years older than me, but she looked forty. Frontier life wasn't easy on women, apparently.

"I'm looking forward to meeting them," I said and patted her hand. I stood and pushed my chair in. "Would you like to come along with me on that walk, Maude?"

Her face settled back into its former grimness. "Oh no, I couldn't. I've got the chickens to tend to and a pie to bake for dinner. Hiram's been wanting a blueberry pie, and I picked some berries up the hill this morning."

"That sounds wonderful," I said. "Is there anything you need from the market?"

Maude made sort of a barking sound, and I realized it was her version of a laugh. "Market? What we got here is general stores and a mercantile or two, Miss James. Folks raise their own, otherwise it's too dear. I'm set with my stores for now. You just go on and see what you find, and you'll get the hang of how things are in Dodge."

That didn't sound promising, but I wanted to look anyway. It couldn't be that different. People needed things, and there was a train, after all. I wished her goodbye and set off down the street, back towards the commercial area.

CHAPTER 3

I walked down Third Avenue, full of houses—mostly one story—and thought how fortunate the Sampsons were, with their tidy little two-storied clapboard. Most had gardens, chicken coops, some pigpens, and an occasional barn housing cows or horses. Maude was right: people raised their own here, right alongside their houses. I turned west onto Walnut and went to Second Avenue, passing a large building called Wright House, clearly a hotel and restaurant. Patrons and customers sat in chairs on the porches and stood on the wooden sidewalks, eyeing me just as I was glancing at them. I passed Chestnut, beginning to get a sense of how things were laid out in Dodge. Tree streets crisscrossed the numbered avenues, but, after Chestnut, things became more commercial, ending at Front Street, where I'd begun this morning in Mr. Zimmerman's wagon. Before I reached Front, a sign caught my eye.

Dodge City Times, it read, and I opened the door and went inside. A pleasant-looking young man in a green-shaded cap sat behind the counter.

"Good afternoon, miss."

"Good afternoon to you," I replied. "I am Miss Chastity James, and I'm the new schoolteacher."

He stood up and held out his hand, which I quickly took in mine. *A thoughtful man.* "Richard Jensen, at your disposal. How fortuitous you stopped in, Miss James."

"Oh, I'm happy you think so," I said, smiling. "I came to get a copy of the paper and learn more about your town."

"Of course, of course," he said and handed me an eight-paged newspaper with his ink-smudged fingers. "But, as long as you're here, perhaps we could do an interview."

I stared at him. "Excuse me?"

He chuckled. "I mean, just a short article to introduce you to the citizens of Dodge. I think you're newsworthy, our first new teacher from back East, for our new school on Boot Hill. Don't you agree?"

"Well ..."

He rummaged around on the desk for a pen and paper. "So, beautiful and accomplished, Miss Chastity James ..." He stopped and peered at me. "Is that your real name?"

"Yes," I said and held up my hand. "But please leave out 'beautiful,' Mr. Jensen. I want to be judged on my merits, not my appearance. I'm sure you see where that could be somewhat controversial."

Contrite, he scribbled on the paper. "Of course, I understand perfectly. But you are, you know, if you don't mind me saying so. Beautiful."

Irritated, I swallowed my retort and smiled at him. "Thank you, Mr. Jensen, but that's not the point here, is it?"

"No, Miss James, you're correct. So, where did you go to school?"

"Vassar," I said, and for the next ten minutes we talked about academics and my hopes for the children of Dodge City and their education. He scribbled away as we talked and finally seemed to have what he needed.

"Thank you."

"Of course," I said. "Now, if you'll excuse me, I want to walk down to Front Street and see a bit more of your town."

He took off his cap and apron. "I'd be delighted if you'd let me accompany you. I can be an informative tour guide." He looked like an eager puppy, and I could hardly say no.

"That would be nice of you." Together we went out to the street. Richard was right. He was most definitely a good tour guide, and I was glad I'd accepted his offer, not just for information but to avoid some missteps I couldn't afford as the new teacher in town. We passed dwellings, a church, and some businesses—a tailor, a harness-maker—and came to Front Street. Nothing had changed much since I'd seen it earlier. It was just as dusty and crowded. The main businesses in Dodge seemed to be saloons, and there were plenty of them, like the Long Branch, the Alhambra, the Alamo, and others with colorful signs. Raucous laughter and piano music filtered onto the wooden sidewalks, which were filled with cowboys, more formally dressed men, and a few women. Some ladies wore simple dresses and carried baskets and boxes, while others were dressed for more interesting pursuits. Their gowns were garish and generally ruffled, replete with plunging necklines and a few pins, flowers, or feathers decorating their hairdos. I glanced at my companion, who smiled at me.

"The hostesses start coming to life in the afternoons, but things get really lively after sundown," he explained. "Respectable women usually find it advisable to stay off Front Street then. It can get pretty rowdy, especially this time of year when the cattle drives are coming in all the time."

Still, nearly every man we passed nodded, tipped a hat, or stepped back to allow me passage, as they did for the other women we encountered. They were a courteous bunch of fellows, not what I would have expected from their appearance. Everyone seemed to be in a good mood, joking and laughing. I remarked on this to Richard.

"Most of the time," he said. "Although, come the night

and even sometimes during the day, things can get out of hand after the cowboys have gotten liquored up, lost some money, or fought over a woman. But we've got very competent lawmen here in Dodge."

I had no doubt he was correct, and I had no intention of ever setting foot on Front Street after dark, I decided. "I'd like to find some penny candy for the schoolchildren," I said as we passed by what looked like a general store. My escort stopped and opened a door, gesturing me inside a cavernous building. It was dim and cool inside, and I blinked a few times after the glare of the afternoon sun outside. A fan turned lazily on the tin ceiling, and, as I looked around, I saw that the store was filled to the rafters with every sort of merchandise imaginable —from bags of flour, sugar, and foodstuffs on loaded shelves to rows of fabric bolts and racks of ready-sewn shirts, pants, and dresses, boots, hats, even leather chaps and bullwhips. I couldn't begin to take it all in.

"Bob Wright, at your service, madam," said a mustachioed man in an apron behind a long wooden counter. "Anything you might want in Dodge City, you can find right here at Wright and Beverly. Good afternoon, Richard."

"Well, there's a couple other establishments that make the same claim," Richard said, "but yours has always been my favorite. Bob, this is Miss James, the new schoolteacher." Wright gave a portly bow and smiled.

"Very pleased to meet you," he said. "What can I do for you?"

"It looks like a person could discover anything they want here," I said, and I meant it. It really was quite amazing. "At the moment, however, I would like some candy for the children."

Wright beamed. "Of course." He directed me down the counter to rows of glass jars, filled to the brim with ribbon candy, peppermints, licorice, and other delights arrayed in a glittering, sugary display. I chose enough candy that I thought it might well last until Christmas, and Bob filled a bag and talked with Richard while I wandered around the place. It was like an advertisement for life in Dodge City, and I could imagine the townspeople wearing, using, and eating all the goods on display. *A good education for one who didn't know much about a place would be to come here,* I thought, and I was glad I had. I picked up a pretty handkerchief with a lace border that I thought Maude might like and added it to the candy on the counter.

I paid for my purchases, which Richard insisted on carrying, and we left. I had considerable cash in my reticule, as well as some in my trunk back at the Sampsons', but I'd need to establish a bank account.

"Richard, where is the nearest bank?"

He laughed. "We aren't quite that advanced yet, Miss James. I asked the same question when I got here two years ago from New York."

"What do people do?"

"The merchants have a private banking exchange service," he explained. "Wright and Beverly do so, as well as Rath's and others, even Zimmerman's. It's very secure and works well, even wiring and so forth. They have safes and strongboxes and handle the drover money, too."

"Zimmerman's? The gentleman who hired me and picked me up at the depot?"

"Yes, I believe so," he said. "In fact, his establishment is just down the block, so let's stop in."

And there he was, Frederick Zimmerman, inside his two-story mercantile, advertising his services, "Gunsmith, Ammunition, Hardware," in all his glory.

"Miss James! I see you're finding your way around town—and with an escort as well." Zimmerman gave me a big smile. "Richard, how nice of you to show our new schoolteacher around."

If there was a subtext here, I wasn't sure, but I chose to ignore it, and Richard seemed unperturbed.

"Yes, I stopped in to the newspaper, and Mr. Jensen was kind enough to show me around a bit," I said. "In fact, he tells me I may do some financial dealings with you."

"Indeed. I'd be delighted to handle your needs, Miss James. I should've mentioned it earlier but I've had a very busy day. Ten guns delivered to Mr. Goodnight today."

"How interesting, Mr. Zimmerman. You certainly have many talents," I said. His was another emporium stocked to the gills, but this one leaned more to the hardware and artillery side of things; nary a bolt of calico was to be seen, to say nothing of penny candy. I thought this was a good place, given the number of guns around, to bank my money. "I'll be back tomorrow, perhaps, and we can set up my account, if that's all right."

"Of course, of course."

Our last stop of the afternoon was the best. Dodge City had an ice cream parlor, right in the middle of everything else. I was ravenous by now and devoured not only a large dish of ice cream but two pastries as well. Richard Jensen gazed at me as I dabbed crumbs from my skirt.

"I like to see a woman with a healthy appetite."

I laughed. "I've certainly got that, especially since this is first thing I've eaten today besides an apple on the train. I'm eager to see what Maude has planned for supper, but this has been a big help."

"Ah, I understand. Maude Sampson? You're staying with them?"

"Yes, for now, until the schoolhouse is finished. I was told there would be quarters there."

Richard looked skeptical. "That's the first I've heard about that. For now, I'm sure you'll be fine at the Sampsons', although I heard—" He broke off. "Are you a churchgoing woman, Miss James?"

I took a last spoonful of ice cream. "Not particularly, Mr. Jensen. Although I get the impression the Sampsons are quite religious."

He nodded. "So I've heard." He shrugged. "Well, I'm sure it'll work out."

I suddenly found myself very tired. This afternoon had gone a bit too long. I pushed back my chair. "Thank you for all your help today, Mr. Jensen, but I need to get back to the Sampsons' and see if I can help with supper preparations."

"Certainly ... of course, I mean." He stood up, a bit flustered, and I hadn't meant to be so precipitous. "I've taken up much of your time, but it's been very enjoyable." He looked at his pocket watch. "I need to get back to the paper myself."

He offered to walk me back to the Sampsons' house but I assured him I could find it on my own, and we parted ways, me heading north on Third. It had been an interesting afternoon. I had a lot to learn about Dodge City and its denizens, but I'd made a start. I heard a gunshot, but I never broke stride. Maybe I was already getting acclimated.

* * *

I FOUND Maude in the kitchen, which was like a steam bath. On the stove, potatoes boiled in one pot and green beans in another, and a large iron skillet held chicken ready for frying. True to her word, Maude had baked a large blueberry pie that was now cooling on the table.

"My goodness, you've been busy, Maude."

She gave a start and whirled around. "Oh, you're back."

"What can I do to help?" I didn't wait for an answer but opened the door to my room and took off my jacket. It was a relief to rid myself of the thing. Although my white shirtwaist was damp, it'd have to do. I stowed the candy in my trunk and took out the handkerchief.

"You don't have to help, really," Maude said. "I can manage. It's what I do."

"And you do it beautifully," I said, "but I want to help. Can I set the table, or anything else?"

She looked uncertain. "If you want, Miss James. The dishes are in the sideboard in the dining room. We'll be five … oops, I mean six. Hiram sent Mary back to say Duane's coming for supper, too. He works for Hiram at the freight office."

"All right, and it's Chastity, please." I smiled. Then I held out the handkerchief. "I thought you might like this, Maude. I saw it at Wright and Beverly's store, and it reminded me of you."

She looked stunned but took the handkerchief, her fingers running over the lace like she'd never seen it before. "It's so pretty. Why would you give me this?"

"Because you've been generous enough to take me in, and I wanted to show you I appreciate it."

A few seconds passed, and she smiled. "Thank you, Chastity. It's very nice." She put the handkerchief behind a canister of flour in the cupboard. "I don't have a lot of pretty things."

"Everybody needs pretty things," I said. "Now, let me get that table set."

Table set, Maude assured me she didn't need my help and shooed me out of the kitchen. I went into the front room and sat on the couch. It was stiff and uncomfortable but good enough to give me a few minutes of quiet contemplation to evaluate everything I'd learned today. In the span of five days, I felt I hadn't simply traveled thousands of miles, but to another world entirely, a town and a people so alien to me it was difficult to process with any objectivity. Maude was an odd one, but I hoped we'd connected. As for the nun's cell … well, it wouldn't be for long, I hoped. Richard hadn't seemed sure about that, so I thought I'd bring it up with Zimmerman tomorrow. I vowed to focus on the job I'd come here to do. With that thought, I put my head back on the hard wooden frame of the sofa and fell asleep.

The slam of the front door woke me, and I sat up, my neck cracking from its awkward position. Two children, a boy and a smaller girl, both dressed in rough, homespun clothes, stood before me, eyeing me like I was a polar bear in the Boston Zoo.

"Pa, she's here," called the boy, and a large man entered the room. He was tall and plain featured, his face unshaven and his hair receding. He had his hands on his hips, and his gaze was no less speculative than that of his children. I jumped up, smiled, and offered my hand to him.

"Good afternoon," I said. "You must be Mr. Sampson." He nodded but didn't take my hand. I turned my attention to the children. "I'm Miss James, and you must be Samuel and Mary. Your mother told me all about you."

The little girl smiled shyly, but the silence stretched awkwardly. Maude entered, wiping her hands on her apron, followed by another man, also tall but younger than Hiram Sampson by a few years. He was equally unshaven but smiling, and his gaze swept over me. I wished I hadn't taken off my suit jacket.

"Hiram, this is Miss James." Maude turned to the man behind her. "And this is Duane Olson, who works for Hiram down at the freight office, come for dinner with us."

"Howdy," said Duane Olson, and Hiram Sampson nodded again. "We been hearin' about the fancy new schoolteacher comin' any day, and here you are." He laughed as though that was amusing. "And you are pretty fancy, that's for sure."

Maude frowned and put her hands on the children's shoulders. "Come on back, and let's get everyone washed up for supper. It's on the table and we don't want it getting cold."

Dutifully, we all followed her to the dining area, me silently trooping at the last, happily avoiding Hiram and Duane's view of my posterior. Finally we sat down, Hiram and Maude at each end, the children on one side, and Duane and me on the other. My stomach growled, but when Hiram clasped his hands and bowed his head, everyone else did, too—including me, even though my routine at Harrowhill had been notably lacking prayers at dinner or anywhere else, for that matter. Hiram was a windy prayer and did a thorough job of thanking God for a great many things, including the food, before the first dish was passed.

My first dinner, or "supper," in Dodge taught me there were two kinds of people at the Sampson table, the quick and the dead. Hiram and Duane laid into that fried chicken like ravenous wolves, and Maude, the children, and I found ourselves with wings, backs, legs, and as many potatoes and green beans as we could salvage between the four of us. Apparently, God favors the working man, especially if he prays beforehand. If I'd been clocking it, the prayer took longer than the eating.

I did my best to start a conversation but quickly gave up when I realized there was no time for that. I concentrated on my plate.

"You got that blueberry pie, Maude?" Hiram said. They were the first words I'd heard him say. Duane looked up eagerly.

Maude bolted the rest of her potatoes. "I surely do, Hiram. I'll just get it." She returned with the pie, cut half of it for the men, and gave the rest of us smaller slices.

Within minutes, that was gone as well. Hiram stood up, as did Duane.

"Good food, Maude. Thanks," Duane said as he followed Hiram out to the front porch, where I soon smelled burning tobacco. Mary and I helped Maude clear the dishes while Samuel melted away to who-knows-where.

"Maude, that was delicious. Thank you," I said as she

piled the dishes into the sink and heated water on the stove. She smiled at me.

"Glad you liked it, Miss … er, Chastity. Now you go set so's I can attend to this."

I knew dismissal when I heard it, and I didn't argue. I went into the front room and took a seat on the couch, Mary trailing behind me. She scrambled up on the sofa and regarded me with big, blue eyes.

"I get to go to school this year."

"I'm very glad, Mary. We're going to learn wonderful things. How to read, how to do sums, and lots of other surprises."

"She don't need to know much," Hiram said, sitting down on the chair next to me. "You going to teach her how to cook and clean a house, too? That's what women need to know." His face was set in a scowl, and he stared at me as though I were an intruder in his home and he wasn't sure how I'd gained entrance.

Duane stood in the doorway, picking his teeth. He chuckled. "Hiram, I swear, you're a hidebound. Times are changin'. There's lotsa things women need to know." He leered at me. "Ain't that right, Miss James?"

"Indeed, Mr. Olson. As the Bard said, 'Ignorance is the curse of God; knowledge is the wing wherewith we fly to heaven.' That is why I've come to teach school in Dodge City. For girls and boys both."

Hiram eyed me suspiciously. "Who's Bard?"

"Shakespeare, Mr. Sampson. I heard there have been performances here by traveling companies. I hope to take the children to one if they return."

"Never heard of 'em." Hiram got up and retrieved the Bible from the top of the piano. "Maude, get out here. Time for scripture."

Duane looked around like a fox caught in a henhouse. "I

have to meet a guy down at the Dodge House. Nice to meet you, Miss James."

"You, too, Mr. Olson." I'm not sure he heard me, he left so fast—which was just as well. Maude came in, and then Samuel appeared like a small ghost, settling down beside his father's chair. My first evening in Dodge City, Kansas, with the Sampsons, scripture, and almighty God began.

I LAY UPON MY BACK, my thin, cotton nightdress damp where it touched my body. The mattress crackled if I so much as moved a muscle. It was hard as a tombstone, and the pillow wasn't much better. I was bone tired, even though the faint glimmer of light under the door attested to the fact that it couldn't be more than eight thirty. In my room, it was fairly dark, but I had no desire to read or light the remnants of the candle on the table. My mind was whirling, trying to make sense of everything I'd seen and heard today. Apparently God, in spite of Hiram Sampson's best efforts, wasn't making things clearer. I needed to justify my decision to come to this place and set myself on the course I had. As always, I fell back upon mentally talking to myself.

Chastity, remember what you want, my inner voice said. You want to teach children about a bigger world than the one they see within four walls. You want to introduce them to a world where they can achieve, grow, and fly. To show them that there are no boundaries to what the mind can absorb or create. That anyone can do so, no matter who they are or where they were born. You want to give them a start, an impetus, a desire to seek more.

You are not here to judge, appraise, or argue with the people who live here or pay your salary, even though that is your inclination and your nature. You were hired to teach and inspire, and that is all you must concentrate your energy on. You wanted that, so deal with it.

That was my positive inner voice. My other one, often suppressed but never far away, said: *Chastity, you've taken on more than you can chew.* (A favorite saying of Leland's.) *Who do you think you are? You're not Athena, Pericles, or Plato; you're just Chastity James. You should get yourself back on that train in the morning and realize that Dodge City is not ready for your tempestuousness, impatience, and disdain. So far you've curbed it, but we know that won't last, not with a temper like yours. Nobody appointed you the arbiter of good marriages, the plight of women, fairness, morality, manners, or religious intolerance. Get out while the getting's good and go home. Besides, you miss your horses.* The negative voice was just getting started.

I turned over and put my hand over my ear, the other already muffled by the pillow. That used to work when I was ten, but it was a long time this night before both voices were silenced and I fell asleep. The gunshots didn't help either.

CHAPTER 4

*N*o morning sunlight greeted me, nor birdsong. I heard movement and dishes clattering on the other side of my door, but the room was nearly black as pitch, except for that sliver of light under the door. *Oh no,* I thought, *breakfast at six a.m.* I considered hastily dressing in the dark, but the idea quickly lost its appeal. I closed my eyes instead.

The next thing I heard was a soft knock on my door. "Chastity? Miss James?"

"Yes?"

"It's Maude. I'm heading to the store. There's coffee on the stove, if you're wanting some."

"Thank you," I mumbled, and I breathed a sigh of relief when I heard the front door shut. Hopefully, the rest of the Sampsons were long gone. I cracked open the door to an empty kitchen and, after waiting a few seconds, didn't hear anyone about. Maude had indeed left a coffeepot on the stove, so I poured a cup of coffee and sat at the kitchen table. It was sunny and silent, just what I'd hoped for.

The coffee was muddy and lukewarm, but it woke me up. I rinsed out my cup and filled my ewer with fresh water, then washed and dressed in a simple shirtwaist and skirt, pulling my hair back once again in its schoolmarmish bun. Another day of the Chastity James Dodge City Tutorial had begun. I gazed into the small polished tin mirror hanging on the wall over the basin. I fancied I looked pretty severe, but tendrils of blonde curls were already escaping their pins, damning my efforts. What I needed, especially in this heat, was a hat to keep my hair in place and give me some shade. First stop, Wright and Beverly.

According to my pocket watch, it was just after nine o'clock by the time I reached Front Street—a beautiful sunny day, the sky a celestial blue. It was amazingly quiet compared to yesterday. Maybe the night's revels had caused the cowboys to sleep late. I traded polite nods and good mornings with more than a dozen cordial people before I reached the store. Dodge City was a friendly town.

The bell jingled as I pushed open the door and stepped into the store. I gazed around, much as I had yesterday, because it truly was fascinating in its floor to ceiling jumble of merchandise, sort of a compendium of people's needs and desires on the frontier.

"Good morning, Miss James!"

Bob Wright stood behind the counter, a toothy smile on his face. He did seem like a nice man. A plump woman bustled up beside him, smiling as well.

"Mary Jane Wright, and I'm so glad to make your acquaintance," she said, coming out from behind the counter. She waved a newspaper. "I was just reading about you, and Bob was telling me how you came in yesterday. How nice to see you in person."

Oh God, I thought. My new friend, Richard the newspaperman, was a quick one. I had no idea I'd be in his paper this morning. The man clearly didn't sleep.

I managed a bright smile. "So nice to meet you, Mrs. Wright," I said, wanting only to get my hands on that paper to see what Richard had written about me. "Your husband was so kind yesterday when I came for candy. How friendly everyone is here in Dodge."

Mary Jane Wright, sausage curls bobbing, grabbed me by the arm and led me to the counter. "Bob and I were just saying how wonderful it is someone with your education and background has come here to teach our children. Our girls are tingling with excitement at the thought of being your students."

"May I see the paper?" I asked. "I'm amazed Mr. Jensen has been so quick with his printing. It's just like a Boston newspaper."

Mary Jane bobbed her head at her husband. "Hear that, Bob? We're just like Boston, can you imagine?" She held out the paper, her pink cheeks flushed, happy as a hen with six chicks. I took it from her and read the article she pointed out.

MISS CHASTITY JAMES, of Massachusetts, a graduate of Vassar College, has arrived in our fair town to teach the children, ages six through sixteen, in our newly built Boot Hill School, a modern marvel of its kind in the West, dedicated to the virtuous education of our youth. Miss James is an expert on reading, mathematics, history, and literature, with an emphasis on William Shakespeare, as she has confided to this newspaper. She is well trained in the arts of elocution and debate as well and plans to introduce our children and even many adults to the joys of theater and the beauty of spoken language. Miss James is currently residing with the Hiram Sampson family on Third Avenue. We are fortunate to have her here in Dodge City, and please make every effort to make her feel welcome.

. . .

YE GODS, I thought. Well, it could have been worse, I suppose, although I wish he'd left out the Shakespeare part. At least he hadn't said "attractive" or some other attention-getter I didn't need. Thankfully, there was no photograph. I smiled rather bleakly at Mary Jane. "Well, isn't that … nice?"

"It certainly is," she said and squeezed my hand. She really was sweet, as nice as her husband.

"I'm not used to having people talk about me, or having my name in a newspaper," I said, "but I guess people do need to know I'm here, given that I'll be in charge of your children's education."

"Absolutely," said Mary Jane. Bob nodded in agreement.

"Well," I said again, feeling like an idiot. "Mr. Wright, you were so kind yesterday, I came back this morning knowing your emporium was just the place I needed."

They both looked up with interest because, of course, they were shopkeepers first and foremost, and that was just what they wanted to hear from potential customers.

"I need a hat."

Mary Jane laughed with delight and took my hand. "You have come to the 'Wright's place.' " She laughed at her own joke and then led me toward the back of the store, where there was quite a display of dresses, shoes, petticoats, shoes, and, yes, hats. I decided upon a wide-brimmed straw one with a white ribbon. It fit perfectly, and I punched the hatpin into my coiled-up curls.

"What do you think, Mary Jane?"

She clapped her hands. "Oh, Miss James, it's perfect for you."

I smiled. "Please, it's Chastity. I feel like I've known you much longer than a day, Mary Jane."

She blushed. "Oh, me, too." She took my elbow and steered me back to the front counter. "Is there anything else we can do for you this morning?"

I paid for the hat and put my reticule on the counter.

"Well, yes, there is. Can I order books and supplies for the school from you? How do we go about that?"

Fifteen minutes later, we had worked out the details of books and supplies ordering from St. Louis, and I turned to go, only to be confronted by a substantial gentleman in a beige waistcoat, his pocket watch dangling from a chain on his vest. He tipped his hat and offered a polite bow.

"Charlie Bassett, at your service. I hear you are Miss James, our new schoolteacher."

"Indeed, I am. How do you do, Mr. Bassett?" I shot a glance at Bob Wright, who I supposed was the supplier of this information. He was busily polishing a glass jar. "And what do you do here in Dodge City?"

He laughed heartily. "As little as I can. That's the nature of the job, but, unfortunately, I don't always succeed. I'm the town marshal here in Dodge."

I laughed, too, as his laugh was infectious. "Ah. That would account for the gunshots I heard last night. I wish you more success, Marshal Bassett."

He eyed me like a hawk. Charlie Bassett had a charming demeanor, but he didn't seem to miss a detail. "Miss James, I think you may be just what we need here. If you're done with your purchases, may I escort you?" He offered his arm.

I took it. "That would be lovely, Mr. Bassett." I turned back to Bob and Mary Jane. "Thank you so much for your help. I have a feeling I'll be saying that often."

"You're very welcome, Miss James," Bob said. "See you next time."

Charlie Bassett and I stepped out onto Front Street. In my time at Wright and Beverly, things had picked up. More people crowded the sidewalks, and wagons and riders on horseback traveled on the hard-packed dirt street, clouds of dust rising in the morning air. The all-pervasive stench of cattle and their leavings was back in full force as well, but somehow it didn't bother me as much as it had yesterday. Maybe Zimmerman was right.

We headed west down Front Street, people melting out of the way when they saw my escort. Charlie Bassett was a presence, as I had already discerned back at the store. *No harm in getting to know the local law authority,* I thought, as I clung to his well-tailored arm.

"Mr. Bassett," I said, "I've not had breakfast this morning. Perhaps you could recommend a restaurant, for that or luncheon, at this late hour?"

"Of course, Miss James."

He led me farther down the street, and we stopped outside the building displaying the sign "Dodge House." In we went with no further ado and were shown into a dining room as elegant as anything I'd seen in Boston. The tables were covered in white linen, set with silver and gleaming crystal, and we were seated near the front windows. A waiter arrived with a pot of coffee and filled our water glasses, depositing menus in front of us.

"How lovely," I said. "This is not what I was expecting."

Bassett smiled. "We are not barbarians, Miss James. I would be honored to order for you."

Of course, I let him do so, and, within minutes, plates full of eggs, sausages, potatoes, and biscuits were delivered to us with a flourish. There were even wild strawberries. Truth be told, I dug in like a farmhand. The food was delicious. Last night's supper had left me with an appetite I couldn't appease until now. I had a feeling that might be normal at the Sampson house, despite Maude's best efforts, and it was good to know there was somewhere I could find sustenance.

"I can't think of anyone more qualified to tell a newcomer about the pleasures and dangers of Dodge City," I said, dribbling honey over a biscuit. "What goes on here?"

Charlie took a sip of coffee. "Dodge is a new town, Miss James, and it has certainly had its growing pains, like any. But it's magnified. First, we had the buffalo hunters and, for some years now, the cattle drives, thanks to the railroad. The big ranches north, west, and south of here bring their herds in as soon as the snow is passable, and it's a constant hive of activity with the cowboys, freighters, ranchers, and brokers. We try to keep a lid on it, but it's not easy."

"Hence the gunshots I hear," I said. "Things get much livelier as the day progresses, I noticed. It's a bit quieter on a farm in Massachusetts."

"I don't doubt that," he laughed. "These boys have been on the trail for weeks, and they arrive here looking to blow off steam, get drunk, gamble, and take up with women, if I may be truthful and not offensive." I waved my hand in dismissal, and he went on. "All those activities sometimes lead to rowdiness and disagreements of one kind or another, and that's where I come in, along with my deputies and the sheriff. It's been a tough year for us."

"How's that?" I scooped up some eggs, wondering if I really wanted to hear the answer.

"I've only been the marshal since April, when Ed Masterson was shot down by a couple of Texans, but things are stabilizing. I've got good men here, and Ford County has a dedicated sheriff in Bat Masterson, Ed's brother." He signaled the waiter for more coffee.

"Good lord," I said, putting down my fork. "I'd no idea about these things."

"One of the reasons I wanted to meet you, Miss James," Charlie said. "I didn't think you had, and it's best to hear about them from somebody who is working to keep citizens safe here in Dodge. I can assure you that you are in no danger, but I think it's wise to be aware what has happened here."

Frankly, I wasn't all that surprised or concerned, but I thought it best not to let Bassett know that. I was a prim schoolteacher dedicated to upholding moral standards, and worldly sophistication was a trait the parents of Dodge City might not embrace. I put on my best meek smile.

"Thank you for your concern, Marshal. It's very kind of you."

A shriek erupted from somewhere upstairs, but Bassett didn't so much as blink an eye as he took another sip of coffee. While I was contemplating how to ask what could be going on, a man lurched unsteadily through the hallway outside the dining room, holding a white napkin speckled with blood over one side of his mouth.

"Looks as though Dr. Holliday has been busy this morning," Bassett said. "We have a very fine dentist here at the Dodge House, in case you ever find yourself in need of tooth repair."

A dapper gentleman strolled languidly into the dining room at that moment and stopped by our table, his slight figure the perfect vehicle for the elegant vest and waistcoat he wore.

"Morning, Doc," Bassett said, glancing up. "I was just telling Miss James here, our new schoolteacher, about your talents. Miss James, Dr. John Holliday."

"How do you do," I said. "I just saw one of your patients depart."

He bowed over my hand. "Delighted to make your acquaintance, my dear. I've been havin' a busy mornin', it's true." His voice was soft, a honeyed Southern drawl, and his handsome face was even more appealing. "I can only hope my patient's yelps didn't disturb y'all at your breakfast. I try to be not only accurate, but quick in my work. If he woke Kate, I'll be hearin' about it half the day."

Charlie laughed. "I'll hope she's still asleep as well. We'll have a noisy enough night at the Long Branch as it is, with the Loving crew in town." He stood up and placed his napkin on the table. "We were just leaving, but I'll see you later."

Dr. Holliday helped me from my chair, a consummate

gentleman. "I can see the children of Dodge City will be in excellent hands, Miss James. A pleasure to meet you."

"Why, thank you," I said. We stood eye to eye, and I couldn't help but smile at the mischievous twinkle in his eye. "Very nice to meet you as well."

We strolled east down Front Street. My planned next stop had been Zimmerman's to set up an account. We passed a saloon whose name I noted. "Is this the Long Branch you were talking about?"

Charlie Bassett stopped. "It is indeed. In fact, I need to stop in, so I must leave you to your own devices, Miss James." He smiled. "In the interest of full disclosure, I used to own the place."

I chuckled. "Mr. Bassett, you are a man of many faces, I see. Thank you so much for breakfast, conversation, and your kindness. I liked your dentist friend as well."

"Most women do," he said, shaking his head. "He has many faces, too, Miss James, and I don't think you'd like the others so much." He gazed at me for a long few seconds. "Just so, I think you perhaps might have experience beyond simply teaching school." I said nothing, looking him pointedly in the eye as a beat passed.

"Well, what I mean is, you're a charming young woman, and we're lucky to have you." He tipped his hat. "Give my regards to Mr. Zimmerman. I've had a delightful morning."

Well. I guess Charlie Bassett wasn't a lawman for nothing. I was pretty sure I'd just passed a test that I hadn't known I was taking, and I wasn't sure if I was angry or not. By the time I got to Zimmerman's, I was still trying to decide if owning a saloon in the town where you're the marshal was a conflict of interest. Law was never my forte. Besides, breakfast had been good.

Setting up an account didn't take long, even though Zimmerman's eyebrows raised when I deposited $800. We discussed my salary, as well as some supplies and furniture for the school that were ready to be moved in as soon as construction was finished. We agreed to meet the next morning to tour the school. I walked slowly back to the Sampson house. I'd had enough acclimating for the day and looked forward to one of the gothic novels I'd packed, if not the room I'd have to read it in.

CHAPTER 5

𝒪𝓂y new hat shielded me from the morning sunlight as I climbed the hill up to the new school building. Sawdust littered the floor as I stepped into the building, and the pleasant smell of fresh-cut lumber dominated the space. I glanced at the rafters still being hammered into place by two workmen far above my head. Fred Zimmerman had taken my arm to help me up into the structure, as no steps were in place yet.

"As you can see, Miss James," he said, "progress is accelerating. We'll be done in no time."

I wasn't sure what "no time" meant in Dodge City, but I was standing on a wooden platform with walls made of boards with four feet of landscape between them and a roof that was yet to provide a ceiling that wasn't made of sky and clouds. Three men outside were cementing bricks into place along the wooden frame, and it seemed they had a long way to go.

"Hmm," I managed, while Zimmerman bustled forward. He didn't have to go far. The entire building was roughly thirty feet by sixty feet. About two thirds of the way in, a man was wrestling an iron woodstove into place on a hole in the floor. If there were "quarters" for a schoolteacher, I don't know where they would have been. I was told there were currently fewer than fifty students, but the number increased all the time. The space as it stood would barely accommodate that—unless there was to be a second floor, in which case this place would take much longer to complete.

Zimmerman was absorbed in conversation with a tall man who seemed to be in charge, judging by the orders he issued towards the other men, both the roofers and the woodstove installer. I'd heard stories about barn raisings accomplished in a day, but it didn't look like they applied here.

I had traversed the length of the building when Zimmerman joined me, beaming.

"Isn't this wonderful, Miss James?"

I coughed. "Absolutely." This time I took his arm, steering him towards the back of the platform. "So where exactly would the teacher's quarters be? I'm no builder, but it doesn't look as though there'd be any room for that."

"Well, that's the thing." He looked around as though someone would arrive to help him explain. "There won't be any quarters for a teacher. We've had some discussions about this recently, and since everyone's been happy with the arrangements we've had in the past, we thought it best to dispense with that and add a second floor, since we have a continuously growing number of students to accommodate." He smiled at me, and I wanted nothing more than to tell him he was a lying skunk. But I was Miss James, mannerly schoolteacher, and I reined in my temper, which had no place in Dodge City. It resided back in Massachusetts.

"Ah, I see." I gazed at him, trying to get him to look me in the eye, which wasn't an easy task. "It seems you were not entirely honest with me. It looks as though I will be living with the Sampsons, then. Is that the gist of it?"

He looked at the floor, the rafters, and finally at me. "Well, yes, even though we had originally planned on you being here,

Miss James. The school board had to make adjustments after you had signed your contract, but really, we believe you will be more comfortable with the Sampsons." He spread his arms. "It's lonely up on this hill and no place for a woman alone. We took that into consideration, your safety and well-being, I mean."

"How kind of you," I said. "I'm sure you have my best interests at heart, Mr. Zimmerman."A muffled cough that could have been choked laughter came from somewhere above, and I took a few paces around the floor. "However, Dodge City seems to be a well-regulated town, and I do value my privacy."

He swallowed and took a sudden intense interest in the workers on the roof.

"So how long until this structure is finished? My under-standing is school starts next week. Where am I to teach?"

He gathered himself, brushing his waistcoat, chin up. "Miss James, we have covered that contingency, of course. The original school building on Walnut Street will suffice until this one is ready. We are prepared, as I assume you are."

Oh my, I thought. *The best defense is an offense. Well, then.* I stepped directly in front of him. "Mr. Zimmerman, I assure you, I am ready to teach in any conditions that may happen. I'm more than happy to begin this school year, my first in Dodge, in whatever building you deem appropriate. It is certainly not my place to dictate architecture to you or anyone else in Dodge City. I am here to educate your children and serve at the pleasure of the school board."

I don't think any mere schoolteacher had ever questioned him before. I was happy to be the first, even if I'd lost round one with the school board.

Mollified, Zimmerman smiled and took my arm, escorting me out of the building. He was a man who had prevailed, or so he thought. Ignorance is bliss. When we reached the bottom of the hill we turned towards Front Street.

"Since we have visited the future, Mr. Zimmerman, I would like to see the present as well," I said. "The current school where I will be teaching."

He frowned. "I have a busy day scheduled, Miss James. Perhaps another time. You'll be there soon enough, after all."

I stopped. "I really must insist, sir. Surely, I am not being unreasonable. In four days' time I will be standing in the building for hours at a stretch. I want to take its measure now. I have preparations of my own to make. And I will need a key."

"Of course, of course," Zimmerman sighed. "You must forgive me, Miss James. I am not good with details, and I have been so busy this time of year." He fumbled a keychain from his pocket and removed a key, handing it to me. "This really belongs to you, now."

I took it and clenched it in my fist, as though he might ask for it back. "Thank you. So, where is the old school?"

"Just follow Walnut here, down to First. You can't miss it. Good day." He turned on his heel and made for Front Street and what I presumed was his very pressing business. I was fine with that; I had pressing business of my own.

I passed the Sampson house down the street and continued on, past residences and the Wright House. A good number of people crowded the front porch, and the savory aroma of roasting meat wafted through the air. My stomach rumbled as usual, not quite content with Maude's watery oatmeal, but I ignored it. I wondered idly if Bob Wright owned that place too. Probably.

On the next corner stood several buildings. One was someone's house, with a small garden in the front yard. A vacant lot was across the street, and another catty-corner. Zimmerman was right. A square clapboard building stood on the only other corner, a bell in the belfry atop it. It looked a bit forlorn and could have used a good coat of paint, but this was definitely a school.

When I went to put the key in the lock, the door opened on its own, hinges squeaking. Dust motes floated in the light shining through the windows on each side, and two small birds flew past my head, taking the opportunity to escape to the open sky.

The stench of dirt, mildew, and worse assailed me instantly. I fished a handkerchief out of my pocket and covered my nose and mouth as I stepped over the threshold. One room, perhaps thirty by forty feet, with a woodstove centered along one wall, a square wooden desk with a chair in the back (presumably for me), while benches and narrow tables took up the rest of the space. Shelves lined the right side, piled with dusty books and slates, and everything, including the floor, was covered in an inch or more of dust and bird and mouse droppings. A broom stood beside the woodstove, along with a pail, but obviously no one had swept or washed the place since spring. I had a sinking feeling those jobs were falling to me. I peered out the back door and saw a water spigot and pump, and, of course, the outhouse—with a door I didn't open. I wasn't up to that task.

I poked through the books on the shelves, finding worn copies of McGuffey readers for different levels, but I could tell at a glance we'd need quite a few more if Zimmerman's estimates of student numbers were accurate. I found a dozen or so slates, but no slate pencils, so I added more of both to my mental list.

"Hello?"

Startled, I spun around. A plump woman in a blue, calico-print dress, her hair firmly bonneted in the same fabric tied beneath her chin, stood smiling in the doorway. "Molly Clarke," she announced. "I'm betting you're the new school-teacher we've been hearing so much about." She bustled in and stopped, studying me closely in the gloom.

"Oh my, you're a pretty one, aren't you?"

I bristled inwardly, but I was getting used to this. "Thank

you. I'm Chastity James, Mrs. Clarke. Nice to meet you." I held out my hand, and she took it firmly.

She put her hands on her hips and looked around the schoolhouse, shaking her head. "This is a right mess, isn't it, Miss James?"

I laughed. "Yes, Mrs. Clarke, it certainly is. Not just the dirt, but lack of supplies as well. I shall have to have a chat with Mr. Zimmerman."

Molly Clarke snorted. "Well, he's tight as a tick, no doubt about that, so I wish you luck. I've got three pupils for you, though, so I'm on your side. We'll go see him together, if you like."

A supporter, my first one. Relief flooded through me. "Your help would be wonderful, Mrs. Clarke. I need so many things to create the educational experience I was hoping for."

She gave me a sharp look. "Do you?" Molly Clarke seemed a clearheaded woman.

"Yes," I said. "We need more readers, more books, more slates, pencils, and, from the look of it"—I glanced around the room—"more desks and benches. It's my understanding enrollment is rising. The new school won't be ready for who-knows-how-long." I stared back at her. "I was up at the new Boot Hill school this morning, and I can't see how that place will be ready for at least three months, maybe more."

She laughed. "You're no fool, are you, Miss James? This town, I swear. People have grandiose plans, but the follow-through is usually lacking. That's what I tell my husband, George, and he agrees with me."

I couldn't imagine George doing anything else. Molly Clarke was a force of nature, and I liked her.

She took one more look around the room and sniffed. Then she took me by the arm. "Let's go over to my house and have coffee and sandwiches. We can lay our plans for the school board and Fred Zimmerman."

I followed her outside and shut and firmly locked the

door behind me. No more birds or anything else were finding their way into my domain. Off we went, down Walnut Street to a well-kept house, where I was ensconced at a kitchen table while Molly brewed coffee and made chicken sandwiches.

"So," she said, taking a bite of tomato and chicken. "Where are you staying, Miss James?"

"With the Sampsons," I managed, swallowing my own large bite of her delicious sandwiches, the best food I'd eaten since I'd left Massachusetts. "This is delightful, Molly, and the bread—you make this?"

"Every morning, my chick," she laughed. "Women who like food have to make their own out here."

"It's wonderful," I said and polished off half my sandwich. "Where are you from, if you don't mind me asking."

"New York," Molly said. "Used to be Molly McCann, Irish through and through. Mum and Da came over with the famine and went west. I met George and came to Dodge with him for the freight business. Now we even have our own store. George specializes in spirits, Miss James, and there's a big call for that here." She laughed, and I did, too, because she sure was right.

"Please, it's Chastity," I said. I had a feeling Molly Clarke and I were going to be good friends.

We moved on to molasses cookies sprinkled with sugar, while making a list of supplies and demands for Fred Zimmerman, gossiping about the town and its inhabitants and sharing a bit of history about both of us.

"Oho, so you met our marshal," she crowed when I told her of my breakfast with Charlie Bassett. "He doesn't miss much, that one, but he's a good man for the most part. Every lawman around here, and most I've ever met, have their fingers in many pies, from saloons to gambling to women. But George trusts Charlie and that deputy of his, Wyatt Earp. Earp's family and some of his friends … well, not so much, but they're an interesting bunch and haven't caused me any trouble. Live and let live, I say."

I agreed with her philosophy. "You ever run into a dentist, Holliday?"

Molly nodded. "One of Earp's friends, like I said. Pretty visible, him and that Kate woman. Seems like a charmer, but we don't exactly run in the same circles." She washed off the plates. "Supplying the whiskey and drinking it with them, well, that's two different things, isn't it?"

Indeed it was. There were at least two sides to this town, as I was beginning to find out, but I had always believed power has a tendency to overlap. My side was firmly on that of family and children, and from the cautions on my contract, if I wanted to keep my job, I'd best be careful who I befriended or shared a meal with. The warnings were explicit: no being seen with gentlemen "friends," never visiting questionable establishments, attending church at least once a week, and going to bed with the birds and getting up with them, too. There were more, but the less I thought about them, the better.

The Clarkes' three children, eight-year-old Fiona and their fourteen-year-old twins, Ben and Liam, all towheads, bounced in and out as we chatted, laughing and disheveled as children should be. They were followed everywhere by a brown mutt named Droop. They were charming and polite, interested in their new teacher but clearly enjoying their last summer days of freedom.

I had thoroughly enjoyed my time at the Clarke household, but I knew I should be getting back to the Sampsons' and letting Molly get on with tending to her family. I said as much, and she took my hand.

"Chastity," she said, gazing into my eyes, "you're an interesting and puzzling young woman, quite a lady and out of your element, if you'll pardon me for saying so, but you got grit, I can tell that. I want you to come to me with any problems you might run into, and I'll help, along with some other friends of mine that you'll be meeting soon. You've taken on a great deal—more than you know, I think, as the number of children is growing every day with new arrivals in Dodge City."

I nodded. "I'm beginning to suspect Mr. Zimmerman was not quite accurate in many of his conclusions, Molly."

She gave that now-familiar Molly snort. "That's for certain. And there's something else. Them Sampsons." She looked at me knowingly. "There's a couple of all-too-pious penny-pinchers. Getting a lot of Bible reading in, are you?"

I flinched. "Well ..." I didn't want to complain so soon about my hosts.

Molly laughed. "They got you in some closet, up at dawn eating nasty oatmeal and buying your own candles, haven't they? I know those two, and, besides, the last couple of school-teachers here have told their tales, believe me." She got up and shook her head, curls bouncing. "I don't know what Zimmerman's thinking, boarding teachers there, but there's likely some favors going on."

I stood up too, brushing my skirts. "Listen, Molly, while it's not ideal, it's not that bad, for now. I'm not helpless, and I do have resources. Believe me, I will make adjustments as the need arises. I appreciate your concern." I hugged her, and she held me warmly. It was a nice feeling, one I wasn't used to, except from Hilda, our cook, and I liked it.

"Thank you so much for everything, Molly," I said. "I'll stop by tomorrow, and we'll go meet up with Mr. Zimmerman." I held up my notes. "We'll get what we need, I'm sure of it."

We would, too, one way or another. I had no doubt about that.

* * *

I BLEW out the candle and lay back on my narrow bed, bunching up the pillow beneath my head. *Oh, for my down pillows and comforter and the open window with a fresh breeze from the forest and meadows,* I thought, but I stifled the longing. *You made choices, Chastity,* I told myself. *Don't whine now.*

It had been another tasteless dinner and a tedious evening of sermonizing under the watchful eyes of Maude and Hiram. I wondered what Leland and Matthias were doing tonight back in Massachusetts. Enjoying their port on the patio after a dinner of roast beef and pudding, no doubt, discussing politics or literature. I missed them terribly, much more so than I had when I went to school. They were just so very far away, and this place felt like another world in comparison to the one they inhabited, the one I knew and loved. Independence had a price; I just hadn't realized it would be so costly.

When the footsteps stopped outside my door, my ears strained to hear the next sound. For many seconds, there was nothing, and all my senses went into high alert. I heard the squeak of the doorknob, but it stopped. For a few minutes, I heard nothing, and then, heavy footfalls—attempting to be stealthy—faded away.

I took a deep breath, not even realizing I'd been holding my breath for what seemed hours. This was a new development and one I'd hoped wouldn't happen, at least not so soon. "By the pricking of my thumbs," I recited in spite of myself, "something wicked this way comes." Tomorrow night, the trunk was going in front of the door—who cared if anyone heard me shoving it aside in the morning.

I did not sleep well.

CHAPTER 6

I rose with the birds, even if I couldn't hear them. I heard feet above my head, and that was enough. I chatted with the children while we ate our oatmeal and Maude scurried about, making bacon for Hiram. He appeared, pulling on his suspenders as though they conveyed authority, and sat down at the table. He glanced at me and looked quickly away, but as we finished the meal I could feel his eyes on me, flicking away if I looked in his direction.

"So, tell me what are your favorite subjects in school?" I directed my question to both Mary and Samuel, and Samuel answered first.

"I like numbers," he said shyly. "They're good for business, Father says."

"Your father is absolutely correct, Samuel," I said. "I'm sure you're a great help to him."

The child beamed at me, but Hiram coughed. "Maybe when he's big enough to carry a bale or a box. Now he's just good for cleaning up horse dung."

Samuel's face fell, and I wanted to swat Hiram. Instead, I smiled at Samuel. "But Mr. Sampson, I'm sure it's wonderful to have your son learning the business, in any capacity, so he may carry on your legacy." I turned to Mary. "And you, Mary, since you go with your father every day, I'm sure you contribute as well. What are your duties?"

Hiram laughed, his small piggy eyes nearly disappearing. "Her? She's good for sweeping and running for lunch and water, that's all. Woman chores and not much else."

Mary's expression didn't change but then I'd noticed it rarely did. The poor child seemed like a porcelain doll, and the only difference was that her eyes blinked and her mouth opened occasionally for food. I don't think I'd heard her say twenty words in four days now.

I smiled at her, regardless. "Mary, you must be a big help."

She nodded and spooned up the last of her oatmeal. If these children did so little, why in the world did they have to go to work with Hiram every day? The question was answered almost as I thought it.

"The Lord requires everyone to do their part, even the little children," said Hiram piously. "And these children are no exception to the rule of God."

I nearly choked on the awful oatmeal, but I held my gorge and my tongue. I thought instead of my upcoming meeting with Zimmerman, and that was enough to keep my mind occupied until Hiram and the children left. Maude smiled rather wanly at me and shooed me away from the breakfast dishes. I didn't argue but instead gathered my portfolio and left to meet Molly Clarke.

Molly opened her door, and, to my surprise, four other women were sitting in her parlor when I stepped in.

"Chastity," Molly said, eyes twinkling, "I thought you might want to meet some of the other ladies whose children will be in your charge. I know they are eager to meet you." And just so, the Dodge City Education Committee was born.

In just over an hour, we came to know each other, laid out our goals and plans for the coming school year, and agreed upon how and what we wanted the children to learn. They were a lively bunch, those women. I realized that meeting Molly yesterday had been no accident, and she affirmed it with a chuckle.

"Oh my, I'd been waiting for you to show up at the school," she said. "We all knew you were here, and likely the school board hadn't told you that the old school was where you'd be, since the new one's nowhere near ready."

I gave her a quick hug. "I'm so glad you did, and the rest of you, too. We're a force to be reckoned with, now."

Four women I hadn't known until this morning sat there. Pam Gowan, thin and rangy, an outspoken rancher's wife with four children, was from St. Louis, where she'd attended St. Agnes School. She had definite ideas about what she wanted her children to learn. Myrtle Carson and her husband ran the livery stable and lived in town with their three children. Myrtle was as no-nonsense as Pam, but her sweet voice made it clear she wanted singing in the curriculum and as much music as Dodge City and I could provide. Sarah Jones was a pretty, dark-haired woman who made no secret of her past as a hostess at the Alhambra Saloon, but she and her cowboy husband were now raising horses just outside of town, and she wanted their daughters to learn everything they could. Beth Williamson was from Chicago. She and her husband had come here to open a freight business like Hiram Sampson's, and it sounded like it was doing very well, bringing in goods from Chicago with superior contacts. They had two children and high expectations. Beth was also a Shakespeare aficionado, which warmed my heart.

"Chastity, you're just what we were hoping for," Beth said, brushing her pale hair back on her shoulders. "This is the first time they've advertised and brought someone with first-class credentials from back East to teach here. The others have been all right, some up and some down, but I think we see eye to eye."

"Agreed," Pam Gowan chimed in, and the others nodded

assent. "We're on the right track, for the first time ever, in my opinion. Are you two ready to take on Zimmerman this morning? We can all go if you like."

Molly shook her head. "Chastity and I can handle this, ladies. I think he'll get his back up if any more of us come. He already knows we haven't been too happy with his latest decisions. Don't worry, we'll get it done. Right?" She turned to me.

"Absolutely," I said. "I'll give you a full report at noon, when we meet back at the schoolhouse." I thought about the volume of work ahead of us. "Are you sure you want to help with this? The place is a mess."

Molly and I had told them of the condition of the schoolhouse, but nobody had seemed surprised, and all had volunteered. I'd dreamed about scrubbing floors last night and was grateful for the help and not having to confront Zimmerman about that, amongst everything else.

"Don't be silly," Myrtle said. "We'll be there."

* * *

MOLLY and I entered Zimmerman's store. It was busy this morning, full of cowboys and ranchers buying ammunition, guns, and other things whose uses I couldn't begin to guess, but I'd never been one for the mechanics of things, only those that involved horses. We idled about, waiting for customers to finish their business. After half an hour or so, there seemed to be a lull, and we approached the counter.

"Good morning, ladies," Fred Zimmerman said—with some apprehension, or so it seemed to me. "What can I do for you?"

"Good morning to you, Mr. Zimmerman," I said brightly. "Mrs. Clarke and I've come with a few requests for school supplies, now that I've had an opportunity to inspect the schoolhouse." I produced my notes, and he sighed. "Thank you so much for the key yesterday, by the way. Perhaps we should have this conversation in private?"

"No need for that, and I can't leave the front counter. What do you need?"

I shoved the notes in front of him. "Three dozen slates, six dozen slate pencils, McGuffey readers"—I pointed at the paper—"in different levels, as I've detailed here, and two dozen copies of Shakespeare's complete works, for starters. I will have additional requests as the school year progresses, as I'm sure you're used to."

I hadn't meant to overwhelm him, but it looked as though I had. "Well, well," he said, staring at the papers. "This is more than any of the other teachers have asked for, Miss James."

I smiled at him. "I do not idly request these items, Mr. Zimmerman. They are the bare essentials. I'm not privy to what other teachers have needed, but this is what I require." I waited a moment. "I'm sure the school board has a budget for supplies. Or, if they do not, we may need to ask for a levy of some sort."

He coughed and looked around as though searching for reinforcements. He didn't have any takers, even though the store was filling up again, but I did. Molly Clarke put her hand on the papers and stared at him.

"The Dodge City Education Committee endorses Miss James's requests, Mr. Zimmerman. We are concerned about the quality of our children's education."

"The Dodge City Education Committee? What the hell, excuse me, is that?"

"Yeah," a man muttered behind us, "what the hell is that? Buncha busybody women, sounds like to me." Murmurs of assent followed this remark.

Molly, nonplussed, smiled at Zimmerman. "The loving parents of Dodge City's children, Mr. Zimmerman. We are certain you have our children's best interests at heart, of course, since you're the head of the school board and that's your sacred responsibility."

I looked over my shoulder. By now, a small crowd had gathered, customers and just those interested in the conversation. Zimmerman harrumphed and gathered up my list. "Ladies, I can assure you the school board has your children's futures in mind. I'll send for these items today." He glared at me. "Keep in mind, it'll take three weeks at least for these items to arrive, Miss James, so you'll have to make do in the meantime."

Low laughter erupted behind us. "Three weeks, my ass. More like three months, serves them right. Can't teach school with what you already have, shouldn't be teaching at all, what I think." The voice sounded familiar.

"Of course," I said graciously. "Thank you so much, Mr. Zimmerman. You're very kind." I ignored the chatter, which had increased. Molly and I turned to leave, and I spotted Hiram Sampson and his friend, Duane Olson, among the men.

"Miss James," Zimmerman called.

I glanced back at him. "Yes?"

"Just to be clear, if any of these items, such as the Shakespeare volumes, prove to be more costly than the school budget can cover, can I assume you will cover the extra charges? I believe you can afford it."

With one remark, Zimmerman had ruined my credibility and divulged that I was not dependent upon the board's salary, as the other teachers had been.

Furious, I clutched Molly's arm, not wanting to give him the satisfaction of knowing how angry I was. "Yes, Zimmerman," I shot back, deliberately leaving out "mister."

"If you find your board is in financial jeopardy because of buying needed books, I'll certainly take care of it."

A hush fell over the store, and we made our way toward the door, the men parting as though we were contaminated.

Uncomplimentary murmurs about "uppity women," and "Eastern know-it-alls" and chuckles surrounded us. I heard Hiram Sampson's voice above the rest. "Thinks she's something special, for sure. Hasn't lifted a finger, poor Maude says …" I shut the door and didn't hear the rest, mercifully.

Tears prickled behind my eyes, threatening to spill over. Molly took a glance at my face and hustled me along the sidewalk, our boot heels clicking smartly on the wooden planks. We turned north toward the Clarke house and slowed a bit.

"That goddamn Zimmerman," Molly said, and I nearly choked. "Don't you worry about a thing, Chastity. That little shit weasel's going to get a talking to when I tell George what happened in there. George is on the board, you know." I began to laugh, which was better than crying.

"Oh God, Molly. Shit weasel?" Now I couldn't stop laughing. Molly joined in, and there we were, two grown women holding onto each other on the street, cackling hysterically. We'd been through a battle, but I hoped there wasn't a war starting.

WITH SIX WOMEN WIELDING MOPS, brooms, rags, soap, and water, and a throng of enthusiastic children eager to stock coal and wood and straighten shelves, by four o'clock the little schoolhouse gleamed like a polished jewel. We women sat on the benches, mopping our sweaty faces and looking at each other and the room with weary satisfaction, while the children ranged outside in the schoolyard in a game of Red Rover. Late afternoon sunlight glinted through the clean windows, bathing all of us in a golden glow. I felt such an affection for these kind women, I thought I'd burst with it.

"That wasn't so bad," Pam Gowan said and gave the table in front of her a last swipe with a damp rag. "Place looks pretty decent."

"I can't even begin to thank all of you," I said. "I would've been at this for days." I got up and wandered over to my desk at the back of the room, running my hand over the dust-free surface. I picked up the now-gleaming brass bell by its wooden handle and rang it for the first time. "School will be in session!" I laughed in delight, and everyone joined in.

Charlie Gowan stopped just inside the door, breathless, with Liam Clarke right behind him. "School's starting?"

"Pretty soon," I said, "but not today."

They ran back outside, and the game resumed. Pretty soon, indeed. Two days from now, nine o'clock Monday morning. I could hardly wait either.

I locked the schoolhouse door and waved goodbye to everyone except Molly, as the women dispersed, children in tow. At the Clarke house, I stopped at the gate, turned to Molly, and gazed into those bright-blue eyes.

"You know something, Molly Clarke? You're a godsend. Without your support and everything you've done, this would have been so difficult—in fact, nearly impossible—for me."

Molly put down the bucket and mop she'd been carrying and hugged me soundly.

"You'll be just fine, my chick. Far as I'm concerned, you're the godsend here. We've needed a teacher with fresh ideas, young and fierce just like you." She pulled back and peered up at me. "I was so proud of you, standing up to that bully, Fred Zimmerman, this morning. Don't give those stupid men or even him another single thought. They aren't worth your spit. This whole town is going to stand behind you."

I could feel my eyes prickling, but I took a deep breath and hugged her again. "Thank you more than I can say." I looked up at the sun slanting lower. "Home to the Sampsons."

Molly picked up her bucket. "That's another thing, Chastity. I heard that Hiram Sampson shooting off his mouth this morning, too. You have any trouble over there, you let me know. I've not heard good things about them; that's all I'm going to say, but mark my words, you be careful. Too much Bible reading can turn people odd."

I waved and walked on down the road. She was right, and I was not looking forward to my evening of tasteless supper and sermons. I heard footsteps behind me and turned to see Liam Clarke, smiling shyly. Both the twins were handsome young men, their blond hair falling across their foreheads, and gangly as adolescents are. I'd noticed Liam, in particular, was always there when I needed anything, and I knew he had a crush on me. I smiled back. It was good to have a knight errant.

"I thought I'd walk you home, Miss James," Liam stammered, his cheeks pink. I took his hand, and they turned even pinker.

"Thank you, Liam. I'm delighted to have your company." We walked on, chatting about books and school, and I was sorry it was such a short way to the Sampsons'.

Maude was in the kitchen when I came in, stirring a pot of soup and cutting bread for supper. I greeted her and went out to the pump to replenish my water supply. I was a sweaty, dirty mess from my exertions this afternoon and likely smelled like a field hand. She glanced at me in curiosity.

"What in the world have you been doing, Chastity?" she said when I came back in and was heading toward my room.

"Cleaning up the schoolhouse, Maude, with help from some of the mothers of my new students," I said. "Actually, we started a committee, and I was just going to ask if you'd like to join us. We talk about what we want the children to study and ask for everyone's suggestions."

She stopped stirring her soup and looked at me like I'd grown two heads. "Why would you do that? Schoolin's just some alphabet and numbers."

"Well, we can talk more about that," I said. I should've known better, but, still, she had two children I was going to be teaching. "Right now, I really need to clean up."

By the time I'd stripped down, gone through two pitchers of water and a lot of soap, and dressed in a simple cotton gown, I heard Hiram and the children arrive and the clattering of dishes. I dashed out to set the table and say hello, and, within minutes, we were sitting down to bowls of soup and a platter of bread.

I was starving, and it looked as though everyone else was hungry as well. We applied ourselves with gusto to the soup, some sort of beef and vegetable mix, and Maude's fresh bread. There was no conversation, but she brought out an apple cobbler that she proceeded to cut up and serve.

Hiram hadn't met my eyes since we'd sat down and I thought, *in for a penny, in for a pound.*

"So, I was telling Maude we cleaned up the schoolhouse and ordered new supplies for the students today."

Hiram snorted. "Half the town knows that, missy. You high and mighty tellin' Fred Zimmerman his business along with that Clarke woman."

Maude froze, her forkful of apple cobbler halfway to her lips. "You didn't mention that, Chastity."

"It didn't exactly go that way," I said. "Like I mentioned earlier, Mrs. Clarke and I met with some of the other mothers of my students this morning. After looking through the books and supplies at the school, I went to Zimmerman's to order more. I believe what the students need is my business, Mr. Sampson. That's why I'm the teacher, not Mr. Zimmerman."

Hiram's face got red. "That's not what I heard, nor anybody else." He turned to Maude, his voice rising. "I hope she ain't been fillin' your head with any nonsense." He glared at me. "Who do you think you are, woman? You been in this town all of a few days, and you're tellin' us how to run things? That don't fly out here. You need to keep to your place."

What an ass. "And what place would that be?" I challenged. Maude stiffened, and the children were quiet as mice.

"Listenin' to men who know best. A handmaiden, like the

Lord decreed," he spat. "I guess you've not been listenin' to what the Bible says. For all I know, you're one of them anti-Christers or something. Fine choice to be filling our children's heads."

This had gone way too far, especially in front of the children, and I knew I had to rein it in. This man would never support me or be my friend, but I was living under his roof for the time being, and he clearly had a big mouth—as he'd demonstrated this morning, as well as right now. If I wanted to stay in Dodge, I didn't need him and his like-minded friends campaigning against me.

I looked down at my plate and raised my eyes with false contrition. "Mr. Sampson, I apologize if I've been too forward for your tastes, but my actions have only been for the sake of the children in my care. If I was too enthusiastic about the needs for the school and the youth of Dodge City, I'm sorry. I only want the best for everyone here. I know I'm an outsider, but I want to belong. It's been a difficult transition for me."

He was silent, staring at me across the table. I actually let a fake tear slide down my cheek for emphasis. Maude looked back and forth at us, her usually pale face even more drawn.

"Well, then." He stood up and pushed back his chair. Maude gave an almost imperceptible sigh. "Maybe so, but we'll be keeping an eye on you." He stomped into the front room, taking down the Bible from the piano. I could only imagine what we'd hear about tonight. Jezebel, likely.

* * *

I LAY sleepless in my narrow bed after moving the trunk to block my door. As I'd expected, tonight we'd heard about Jezebel and Sheba, and the children's eyes had grown wide. I didn't know a lot of Bible stories, but Leland had included most of them as a sort of curriculum of current thought, given that so many people listened to them every Sunday.

Women who didn't behave as handmaidens or proper wives were likely to meet a sorry end, so they told, and I felt pretty sure I was in a suspicious category in Hiram's mind after today.

I went over the events of the day, running them back through my mind, and I don't think I would've changed a thing. After an hour or so, my eyelids closed as a response to my aching muscles, and I began to drift off.

They flew wide open at the squeak of the doorknob and the soft clunk of the door hitting the heavy trunk. My body went rigid, and my heart thumped in my chest.

"Bitch."

The door shut softly, and it was a long time before I closed my eyes again.

CHAPTER 7

I missed breakfast, deliberately so. When I emerged, Maude was in the kitchen, kneading bread dough, her apron dusty with flour.

"Morning," I said. She nodded in reply, not taking her eyes off the dough.

"I'm headed over to the schoolhouse. Thought I might take some books over there. Do you happen to have a cart or wagon I could borrow?"

"No."

"Oh. Well, perhaps the Clarkes have one. I thought you might want to come with me," I said. "The schoolhouse looks really nice, and you can see where the children will be during the day."

Fists pounded into the dough. I was starting to see where Maude takes out her anger. I wasn't surprised she had some, but I hoped it wasn't directed at me but at her lout of a husband. When she finally looked at me, though, that didn't seem to be the case.

"I don't want to be seen with you, Miss James, and have people think I'm like you or that Molly Clarke woman. I'm a God-fearing woman who knows her place."

"Ah." It seemed my apprehensions were well founded. "Look, Maude, I haven't done anything wrong, to my mind, and I apologize if I've offended you somehow."

She spun around, eyes flashing. "Hiram told me, you know."

"What?" I was baffled, but the woman was shaking with anger.

"How you try to entice him every time my back is turned, and how you flirt with any man you see. Just like that other harlot who used to stay here. You were so nice at first, I thought you were different. But now you've shown your true colors, may God forgive you."

"Maude, that's not true," I said. "I've never done anything of the sort. Hiram is lying to you."

"Don't you dare speak to me like that!" she screeched. "You are a liar and a whore. My husband wouldn't lie." Her fists, white with flour, were clenched.

The best defense is to accuse someone before they can accuse you, and I should've had the sense to know Hiram would do just that since he'd found the door blocked last night. I couldn't stay here. I'd be moving a lot more than books today, obviously. I turned on my heel, went back to my room, collected my reticule and hat, and walked out the front door without another word.

It was just two blocks to the Clarkes' house, and I was still trembling with suppressed fury when I stepped into Molly's kitchen. She took one look at my face and sat me down at the kitchen table, pouring me a cup of coffee without saying a word.

I finished the coffee, wishing I had a shot of Leland's brandy to put in it. Molly poured me another and sat across the table.

"The Sampsons?"

I nodded. "I have to find a place to live; I can't stay there another day. Or night, which is a lot worse, frankly."

"I'm not surprised. Anne Gleason, the last teacher, had a problem there, too, and I suspect she wasn't the first," Molly said. "I can't imagine Zimmerman and others don't know, but he keeps getting away with it, and that poor wife of his defends him."

"She certainly does," I said. "So, is there a nice boarding-house or hotel available?"

Molly laughed and then looked despondent. "On a school-teacher's salary? Oh, honey, I doubt it."

I gazed silently at her over the rim of my coffee mug and raised an eyebrow slightly.

She looked at me quizzically and then I could see comprehension dawning. "Oooh, you little devil. Zimmerman wasn't just talking mean when he said you could pay for those books, was he? You come from money back there, Chastity?"

"Well, sort of, but that doesn't mean I'm rich, you understand?" I sighed and sat back on my chair. "I never meant to fly under false flags, Molly. I just never thought it could ever be an issue. Let me explain."

So I told her about Harrowhill, Leland, Matthias, all of it. How I never really knew my mother, had grown up with men and horses, and hadn't discovered what being a girl was until I was fourteen and Mrs. Riley told me why I was bleeding. About going away to school and learning there was a great deal more to the world than I'd ever thought about—that there was a West, with brave people who'd gone and made new lives for themselves, and how I wanted to be a small part of that, doing the only thing I'd been educated to do: teach what I knew.

Molly squeezed my hand. "Chastity, you've got some grit."

I smiled ruefully. "I'm no saint, Molly. I'm willful, opinionated, and, yes, spoiled by many standards. I want to be independent and show Leland that I can make it on my own, but he was smart enough to make me sell my colts to him so I'd have some seed money in case life in Dodge City wasn't exactly how I'd dreamed it would be, and he was right."

"Your father sounds like a smart man, my chick," Molly said and put a plate of cinnamon rolls on the table.

I nodded. "He is, Molly. And, that is why I can afford to buy books and move out of the Sampsons'. Neither of which I'd planned to have to do, and certainly not this soon." I took a bite of warm cinnamon roll and sighed with pleasure. "All that said, he was quite clear he wouldn't be sending me money, and I'd have to work things out on my own. He and Matthias both were strongly against this whole idea." I popped the last bit of roll in my mouth and swallowed it along with doubt. "But, I'm here and I'm staying. Will you help me?"

"You know I will." She sighed and put her arms around me. "You'll need it."

"I know I will. Thank you."

"You ever scrub a floor before yesterday, Chastity?"

I laughed. "No, Molly, but I can go you one better. I've mucked out horse stalls since I was five."

Molly took off her apron and hung it on the back of the chair. "Come on, girl. Time's a-wastin'. We're going to see George. He knows everybody in this town and is apt to know just where you can find a place to live."

* * *

MOLLY WAS RIGHT. George Clarke did know everybody, especially people who owned restaurants, saloons, and hotels. I liked him as soon as he smiled at me, as kind and charming as his wife, and I knew how lucky I was to have met both of them. He called his clerk, and, within minutes of Molly filling him in on my difficulties, the three of us were walking down Front Street while he gave me a running commentary on which restaurants and hotels were owned by whom, who patronized each of them, and which to avoid. The man who supplies the liquor knows all the secrets, I found, and that most likely holds true anywhere. Up Second Avenue we went, and into Wright House, the nice looking hotel I'd passed the other day.

"Oh, George," I said, "this is lovely, but I don't know if I can afford to live here."

The lobby was spacious and quiet, with grey wallpaper and a chandelier in the center of the high ceiling. A few men sat in the adjoining dining room, lingering over their breakfasts, most with cowboy hats crown down on the tables. A place where ranchers and cattle brokers stayed, then.

George winked and patted my arm. "Don't worry, I think we can work something out. Besides," he pointed back towards the doorway, "the school is just a block away, and we're close by as well."

He spoke with the desk clerk and disappeared through a door. Within a few minutes, George was back—with a smiling Bob Wright. Of course, I thought, I should've known.

"Hello again, Miss James," he said. "I see you're wearing the lovely hat you bought from us. You do it justice. George here tells me you're in need of permanent and more suitable lodgings, and I think I have just the thing. Please?" He gestured toward a staircase, and up we went. He led us down a hallway toward the back of the building and opened a door.

Morning sunlight poured into a good-sized room through a large window hung with crisp white curtains. Even with the white-ruffle-covered bed, a dresser, two chairs, and a table beside the window, there was room for a wardrobe and a desk. A screen stood in one corner, and there was a tin bathtub, its flower-painted sides peeping discreetly from behind it. I suddenly wanted to live here beyond common sense.

"I keep this room for the occasional ranch wife who

accompanies her husband up to Dodge. Do you think this might do?"

"Oh, Mr. Wright, this will do splendidly," I said. "But I'm on a rather tight budget, and I doubt I can afford it."

"Not to worry, Miss James," Bob Wright said. "You're a charming young woman, and the children of Dodge City are fortunate to have you as a mentor. I think we can work something out. Let's go down to my office." He smiled at George, and we all trooped back downstairs.

Politics were everywhere. Leland always said it, but I'd never witnessed it in action before today. Bob Wright gave me the room, which he said was mostly vacant all winter anyway, for a ridiculously low price, and he arranged for me to take my meals in his restaurant for one even lower. It seemed he was on the school board and wasn't terribly happy with the decisions that had been made up to this point. To have me installed safe and sound in his hotel made good sense, he said, and while I didn't care about the machinations of the movers and shakers in Dodge City, I couldn't have agreed more.

I went back to the Sampsons' with a wagon supplied by the hotel and told my pinched-face hostess, Maude, I was departing and not to count on me for dinner. It was difficult to say what she thought because she turned her face away while my trunks were loaded, but I wished her a good day anyway. I've never been so happy to leave a place as that mean, dark room.

I asked the Wright House restaurant to make me a cake, the most magnificent one they could concoct, which I would take to the Clarkes for their dessert, just a small repayment for changing my life. While I waited for the chef to work his magic, I unpacked my trunks, sorted through the books I'd take to the school the next morning, and then sat blissfully in a chair beside the window, blessing Molly and George Clarke and the generous Bob Wright. I opened the window, and when the afternoon breeze wafted in, I didn't even notice the stench of cattle. Today, that was the smell of hope.

CHAPTER 8

$\mathcal{F}$ ifty-eight eager faces turned towards me as I stood beside my desk. I was so happy, I thought my heart would burst beneath my stiffly starched shirtwaist.

I clapped my hands and grinned. "Good morning! I'm Miss James, and I can't wait to get to know your names." I pointed at a little red-haired boy in the front row who squirmed with excitement. "Let's start with you."

I had a good memory, but, even so, it was going to take me a few days at least to learn every child's name. Some I knew, and I was frankly surprised to see Mary and Samuel Sampson among the benches, dour-faced but there. I hoped to instill curiosity and a desire to learn, even a sense of wonder—lofty goals, perhaps, but that was why I'd come.

After introductions, I divided the students into more or less permanent seats, according to ages, which ranged from five to fifteen. But when we started with alphabet and reading, I quickly discovered that ages and experience were vastly different, depending if they'd been to school before and what they'd learned at home. I found that having the older or more accomplished children help the younger ones worked very well, since I couldn't be everywhere at once. We did math, played games, and I began reading *Swiss Family Robinson,* which they immediately loved. More advanced subjects would come later.

Our day began at nine and ended at three, with breaks for lunch and recesses. There were a few children who didn't bring any food with them, and I made a note to have the cook at Wright House pack some extra sandwiches and fruit each day.

I watched the students file out at three o'clock, saying goodbye to each one. I was exhausted but happy, and most of them were as well. A few of the younger children had fallen asleep earlier in the afternoon, so I thought it was a good idea to schedule some quiet time for everyone. Then they could read, sleep, or practice penmanship or sums with no fear of being teased by their peers.

We fell into our routines, the children and I, becoming familiar with each other as summer passed into autumn, and no further melodrama arose from the community. I was delighted with my lodgings at Wright House, just a short walk from the school.

Fred Zimmerman stopped by one afternoon to observe the children—and presumably my teaching abilities. After the children left, he sat down on one of the benches.

"Well, Miss James, it seems you have things well in hand," he said. "The children have nothing but good tidings for their parents."

"I'm happy to hear so," I said. "We are a bit crowded in here. How are things coming along at Boot Hill?"

Zimmerman frowned. "Not so well, frankly. It's taking much longer than we thought. We keep finding bones every time it rains. We relocated the remains, but I guess we missed some. If we don't get the roof finished before the snow comes, it could well be spring before it's ready."

I wasn't surprised but was disturbed nonetheless. "Hmm. Bones aside, that's not ideal, is it? We're very crowded down here. We started with fifty-eight, and now we're up to sixty students. Some of the children take turns sitting on the floor. Perhaps we could find a few more benches and tables? We could squeeze them in."

"I'll see what I can do, Miss James," he said, brushing off his trousers as he rose. "By the way, the supplies you ordered are here. I can have a boy bring them over tomorrow."

"Wonderful. I'd appreciate that. We certainly need them. How much do I owe you?"

He coughed. "Not a penny. The school levy will take care of it. I apologize if there was any misunderstanding there." He gazed at me, eyes sharp. "Also, it was a pity things didn't work out for you at the Sampsons', but I understand you've found something suitable?"

Took you long enough to get around to that, I thought, but I smiled graciously. "Well, sometimes people don't always see eye to eye, do they? I think it's best for everyone concerned."

He nodded. "I hope so. There was some talk, but the matter seems resolved. Keep in mind, Miss James, that you are living in a building where alcohol is served, and one of the rules for our teachers is that they do not patronize that sort of place."

I stifled a dangerously inappropriate laugh, but I couldn't stop myself from saying, "I don't have a kitchen. Are you telling me I can't have dinner at Delmonico's, the Dodge House, or even my own hotel? That seems prohibitive, to say nothing of leading to malnutrition, Mr. Zimmerman."

He flushed. "This isn't a situation that's come up before, Miss James. All I'm saying is we expect a certain level of behavior on the part of our teachers. Of course, these are somewhat different circumstances."

"I would never behave in any way that would reflect badly on the school board, my students, or myself," I said. "I can assure you of that."

He made his way to the door. "Good afternoon, Miss James."

"And to you." I wanted to ring my bell to let him know class was dismissed, but that would likely launch him into apoplexy. On the other hand, dinner at Delmonico's tonight sounded like a grand idea.

* * *

DELMONICO'S HAD a way with steak, I had to admit, even if they'd just copied the name. Someone besides me must've eaten at the New York restaurant, because even the potatoes were similar. I took a last cheesy bite and smiled at the waiter who poured my coffee. It was early, and the restaurant was half empty. I didn't want to be out after dark, besmirching my strait-laced reputation, but after my Zimmerman encounter this afternoon, I couldn't resist a defiant and celebratory dinner for myself. I had taken care to don a high-necked, black dress with lace cuffs, and I thought I looked as prim as I ever had.

"Miss James, how nice to see you," said Charlie Bassett, with a big grin on his face. A tall man with intense blue eyes and an imposing handlebar mustache stood beside him. "You've been so busy with your duties, you hardly ever surface on Front Street these days."

"Lovely to see you as well, Mr. Bassett." I dabbed my lips with my napkin.

"Let me introduce you to my assistant marshal, Mr. Wyatt Earp," Charlie said, stepping aside slightly for the tall man. "This is Miss Chastity James, our new schoolteacher, Wyatt."

He actually took my hand and gave a slight bow. "Delighted," he murmured in a deep voice. Quite the gentleman in his black suit.

"Nice to meet you," I said, suppressing a smile. "I understand you gentlemen have been very busy yourselves, what with the president stopping in, Indians on the warpath, and that terrible business with Dora Hand."

President Hayes had indeed come to Dodge City on the train in September. With help from the Dodge City Education Committee, I had taken the children to see him. A dust storm had blown enough grit onto the crowd and the president himself that he retired to his railroad car, and we mostly heard General Sherman instead, but the children had been thrilled.

Wyatt Earp looked annoyed at my mention of Dora Hand, a poor woman who was shot in her bed, to say nothing of the so-called Indian attack, which hadn't ever materialized but had terrified Dodge City residents, including me, for days. I hadn't been expecting this excitement, but, as Leland had warned me, it was the wild frontier.

Charlie laughed. "You keep up on local events, don't you, Miss James? I hear you're living at Wright House, so you must hear lots of news on a daily basis."

"Indeed I do, Mr. Bassett." I smiled innocently. "In your line of work, you gentlemen know all the secrets—who's who, who's where, and who's likely to do what. I'll have to keep that in mind."

This time Wyatt actually cracked a smile. "I wish I'd had a schoolteacher as well informed as you, Miss James. I might have avoided a misspent youth."

"Possibly, Mr. Earp." I put down my napkin, and Wyatt courteously pulled back my chair. "I was just leaving; we teachers have more work to do when the day is done. If you'll excuse me, gentlemen?"

"Of course. I hope we see you soon, Miss James," Charlie said, and Wyatt nodded.

I could feel their eyes on my back as I left, but it didn't bother me in the least. Being watched by the eyes of the law in Dodge City was a plus for me, not a threat. Perhaps I could convince one of them to come give a lecture to the children one of these days. Probably Charlie, since Wyatt wasn't much of a talker.

* * *

SATURDAY MORNING I brought cinnamon rolls to Molly Clarke's kitchen, as was my custom now. I chatted with the Clarke children, a sure barometer on how I was doing as a teacher. They were unfailing in their criticisms and forthright in their wishes, so it kept me on track.

Molly shooed them outside to play after a time and poured us more coffee.

"So I hear you had dinner at Delmonico's and met our assistant marshal the other night."

News flew around this town like swallows. "Yes, I did. I'd just had a visit from our school board president that after-noon, and I deserved a steak dinner after that."

She laughed. "I don't doubt you needed it, Chastity. What did he have to say?"

"Oh, that I shouldn't eat in establishments or live in places that serve alcohol,"

I said. "I mentioned I could starve or be on the street, and he amended his judgment for the time being."

"George will love this." Molly broke off another piece of cinnamon roll and rolled her eyes in appreciation. "I like these raisins; I'll have to try that."

"They can't hold a candle to yours, raisins or no."

"They're good, though." She munched away for a moment. "You know, you can't trust those Earps."

"Those Earps? I only met one, I think."

Molly snorted. "Count yourself lucky; he's got a yen for the ladies. His brother runs a whorehouse, another brother gambles the night away at the Long Branch, and Wyatt himself is usually at a table when he can tear himself away from peacekeeping. Besides, his best friend is Doc Holliday, and that's trouble."

"Well, that's interesting." *Did everybody in Dodge City have at least two vocations? It seemed so.* "Don't worry, I wasn't planning on seeing him again. At least, I hope not. The only way I'd see Wyatt Earp again is to get arrested."

We both laughed heartily at that notion and set to packing a picnic lunch for the children so we could take them down to the river for a little fishing. That would be fun, but what I really missed was being able to go riding. I would have to see Myrtle Carson about getting a horse to ride sometimes. Even schoolteachers could do that without fear of recrimination, one would think.

* * *

I PULLED Bella up short and gazed around me. We weren't that far outside Dodge City, but it might as well have been a hundred miles. A crisp wind blew the prairie grass in patterns like waves on a yellow-green sea, and I took a deep breath. No cattle, no dust, just clean, fresh air. Even better, no people and no Dodge City. I mentally kicked myself for not doing this before.

Bella was a sweet and spirited buckskin mare, and Myrtle's husband, Joe, kept her "just for ladies who know how to ride," as he put it. He watched me ride her before he gave his approval and allowed me to take her out of town. This was the third Sunday morning Bella and I had toured the countryside, and I was hoping the foretold snows would hold off forever.

I'd been warned not to go too far unaccompanied, and I'm sure everyone meant well, talking of stray Indians, outlaws, or even a rattlesnake, but the whole point was to be alone, which was hard to explain. So I'd nod agreeably and let people think I was meeting up with one person or another. No dire straits had overtaken me, and, while I felt a little guilty about deception, it was worth it.

The wind had picked up, and dark clouds were massing to the north, so I whispered to Bella, and we picked up the pace. All too soon, Boot Hill was rising before me. A man on a horse was headed straight for me at a pretty good clip, so I halted Bella to wait for him to pass by.

Duane Olson didn't pass by. Instead, he yanked on his reins, stopping in a cloud of dust beside me. I'd seen him here and there since we'd met at the Sampsons', an unpleasant experience I had no intention of repeating, and occasionally I wondered if he was following me, but I'd dismissed the thought. I may have been mistaken.

"Well, well, it's Miss James," he said, settling his dirty cowboy hat firmly on his unkempt hair. "What you doing out here all by yourself? This is no place for a lady." He grinned. "There could be outlaws with trouble on their minds."

"Hello, Mr. Olson." I didn't smile. "I'm perfectly fine, as you can see. I'll let you get on with your business." I lifted Bella's reins, and, quick as a snake, he grabbed them out of my hands.

"Come on, now, don't be in such a hurry," he said. "We haven't had much of a chance to get to know each other. Maybe we can take a little ride together."

I never carried a riding crop, but if I'd had one, I'd have used it on his smirking face. Instead, even faster than he had been, I grabbed the reins back. "How dare you?"

I kicked Bella, and she took off towards the buildings on Front Street at a gallop. I could hear Olson's mocking laughter behind me.

I was still shaking with fury by the time I reached the front porch of Wright House, almost as angry at myself as I was at Duane Olson. Molly and the others had been right. There were dangers for an unaccompanied woman in Dodge City. Riding alone was the least of them, but it obviously provided an avenue of opportunity for a lout like Olson.

I stomped up the stairs to my room. The desk clerk, Stephen, raised his eyebrows as he watched me ascend the stairs, but I ignored him. I certainly didn't need this news to get around town. Dodge was like a witches' cauldron that swirled with gossip, and there was likely plenty of it about me anyway: the teacher who lives at a hotel, eats at restaurants, rides alone, and God knows what else. Next thing you knew, I'd be riding a broom over the prairie on full moons or some other nonsense.

The maddening thing was, most of the men I'd met here, from the rowdiest cowboys to supposedly dangerous gamblers, were unfailingly polite and deferential to me and to all women who crossed their paths. The Duane Olsons and Hiram Sampsons of the world were anomalies that crawled out from beneath rocks or hid between the pages of the Bible, misinterpreting it for their own ends. People like those were the ones who were truly dangerous. I'd been naïve to believe that everyone thought my actions were acceptable and that none harbored ill will or evil intentions towards me.

Keys jingled in the hallway, and I opened the door to call to Greta, the hotel maid. I was glad to see her so late in the day. "Greta, could you have hot water for a bath sent up, please?" I needed to wash off not just horse and dust, but the nasty encounter with Olson.

I went back in my room and pulled out the tin tub to wait for the boy to bring up the water. I settled down in my chair at the desk and wrote Leland and Matthias a short letter, in addition to the one I'd already sent this week. I didn't mention today's incident, but simply communicating with them, even at a distance, eased my mind. As I addressed the envelope, I resolved to be much more observant and much more careful than I had been. I wouldn't always have the option of a fast horse.

I mused about telling Charlie Bassett about the encounter and dismissed the thought. I could only imagine the amusement on his and Wyatt Earp's face. Fanciful, pretty woman complains about a man that's interested in her. Old story, and one they didn't have time for and didn't want to hear. I wasn't Dora Hand or a gambler that'd gotten shot in a barroom brawl. They had other things to do.

So did I. From the false bottom of the smaller of two trunks, I pulled out the derringer and a box of bullets, nestled between packets of the cash money I had left. Leland had insisted I take the gun with me, and I hadn't given it much thought until today. My father was a smart man who thought ahead. As his daughter, I could do no less.

CHAPTER 9

Snow. Covering the dirt, the brambles, the dust-scoured buildings, maybe even the darkest heart, in a magical blanket of purity. I sensed it before I even tiptoed to the window—its vacant silence, transcending the normal bustle of a morning. Pulling back the curtain, I could see nothing except a curtain of white snowflakes hurling themselves in flurries of wind against the glass.

Tomorrow was Thanksgiving, and school would be out for four days. But not today, I hoped, because I would walk there, blizzard or no, and I hoped most of my students could make it as well. We had things to do: our paintings, paper turkey sculptures decorated with feathers the children had found, the flowers we had dried to fashion into table centerpieces—all gifts for their families for the holiday.

I dressed warmly, pulling on the long underwear and wool socks I'd purchased at Wright and Beverly from Mary Jane, bless her advice. Atop those went my green wool suit and the heavy boots I'd also purchased, anointed with what Mary Jane swore was bear fat. Now that it'd dried, the smell was faint, even to my nose, which admittedly was immune after a Dodge City summer. I topped it with my heavy wool

84

coat and wound a matching scarf around my neck and head.

I stopped by the kitchen and picked up my usual lunches and a large box of pumpkin tarts, thanking the chef with three dollars for his extra kindness, and headed out into the storm. It was still early, not many people about yet, especially in this weather. As I stepped into the road, a bulky, snow-covered figure detached itself from a chair on the hotel's porch. I glanced back, but with the snow I couldn't get a good look at him. I could have sworn it was Duane Olson, but then every man I'd seen behind me in weeks looked like him. *Stop acting like a spooked horse,* I chided myself. Likely some poor cowboy who couldn't get a room last night. I strode briskly into the wind, and the man didn't follow.

I stoked the woodstove and lit some lamps. Not taking off my coat and scarf, I grabbed the broom and cleared a path towards the schoolhouse steps, thinking if this kept up, we'd have to get out the shovel soon. By then, I hoped, the older boys would show up.

The little schoolhouse began to warm, and I took off my coat and scarf, hanging them on the pegs George Clarke and his brother had installed on the south wall. The snow quickly melted, leaving damp splotches on the floor. Many more would follow, I hoped.

By nine, the usual time, maybe two-thirds of the class had shown up, braving the snow, some with their parents, all covered with snow and laughing as they stumbled in, stamping their boots.

"Good morning," I said over and over, helping them with their coats and settling them in. I was happy so many had made it, and sorry others couldn't, but not everyone lived as close as I did. The parents and I chatted and agreed that, if the snow kept up, we'd close at noon, and they'd be back to ensure their children got home safely in the storm.

A lovely time we had—all the decorations completed,

pumpkin tarts devoured, and pilgrims and Indians thoroughly discussed. Then I read aloud the first chapter of *Alice in Wonderland*, and the children, thoroughly enchanted, left with visions of white rabbits with pocket watches dancing in their heads. For six of the older children, I passed out copies of Shakespeare to take home for the holiday. I'd decided on *Macbeth* for starters. These children were no strangers to violence, and of all the plays, this was the easiest to entice a reader, I'd always thought. I know it had been for me.

Molly Clarke was the last to depart, bundling up her three. We agreed I'd be at the Clarkes' by two the next day for Thanksgiving dinner, and I was charged with bringing pecan and pumpkin pies. I assured her I wouldn't disappoint.

I banked the stove, straightened the benches and tables, and blew out the lamps. School was over for a few days, and I was looking forward to the respite as much as the children. I had a lot of reading to catch up on. I bundled up and left the school, locking the door.

It was only one o'clock, but it might as well have been evening. The snow still fell, and the wind was blowing it into drifts against the buildings, leaving bare patches here and there and huge waves elsewhere, changing the familiar landscape into an unknown territory.

Weather or no, quite a few people were in the chairs in front of the hotel, likely commiserating on the storm and when it would end. As I stepped into the lobby, I heard someone call my name. I glanced around.

Duane Olson stood there, a big smile on his fleshy face. "Miss James, I'm so glad you managed to teach school today throughout this snowstorm. The Lord truly blesses you, doesn't he?"

A chill ran up my spine that had nothing to do with the temperature. I turned away and entered Wright House, but I could hear his chuckle as I made my way inside.

I threw off my outerwear and stood in my room—shaking,

but not from the storm. This was not to be borne. I was going to have to tell someone, do something, only I wasn't sure what. Was I wrong to perceive this man as a threat? Or was this just my imaginings and he was truly harmless? Maybe I should inform Marshal Bassett. By the time I went to bed, my mind was still swirling. I'd talk to Molly and George tomorrow and see what they thought. Despite my fears, I slept soundly that night, exhausted by the day.

* * *

THE TABLE WAS resplendent with its decorations: the flowers and paper turkey the children had made, the white candles in their pewter holders, and the magnificent roast turkey that was the centerpiece. I don't know where George had procured a turkey in Kansas, but he had his ways. Most tables in town were likely sporting game hens, partridges, chickens, or grouse, but Molly had been up since dawn making stuffing and roasting the bird. It was like Harrowhill to me, and I missed it so much—with a pang that settled somewhere near my breastbone and nearly brought me to tears. Molly could tell, and she enfolded me in her arms where we stood in the kitchen, spooning mashed potatoes into a large bowl.

"I know this is your first Thanksgiving away from home, Chastity." She tightened her arms around me. "I wanted to make it as special as I could."

God, I adored this formidable and kind woman. She'd made all the difference in my time here. "Molly Clarke, I love you. You've made my life here everything that I could've wanted, and you've helped me in so many ways. This is truly a thanksgiving for me, because of you."

George passed us, grinning as he held up a knife and a carving fork. "And the inestimable George. He's a wonder."

Dinner was delicious. Molly was a cook beyond compare.

We all sat back, holding our stomachs in pleasure and deciding to wait a bit for pies. I turned to the Clarke children.

"I have to give my thanks, not only to your parents, but to you," I said. "Ben and Liam, you've been the best help I could have ever envisioned. You stockpile the wood, the coal, and the lanterns, and you keep the school running. I don't know what I'd do without you both. You're amazing."

The boys' faces flushed with embarrassment but also with delight. "And Fiona, my dear." Fiona giggled and sat up straighter in her chair. "You are my barometer." I wasn't sure she knew what a barometer was, so I expounded. "If I wonder how I'm being received, if the children understand what I'm saying, I look at your face, and you never fail me." She jumped from her chair and hugged me.

"I love you, Miss James."

I laughed. "I love you, too, Fiona." I looked around the table. "I love all of you Clarkes. People like you are a gift and the reason I came here. Happy Thanksgiving."

Dusk had fallen by the time Molly and I finished cleaning up. George was still in the parlor, reading more of the *Alice in Wonderland* I'd brought to the children. Molly and I sat down at the kitchen table, as always, and sipped our tea.

"Something's on your mind, so you might as well spit it out," Molly said.

I smiled ruefully. "You know me too well."

Words spilled out of me in a torrent—all my encounters with Olson, not leaving out anything. It was a relief to finally lay it out and see what someone else made of this. When I finished, we sat in silence for a moment. Molly got up and patted me on the shoulder. "I'll be right back."

A minute later, she was back with George. "Tell him what you told me."

I hesitated for a second, and George sat down. "Go ahead, Chastity."

So I reiterated everything I'd told Molly. George shook his head.

"This is a right mess, ladies." He stared hard at both of us. "Chastity, first of all, I believe every word you said. Duane Olson is a lout, just like Hiram Sampson and all the men that work for him. One reason I opened the store and mostly got out of the freight business here is because of Sampson." He leaned back on his chair. "He's a crook, in my opinion, and that leads people to think everybody in his line of work could be some like him. But, so far, he's gotten away with it ... or at least nobody who's ever complained has gone to the law.

"He hides behind that churchgoing façade of his, just like the men that work for him, and I think there's a good number of folks scared of them. His freight business does well and it would be a blow to the community if it got shut down, is what I figure."

I squirmed in my chair. "So, what should I do, in your opinion, George?"

He sat quietly for a minute. "If you go to the law and complain about Olson, I don't think anything good will come of it. He hasn't really done anything he can be arrested for." Now it was his turn to squirm a little. "And, I don't know quite how to say this, but the fact is, you"—here he looked at Molly —"and the Dodge City Education Committee ladies have been pretty visible for months now."

Molly opened her mouth to protest, but George held up a hand. "I'm proud of you all, and things needed to be said. Still, not everyone agrees with women being so forward about things. You are the figurehead, Chastity. You're a beautiful lady, like it or not, and people notice you. You're also the first schoolteacher in Dodge, maybe anywhere out here, who lives in a hotel, and that's caused some talk."

Molly couldn't take it a minute more. "Now listen here, George. We haven't done anything wrong, and you know it. As for Chastity, she doesn't flaunt herself or do one thing that could be considered unladylike. She doesn't deserve this unwanted attention and shouldn't have to feel threatened. So there." She glared at him.

I wanted to crawl under the table, and I sincerely wished I'd kept my mouth shut, not mentioning anything to Molly and especially not George. This was turning into a debacle, and the last thing I wanted was for them to be arguing on Thanksgiving.

I held up my hands. "Please. Stop. I never wanted this to be contentious. I'm sorry; I should've kept my misgivings quiet, and you're right, George, I've brought too much attention to myself. It's likely just my overactive imagination in the first place, and I feel terrible about involving you in my worries. I'll be fine."

"No," George said. "You've a right to be concerned, Chastity. I'm just pointing out, being a devil's advocate here, that there might be differing opinions out there. That doesn't mean we aren't concerned, too."

Molly shot him a look, but she nodded. "All right, I see what you're doing, George, and you have some points." She actually grinned at me. "But, we Dodge City ladies speak our minds, and we aren't stopping. That doesn't give Olson or any other man in this town the right to harass you."

George sighed. "No, it surely does not." He gazed at me, his eyes troubled. "You must be on your guard, Chastity. If Olson comes near you again, I want you to let me know right away. There are people who might have a talk with him, and the law doesn't have to be involved at all."

Molly and he exchanged a look at that comment, and she nodded. "Now, I suggest we keep this conversation to ourselves for the present and get on with Thanksgiving pies. Chastity, you get the plates, and I'll cut portions."

I jumped up and threw my arms around both of them. "Thank you both." I kissed Molly and George on their cheeks. "You're quite wonderful, and I appreciate you more than I can say." Over Molly's head I saw Liam just beyond the doorway, his face pale. I don't know how long he'd been there, but I quickly put my finger to my lips, and he nodded. There was no need for his parents to worry.

I promised to be careful, but I vowed to do more than that. No one needed to be put at risk to defend me. I could do that for myself.

CHAPTER 10

The next weeks passed uneventfully, if you didn't count the occasional snowstorm. There were a couple of those. Afterward, the skies cleared and turned a cerulean blue, clouds scudding across like sailboats on an oceangoing mission. Most of the snow melted within a few days, the muddy streets waiting for the next cover. I came to appreciate the colder temperatures and even the snow, one making the mud solid and the other covering it up as well.

I'd ordered oranges, peppermint sticks, bonbons, red-and-white striped bags, and sixty copies of "A Visit from Saint Nicholas" from Bob Wright, and today I stopped in to find they were here, except for the books. I toted the boxes back to Wright House with the help of a boy from the store and spent two evenings making Christmas gift bags for my students. I hoped the books would arrive soon. I'd read the poem to the children, and visions of sugarplums were indeed dancing in their heads, so I wanted them to have their own books.

A Christmas tree in the lobby of Wright House was a cheery reminder of times past at Harrowhill. A package of the latest novels and newspapers had arrived from Leland, along with a bottle of French perfume and an incredibly soft white scarf from Matthias. I opened their gift early and enjoyed the scent and the feel of the scarf around my neck every morning when I set out for school. How I missed them. It was a constant ache in my heart if I thought about them too much. I'd sent them both leather vests made by a Lakota woman Bob Wright traded with—vests that were buttery soft and fringed, like nothing I'd ever seen in Massachusetts. I pictured both of them sporting those vests and smiled at the thought.

I'd already decided that I wouldn't be renewing my contract when the school year ended, but I saw no point in enlightening Fred Zimmerman about that fact yet. Although I'd made good friends here and loved the children of Dodge, this wasn't my place. I'd brought my vaunted education to the children of Dodge City, but someone else was better suited to continue that work. If I still had the desire to teach, I could do that in Massachusetts. As for proving myself, I'd come to see that, of course, I'd always had whatever independence I wanted, and returning to my beloved Harrowhill, working with my horses alongside Leland and Matthias, was what I truly wanted.

Still, I regretted none of it, in spite of the difficulties I'd encountered. I had learned more in five months than I'd thought possible and had gotten a good look at the rest of the vast country we lived in. I don't think people back East could ever appreciate how big our country is unless they experienced it, and I'd been lucky enough to do that firsthand. That empty sky and the vast prairie thrilled my soul every time I saw it.

I decided to treat myself to dinner at Delmonico's that night. It was quiet this time of year in Dodge, the cattle drives done for the season, and I kept remembering how delicious the steak I'd had there had been. I set off early. The weather was cold but the sky clear. I'd taken to carrying the loaded derringer in my reticule.

I was settled at a table near the window and had ordered dinner when a shadow passed by outside, lingering for a moment to glance in. It looked like Duane Olson, but I discounted it. He'd not been around for weeks now, and I didn't like it when my thoughts turned in that direction— almost as though I might conjure him up.

Delmonico's was crowded this evening, even though it was early. Just after the waiter delivered my food, a man bowed before me, an elegantly dressed woman behind him.

"Miss James, forgive me for intrudin'," said a soft Southern voice. I looked up to see Dr. Holliday, the dentist, beside my table. "Do you remember me?"

"Of course. How are you?" His blue eyes were intense but his smile charming.

"Well, badly in need of a table, and, forgive me again for askin', but since yours is a table for four, and the only one available in this fine establishment, may we join you this evenin'?"

I could hardly refuse without seeming rude, and he and his lady friend sat down. My reputation was close to tatters anyway, from what George had said at Thanksgiving, so having dinner with a gambling gunfighter wasn't likely to damage it much further. The school board wasn't likely to fire me in the middle of the year. The waiter was instantly in evidence and took their orders, the same as mine.

"I can't thank you enough for allowin' us to intrude upon you, Miss James. This is my dear friend, Miss Kate Haroney."

The lady offered her hand, which was firm in mine. She gazed at me appraisingly. "Doc mentioned meeting you a time back, Miss James. I'm impressed you've come from so far away to teach school here. I, too, am far from home." Her voice was soft but strong, her English correct but heavily accented. Her honey-blonde hair was swept up in an elaborate coiffure, and, while not beautiful, she was one of the most striking women I'd ever seen.

Our steaks arrived, and Dr. Holliday ordered a bottle of

burgundy, but when he went to pour some for me, I covered my empty wineglass and shook my head.

He chuckled. "Darlin', you'll be hung for a sheep as a lamb just by dinin' with us, so you may as well enjoy it." He glanced around the room. "Not that anyone here tonight cares, I'd say."

I followed his eyes, and he was right. No one was paying us the slightest attention, so I shrugged and removed my hand from the glass. It was a very good wine, likely one George had brought in. The next hour was filled with the most interesting conversation I'd had since leaving Harrowhill. We discussed literature, music, and politics, and both Holliday and Kate shared anecdotes that made me laugh, all sprinkled with observations about the denizens of Dodge—sometimes in French or Hungarian, which I came to learn was Kate's nationality. We were an unlikely trio in an unlikely place, a fact that wasn't lost on any of us. Doc insisted on paying the check, and, even though I knew it wasn't likely or certainly wise to dine with them again, I was regretful as we left the restaurant.

"We are off to the tables to fill our pockets," Doc said, as we took our leave outside. "Pullin' teeth doesn't pay nearly as well as poker, I find."

Kate smiled. "It does not, my man, and I don't usually have to listen to people scream when I deal cards, so there are many benefits." She took my hand. "You take care of yourself, Miss James. It was lovely to share time with you."

"Thank you," I said. "For dinner and the company. Best conversations I've had in months." I meant it, too, and they both laughed softly.

"How well I know, my dear," Kate said. "That's why I hang onto this one." She put her arm through Doc's, and down the street they went. I watched them go for a few seconds and then turned the other way, back up to Wright House, musing as I went. The schoolteacher had a lesson tonight. When the most sophisticated and likable people in Dodge City have the most scandalous reputations, it was highly probable I was in the wrong profession and the wrong place. Oh, Leland, how right you were.

It had been a lovely evening. Even better, there was no one in the shadows behind me or on the porch as I entered Wright House. That was an early Christmas gift I could really appreciate.

* * *

THREE DAYS BEFORE CHRISTMAS, Bob Wright's boy delivered the Christmas books to me at school just as the children were leaving. Delighted, I knew I was going to have a busy evening. After a hasty dinner at the hotel, I hired a kitchen boy to bring the bags of candy over to the school with me, handing him one of the striped bags for his own.

I stoked up the woodstove, and soon the little schoolhouse was toasty warm. I sat at my desk, the boxes piled around me, and set to making up the gift bags with the books. I wanted to be sure everything was ready, because tomorrow was the last day of school before Christmas. I thought how lucky it was that the books had arrived at the very last minute. Everything seemed to be going so well; maybe it was Christmas magic, I mused.

I finished the last bag and was debating whether to distribute them onto the tables or keep them hidden in the boxes beside my desk until the last minute, when the door burst open.

Duane Olson stood in the doorway, the cold air blowing in around him. He shut the door and swaggered up to my desk, thumbs hooked in his gun belt. He reeked of whiskey, and his smile bared his teeth, a mossy vista that did little to reassure me.

He stopped in front of my desk.

"Well, lookee here." Olson flung out his arms. "My sweet-heart and I are having an evening." The whiskey was cloying, although it hardly masked the smell of the man himself—unwashed sweat and something even worse, judging by the stains on his boots and trousers. I recoiled as though he were a rattlesnake, and, to me, he was just as dangerous.

"Get out." I was surprised there was no tremor in my voice. I was terrified.

His laugh echoed off the walls. "Honey, I'm here to stay. Don't be standoffish." He sat down on the nearest bench and gazed around.

"Mr. Olson, this is a schoolhouse, and we are not having an evening. If you leave now, we can forget this ever happened. Otherwise, I'm going straight to Marshal Bassett." I stood up, eyeing my reticule, where it rested beneath the desk.

He laughed. "Honey, you ain't going nowhere." He moved fast for a heavyset man, walking around the desk, enveloping me in a bear hug, and pinning my arms to my sides. His mouth came down on mine, and I nearly gagged at the rank taste as I struggled to free myself to no avail. He pulled me to the floor, throwing my skirts over my head and pulling down my pantaloons. I screamed, even though no one was likely to hear, but Duane punched me in the face twice to put a stop to that and went back to his work.

It hurt a lot, both my nose spurting blood and his assault on my privates, but I was half conscious at that point, not able to do much about either one. Finally, he grunted and rolled off me. He sat up and lit a cheroot, appraising me with a grin.

"Nice, uh, darlin'? Give ole Duane a couple minutes, and we'll go for round two. You seem to like it." He blew out some smoke. "Whyncha wipe that blood off your face so I don't git it all over my shirt. If you're nicer next time, I'll kill you quick, since we can't have you tellin' your fancy friend, Holliday, about this."

I sat up as well and silently did as he suggested, wiping blood off my face with my full skirts—and also shielding his view of my hand as I reached under the desk and retrieved the derringer. I shot ole Duane in the face and hit the cheroot, too.

I thought it'd done the job, but those are small bullets, and my hand was shaking. He shrieked like a pig, blood pouring down his cheek, but staggered up, fumbling for his Colt 45. He also carried a Bowie knife, and, before he could pull the Colt, I reached up and grabbed the knife. Just like Matthias had taught me to gut a deer, I stabbed him low in the chest and drove the knife down past his navel, conveniently exposed since his trousers were undone.

He fell back onto the floor, his face a mask of disbelief and his hands scrabbling frantically to stop the blood. I pulled out the knife and watched as the blood pooled beneath him and he quit breathing. His eyes gazed blankly upward, but I don't think Duane was looking at redemption.

I leaned back against the desk. I'd just killed a man, a thing I could've never imagined happening. In the course of a few minutes, his life was forfeit and mine was changed forever. I should have felt horrified, but all I felt was justification.

Some instinct I couldn't name led me to unbuckle his gun belt and hide both it and the Colt beneath the woodpile. It was a nice gun and likely much more effective than the derringer. I sat back down on the floor beside Duane, smoothing my skirts. I liked the knife a lot, too, but I wasn't sure about holding onto it, so I dropped it into my bag. I didn't feel so well, and I was really tired.

"Chastity?" I heard the door open, George Clarke's voice, footsteps, and a groan. "Aw, goddamn, goddamn."

Strong arms lifted me off the floor and settled me on one of the benches, and that was the last thing I remember.

* * *

STRIDENT VOICES from the next room woke me. I blinked and looked around in the grey dawn light. I was in a nightgown in an unfamiliar bed in an unfamiliar room. I sat up and moaned softly. I hurt everywhere. I fell back down on the pillows just as the door flew open.

Wyatt Earp stood in the doorway. "Chastity James, you're under arrest for the murder of Duane Olson."

PART II

It's no use going back to yesterday, because I was a different person then.
--Lewis Carroll, *Alice in Wonderland*

CHAPTER 11

$\mathcal{I}$ sat in my room at Wright House and watched the snow falling outside, melting as it slid down the glass. The sun would not come out today, and I was starting to think I'd never see it again. Mornings and evenings had melded into days of misery. I was a prisoner. A deputy marshal sat outside my room with a rifle and a bad attitude, and I sat inside awaiting my trial. My lawyer, a rabbity-looking young man who knew less about the law than I did, assured me we'd fight until the end. Which, if the law in Dodge City had anything to say about it, wasn't far off. I'd already been informed I was going to hang.

The only favorable thing was that I'd been confined to my room at the hotel, rather than the jail, mainly because they were full and also that ladies had tender sensibilities. My tender sensibilities had been used up the night Olson raped me, but pointing that out could lead to concrete floors and bars, so I refrained from doing so.

George Clarke had carried me to his house, where Molly cleaned me up and put me to bed while they figured out what to do. Since Duane Olson lay dead on the schoolhouse floor, there wasn't much choice, and George went to Charlie

Bassett. It seemed a clear case of self-defense: Olson had been stalking me for weeks, had beaten, raped, and planned to kill me to cover up his crime. But that's not how the law decided to see things.

More than a few good citizens convinced Bassett I'd been hiding my true evil nature since my arrival, and I was a danger to society. That a woman could wield a knife to dispatch an attacker with such brutality and precision had dubbed me a vicious and crazed killer who seduced an innocent man. With further flawed logic, since Olson hadn't been wearing a gun, they concluded he hadn't planned to shoot me. They seemed to overlook the fact that Olson was the size of a buffalo and certainly didn't need a gun to kill me, to say nothing of the Bowie knife. They also seemed reluctant to believe I'd been raped, even though Molly had stated so, and the bruises on my face were glaringly evident. My guard, with some glee, showed me a newspaper headline this morning: "Savage Schoolteacher Slaughters Suitor."

I was scared down to my bones. Things were moving so fast, there was no time for Leland to send a lawyer or provide any help, and I hadn't asked for any. I was so ashamed and humiliated that somehow I'd invited this horror into my life that I couldn't reach out to the two people that I revered above all others. I had killed the man. The blazing rage that'd coursed through me blinded me from anything but vengeance against the man who'd not only destroyed my dreams but would've taken my life .In an instant, I'd become a murderess. Whatever capacity I'd had for remorse fled when I realized that, if I had to relive it, I'd do the same thing again. I kept thinking about what Doc Holliday had said: "You may as well be hung for a sheep as a lamb." If I were going to survive this, I might have to do other things that seemed just as impossible a week ago. I didn't have a plan yet, but involving Leland or Matthias just wasn't something I was even willing to contemplate.

There was a quick knock, and the door was flung open, as usual with my guard. So far, he hadn't caught me half dressed, but I could tell he wanted to.

"Visitor. Five minutes."

To my surprise, Kate Haroney shoved her way past him and shut the door in his face dismissively. She quickly threw off the heavy, fur-lined wool cape she wore, hanging it over the bathing screen, and sat down on my bed, the scent of her expensive French perfume wafting through the room.

"Good afternoon, Chastity James. Doc sends his regards."

"Good afternoon to you, Kate." I was grateful for the visit, but puzzled she would come; we hardly knew each other.

She stared at me for a few seconds. "Wyatt and Doc are having a difference of opinion on you, as am I. Let me tell you a story, my dear. It may have some relevance, and it will tell you why Doc and I are in Dodge City. I'll be succinct since we have little time."

In the next four minutes she told me a story, all right. One night, Doc had been arrested and confined in a hotel room as I was, in Fort Griffin, Texas. He had stabbed a man who was about to kill him, but the sheriff hadn't seen it Doc's way. Kate broke him out, and they'd come through Texas and Oklahoma in the dead of winter to Dodge City. She recounted the perils they had faced, and I listened avidly. When she was through, she clasped my hand in hers. "There is more than one way to ensure justice, Chastity James. Sometimes we have to take charge of our destiny." She gazed into my eyes, and I nodded. "You are a young woman who has a future far beyond Dodge City, Kansas, and I believe in your ability to help yourself."

She rose from her chair and walked to the door, looking back at me. "Wednesday evenings have always been quiet in Dodge, but who knows what sort of emergency might break out around midnight." Her eyes flicked to the bathing screen. "That's a very warm cloak."

I nodded my understanding and impulsively embraced her, formidable as she was. She smiled and caressed my cheek. "I'm happy we've met. Good fortune to you." With that, she was gone, her cloak left behind. I had a lot to think about, and, thanks to Kate Haroney, I had some real hope for the first time in many days.

I'd been lucky; they'd been stupid to leave me in my own hotel room as incarceration. Even if they thought of me as some psychotic killer, the search they'd done of my room had failed to find the false bottom in my trunk or the trousers and boots that also resided in its cedar-scented depths. I spent the rest of the morning and a good portion of the afternoon making plans. Around four o'clock, a knock signaled another visitor, and I sat back in my chair, a book in my lap, as though I didn't have a care in the world.

Molly Clarke bustled in, holding a basket with fried chicken and biscuits, judging from the lovely aroma that filled the room. She set it on the desk and rushed to hug me.

"How you doing, Chastity?" She smelled of snow and lilacs. I clung to her, reluctant to let her go. She and George, along with Pam and Myrtle, had been my mainstays against despair. We sat in the two chairs by the window.

"I'm fine," I lied, and we both laughed, on the verge of tears. "My lawyer was here earlier. Looks like trial is set for next week, and he didn't offer much in the way of hope, honestly."

Molly nodded. "I heard." She looked down. "The kids send love. They are so sad, and we can't do much to cheer them up." She looked back up at me, and her eyes were bleak.

We sat in silence for a minute, until I grabbed her hands. "Molly, I need your help."

"Anything you want, Chastity, you know that," she said.

I squeezed her hands. "I know, but this is different. I'm getting out of here. Tomorrow night, and you can help me, if you will."

She gasped. "What are you talking about? Getting out of here? How is that possible?"

"I've got a plan. What I need from you is food, saddlebags, and Duane Olson's Colt I hid under the woodpile at the schoolhouse." I was taking a terrible chance, but one I thought was worth it. "I also need a knife, a Bowie if you can get it, some thick gloves, a canteen, matches, a couple blankets, bullets, and a small cooking pot."

Molly's mouth flew open. "You're going to make a run for it? In this weather? Chastity, you'll die out there."

I laughed grimly. "Molly, I'll die here for sure, and we both know it."

We sat in silence for a precious minute. I didn't want to push her. A tear ran down her cheek when she lifted her head, but her face was set. "When?"

"Tomorrow night, before ten. Bring everything to Carson's Livery and put it in the first stall near the door. Can you do it?"

"Of course. Are you sure about this, Chastity?"

"I've never been more sure of anything in my life," I said. That was a lie.

* * *

WEDNESDAY MORNING DAWNED clear and cold. I kept watching out the window, hoping for snow, since it's much harder to track in a snowstorm, but, by mid-afternoon, it still hadn't come. I'm not much for praying, but I did now. I wasn't sure where I was going. Away from Dodge was all I cared about, but the more I thought about it, I knew I had to have a specific plan, or I was likely to wander around out there until I died of exposure. I knew how to hunt, make a fire, ride in the right direction. East was where I wanted to go, but that could be obvious to my pursuers. I decided to lay a false trail and began scribbling notes and a crude map about Texas on the blank pages of my journal, folding the papers and shoving them in the desk drawer as though I'd forgotten to take them. It wasn't much, but they thought I was distraught, crazy, and stupid, so it might work.

I fidgeted and paced, plotting and re-plotting until I was tired to the bone from thinking about it. I lay on the bed, knowing I'd need rest, and surprised myself by falling asleep in spite of it all.

The usual quick knock woke me, and the night-shift guard, one Jimmy Watkins, came in and set my dinner tray on the desk, his leer ever present.

"Dinner," he announced unnecessarily. He stood there for a few seconds.

"You waiting for a tip?" I sat up on my elbows and glared at him. "I'm not planning on sharing either."

Red faced, he backed out and shut the door. I took the cover off the tray. Roast beef, potatoes, biscuits, and—glory be —a knife to cut it with. They really did think I was stupid. I took my time. The cook at Wright House had become a friend, and the food he sent up was very good. I ate every bite. It could be the last good meal I'd have for some time. I wanted that knife but I couldn't chance Jimmy checking. I reluctantly put it back on the tray, knocking on the door to let Jimmy know he could take it away. Outside, it began to snow, and my nerves jittered in anticipation.

At 11:30, I started moaning, then crying out occasionally. I heard Jimmy's chair creak against the floorboards outside, and, after a particularly loud groan, he knocked on the door.

"You all right in there?"

"No, I … oh, God." I made retching noises. "Help me, please."

He unlocked the door and peered in, rifle in his hand. I was on the floor, clutching my stomach, my hair undone, dress half unbuttoned, moaning softly. He shut the door and stood there, wary.

"Jimmy, please …" I held out my hand. "Can you help me to the bed?"

He smirked a little, leaning the rifle butt against the wall. "I surely can." When he leaned down and put his arms under me, I hit him with the chamber pot. He staggered back, clutching his head, and I hit him again before he could yell. He went down, eyes closed. I stood over him, holding the broken half of the chamber pot.

After dragging him out of the way, I secured his wrists behind him with the handcuffs he wore on his belt, bound his feet with one of the tasseled curtain tiebacks, and, lastly, shoved a handkerchief in his mouth, securing that with the other tieback. He was still unconscious, but breathing, which was good. I didn't need another murder charge.

I dressed quickly in my old pair of heavy riding trousers and high boots and layers of as much clothing as I could wear and still run. Then I picked up my satchel with the cash I'd hidden in the false bottom of my trunk. Jimmy's cowboy hat lay on the floor next to him, and I pinned up my hair and jammed it on. *Perfect.* I put on Kate's cloak, grabbed the Winchester, blew out the lamp, and looked out the window. She'd said midnight, and here it was.

All was quiet, no distraction out there anywhere. Late as it was, I'd have to chance it and just hope no one caught sight of me. Then, I heard a shout outside, followed by people running westward, and I could see the reflection of flames shooting skyward. I grinned. *Bless Kate Haroney.*

I encountered nary a soul in the hotel as I crept down the hall and back stairway. I eased open the back door in the kitchen and stepped into the alleyway.

"Hold it." My heart thumped, and I swung around, the Winchester at hip level.

"Whoa, girl." Eddie Melvin, the Wright House cook, held out a burlap sack. "I been packing one of these the last couple nights, just in case you did what I'd do if I was you."

I stared at him, open mouthed. "What?"

He shoved the sack at me. "Good luck, and git goin'. Olson had it coming." He grinned and shut the door quietly. I hefted the heavy sack and ran down the alley towards the livery stable, three long blocks away.

Molly was as good as her word. I buckled on the gun belt and appraised the horses available. I loved my little mare, but I needed raw power for this. I saddled the big black gelding Carson called Rufus, who rolled his eyes threateningly at being taken from his snug stall on this snowy night. I loaded the supplies Molly had left, tying on the blankets and taking some extra ropes hanging from the tack wall, along with a bag of oats. I left a hundred dollars under the lantern for the horse and tack, knowing they'd find it in the morning. I didn't need to be charged with horse theft either.

I walked Rufus out onto the east end of Front Street but didn't get on his back until we'd passed the last house. I looked back at Dodge City and saw the flames from an empty structure still burning in the night sky. My only regret was leaving the children I'd nurtured—I hoped they wouldn't remember me with condemnation, but with gratefulness for opening new doors for them. I rode away through my own new doorway, into a future I couldn't have imagined six months ago.

CHAPTER 12

here the hell was I?
All I knew for sure was that it was a day and
two nights' ride east of Dodge City. The snow had stopped
sometime yesterday, thank God. It had lasted long enough to
cover my tracks before they'd known I was gone, but it had
been hard going, especially out on the prairie. I'd tried to
follow the river or the railroad tracks as best I could, but the
snow prevented me from seeing much. Just as I was going to
stop last night and get some rest, I paused at the top of a butte
and saw lights in the distance. If there was a posse following
me, and it sure looked like there was, I couldn't stop.

Continuing on through the night had been hazardous,
and, more times than I wanted, we'd stumbled and nearly
gone down in the half-moon light. If Rufus broke a leg, I was
doomed. Now, tired to the bone, I knew I had no choice but to
rest, and so did Rufus. We were both ready to drop.

As dawn broke, I found higher ground, so I had a view of
anyone coming. There had been no more lights for the last
few hours. I unsaddled Rufus. That was dangerous, because
I'd be slow to get going if I needed to, but the gelding needed
the break, too. I rubbed him down and gave him water and a

handful of oats, and then I hobbled him so he couldn't wander far. I lay my head down on the saddle, pulled the fur-lined cloak around me, and immediately fell asleep.

I jerked awake, the sun on my face. Rufus stood over me, munching on some dry winter grass. The horse looked at me as if to say, "Let's get going, woman." He was likely right. I stood up and staggered a few steps. My body ached like I'd been trampled by buffalo during the night. I took care of business, saddled Rufus, and rummaged through my sacks of food. Eddie had given me apples and oranges and loaves of bread, among other things, and I tore off half a loaf and wolfed it down. I wished I had binoculars so I could see farther, but my initial gaze down into the valley below showed no movement, nor any glimpses of sun reflecting off metal. That said, I didn't think they'd given up so soon. Wyatt Earp seemed the determined sort. Maybe they'd veered off, or camped the night before and were far behind, which could be.

I pulled my hat brim down to reduce the snow glare, which dazzled in the winter sunlight. I was still in the river flatlands, but the country was made up of rolling hills littered with rocks, small and large. Once out here, I found it nowhere near as flat as I'd thought. South of me, I saw the sun winking off the water of the river, and almost like I'd planned it, the whistle of a train headed east, where I wanted to be. Matthias had taught me how to navigate with stars, sun, and moon, but with the snow I'd been riding blind—in more ways than one. I turned Rufus in the same direction as the train, and we set off, the only sound the creak of saddle leather.

Traveling in daylight was much preferable, in some ways, and certainly safer. I estimated it was around noon, which made me a little nervous. I'd slept too long, and, if there was a posse, I was sure they hadn't. I pushed Rufus as hard as I dared, but, by nightfall, he was balking, and I couldn't blame him. We stopped, and I fed him some oats and water, but we pressed onward. The moon was up, and neither of us was as tired as before. I wanted more miles between us and Dodge.

Sometime around midnight, by my estimate, we stopped at an empty, broken-down cabin. I unsaddled and hobbled Rufus and threw my cloak onto an iron bedstead, the slats half broke but holding, and fell asleep again, determined to wake by dawn. I hadn't taken off the Colt since we started and didn't see any reason to start now. Maybe if I rolled over on it, which I had a tendency to do before morning, I'd wake up in time.

It wasn't the gun that woke me up, it was the cold. *Christ Jesus*, I thought. *I can't feel my toes.* I wasn't much of a swearer, but growing up with Leland I certainly knew curses, and, in the last few days, I'd taken it up myself, both mentally and chatting with Rufus, who didn't seem to mind. I rather liked it. *Chastity*, I said to myself, *you're becoming a new woman* …and I laughed out loud.

I took off my boots and rubbed my feet with snow, along with my face. I changed my socks and thought longingly of hot coffee. I didn't dare light a fire, not yet. We had miles to go before that would be possible. Maybe I was being too cautious, but I had a sense that wasn't necessarily true. I felt shaky, so I found some jerky in Molly's provisions sack and chewed on that, an orange, an apple, and more bread, and I felt better. Hot food seemed a distant memory. I thank Matthias for his years of teaching me woodcraft and gifting me with the ideal of Mohawk stoicism. You do what you have to do.

We rode on. I hadn't formulated a plan, except to just get out of Dodge and follow the railroad east and north. I had enough money to buy a train ticket and leave Kansas alto-gether at some point, which was my wish. Once I was home, Leland would get me a lawyer, and we'd figure out how to get out of the mess I'd made. It had been self defense, and maybe, in a more civilized part of the country, they'd under-stand that. Perhaps the fact that I'd had to stab the bastard had made people squeamish, but I'd worked with what I had and what I knew. Had I not done exactly that, Duane Olson would have shot me dead. If I felt remorse about anything, it was not telling Charlie Bassett about him earlier.

By late afternoon, there were still no signs of pursuit. I couldn't be complacent, but maybe I could stop for most of the night. Rufus and I could both use a longer rest. I asked the horse what he thought, and the twitch of his ears convinced me. Up ahead a mile or two, I saw the bare tops of cotton-wood trees, so maybe I'd find water nearby—if it wasn't frozen solid.

We crested a low hill and came upon the grove of trees. It looked as though I wasn't the first traveler to camp here, as there were the remains of more than one campfire ringed with small stones. I drew Rufus to a halt and gazed around but saw no sign of anyone. The wind, which picked up around twilight, rustled the naked branches of the trees like the rattling of bones. Rufus crow-hopped, clearly uncomfortable. We waited a few minutes but didn't sense anything else, so I dismounted, holding on to the reins.

Rufus's eyes rolled just as I heard a soft moan, and he pulled sharply, nearly knocking me over. I settled him, but I was just as nervous. What had made that sound? A wounded animal or a human? Either one could be just as dangerous. I tied Rufus to the trunk of a cottonwood and pulled the Colt from its holster. Maybe the smart course would be to ride on, but I liked the look of this place, and, besides, whatever was here, I didn't want it behind me.

It didn't take me long to find him. At first I thought it was a pile of old clothes, but then a hand twitched where it lay in the trampled snow and brush. A young man, the whiskers downy on his cheeks, was covered in dried blood from a wound on his head. He groaned, and his eyelids fluttered open in alarm as I approached, my boots crackling in the brush. I knelt down and put my hand on his shoulder.

"It's all right," I said. "I'm not going to hurt you."

I needed to work fast while there was daylight, since I still wasn't comfortable with a fire. I dragged him up against a tree and retrieved Rufus. There was indeed a small creek, not yet completely frozen over. I brushed his long, blond hair aside and cleaned out his head wound, which looked worse than it was, a bullet graze along the left side of his skull. The wonderful Eddie had included a bottle of whiskey, and I poured a little onto the gash and bound it up with a strip from the bottom of my shirt. He twitched a bit during my ministrations but subsided back into unconsciousness by the time I finished. I covered him with a blanket and sat back on my heels and watched him, but he slept on. I made camp, such as it was, hobbled Rufus, chewed on some jerky, and, in spite of myself, fell asleep.

It was full dark when I woke. Pale moonlight still filtered through the cottonwood branches, ghostly stripes of black and grey. I could hear him breathing, and when I looked up, his eyes were open, gleaming in the shadows.

"Thank you, mister." His voice was low-pitched, soft with a Southern accent. "I was about done in there."

I answered, trying to keep my own voice as deep as I could. "You're welcome. Feel up to telling me how you got here?"

He tried to laugh, but it came out a wincing groan. "That's a long story. You got any water?"

I handed him the canteen. He took a long drink and sat back, grimacing as his back touched the bark. I'd noticed the bruises and cuts on his torso when I'd checked him over for wounds. Someone had beaten him badly—and left him for dead, from the looks of it.

"No wood around here?" He nodded towards the cold fire ring. "It's damn cold."

"That's a long story, too. Why don't we start with yours?" I handed him a hunk of bread. "What's your name?"

"James Beauregard Durant," he said, "but folks call me Beau."

I chuckled. "I can see why. That's quite a mouthful."

"My mama named me after the greatest general in the war. His place was only five miles from ours in St. Bernard Parish. 'Course it was a mite bigger 'n' all."

"You're a long way from home, Beau."

"That's the long story," he said, chewing on the bread, which was none too soft now.

He grew up outside New Orleans, the youngest son of a farmer, he said. His father and brothers were killed in the Civil War, and for years his mother had struggled to keep the farm going, but, by the time he was eighteen, she'd died of consumption, and the bank had taken the farm. Beau headed north, planning to live with his mother's sister in Kansas City, but he never got that far. He was passing through Tulsa, Oklahoma, one afternoon when three men paid him five dollars to hold their horses while they did some banking. Beau gave his croaking, painful laugh.

"They did some bankin', all right. They robbed the place, and, when they come out, I had to ride away with 'em, since the sheriff already thought I was part of it." He shook his head. "They shot a man in that bank, and from then on, I was stuck with the bastards. They made me take a share of the money so's they could say I was in on it, too, and told me straight out they'd kill me if I left. So I stayed. I figured I'd find a way out as time went on, but I never did, with one thing and another.

"It's the Ridley brothers: Tom, Ed, and Whitey. You probably heard of 'em. We'd go into some town, where they'd get drunk and go with some whores, and after the first few times, they made sure I did the same. We robbed us more banks here and there, a few stagecoaches, even a train once, but that didn't go too well, and Tom got shot. We had to hole up at a ranch, and, when we left, they killed the rancher and his wife so they couldn't identify us."

He paused again and looked at me. "I'm a bad person, mister, and a coward, but I'm no killer. I hate those men for a lot of things they did, but they was good to me in some ways, too. But that rancher and what they did to his wife, that was it for me, and I told them so. That was three days ago and 'bout the worst mistake I made yet. They was going to hang me, but they couldn't find a big enough tree limb." He glanced up at the spindly cottonwood branches. "So they beat the hell outta me and thought they shot me dead. Tom always had bad aim, but since he lost his eye in a train robbery, it's been worse. He's the best shot of the three, and maybe he knew he hadn't killed me dead, but I don't know. I do know if you hadn't come along last night, I'd likely not be seeing another sunrise. So I thank you, and I hope you don't think I'm a reprobate, no good, 'cause I never meant to be." He pronounced it "ree-probit," and I smiled, knowing he couldn't see me in the dark. Southerners.

He finished his story and leaned back, exhausted, his eyes closed. I pulled the blanket up around him and patted his shoulder. There'd be plenty of time for my long story. Poor Beau. He might not be a killer, but he was with one now. I'd have to see how he felt about that and just how bad a person he really was.

* * *

MORNING LIGHT WASN'T KIND to any of us but was more honest, at least in my case. Beau's face was swollen and bruised, and even Rufus looked dirty and sore, which he was. I pinned and stuffed my hair more carefully under my hat and rubbed some soot from the old campfire ashes on my face. We washed up as best we could, and set out. Beau swung up behind me, as there was little choice, and he needed the body warmth. I had to move faster than he could walk, and I doubted he could walk far anyway. Rufus was a big horse, and, once again, I was grateful I hadn't taken Bella as my fugitive equine partner.

There was no question we needed to find more shelter than bare trees, and we both needed warmth and hot food. I had no idea what towns might lie ahead or how far they were, so I asked Beau. Maybe picking up a stray would be useful, after all.

"There's that ranch we was at," he said, his breath warm on my neck. "But it's got some dead bodies we'd hafta move."

That didn't sound particularly appealing. On the other hand, it was a house, and it likely had a stove. That did sound appealing. I shifted my sore butt in the saddle.

"Got a barn?"

"Yep. It's about fifteen miles north of here."

"Any chance your old friends would've doubled back?" That I didn't need. Besides, I wasn't sure how much I trusted Beau yet.

"I surely do not think so, mister. They said they was headed to Texas."

They wouldn't expect me to head north, and the sound of shelter was appealing. Following his somewhat sketchy directions, we rode through the day, and, just as I was beginning to think he had no idea where we were going, I saw a couple of buildings not far ahead.

I nudged him awake. His head had fallen onto my neck, and he was snoring softly. "That it?"

"I think so. I'll know for sure when we get closer. A lot of these farms look the same to me."

We got closer, and he decided it was the same place. It consisted of a small clapboard house, a ramshackle shed that Beau said was the barn, and a corral with a mule standing forlornly inside. The front door of the house hung open, not a good sign, but I didn't see any bodies yet.

I tied Rufus up to a corral post, and we approached the house. The smell hit us before we got to the open door, but had it been summer, it would have been much worse. As it was, we pulled our shirts over our mouths and noses and went in. The farmer and his wife lay beside a wooden table, both shot in the head. It was quite sad, the poor man in his linsey trousers and shirt and her in her calico dress, the toes of her worn boots sticking up like small signposts, but we had no time for mourning. We dragged the bodies out into the yard and stood there, looking at each other. It was pretty awful, and neither of us was sure what to do next. It would be dark soon, and I didn't want to waste the light digging graves. I didn't know exactly how to go about that or even if we had a shovel. Beau's eyes didn't seem to be focusing well. He was staggering, so I got him into the house and sat him down on a chair.

"Stay here. I'll see what I can find out there and take care of Rufus and the mule. When you feel up to it, look around and see if there's any food they didn't take."

He nodded, and I went outside, drawing a deep breath of fresh air. I hoped the small cabin aired out before we had to sleep in it tonight. I found some hay in the shed, unsaddled Rufus, and filled the water trough from a pump in the yard. I rubbed Rufus down and gave him the last of the oats. I'd come to love this bighearted, strong horse, and I told him so. There was a chicken coop with four hens, and I gathered up half a dozen eggs. By the time I finished that and hauled my saddlebags inside, Beau had lit a lantern and was foraging in the cupboards. So far, a half bag of flour and a canister with some sugar sat on the table.

I was so hungry, my stomach felt hollow, and I knew Beau must be starved, too, even groggy as he was. He'd even started a fire in the woodstove and put water on to boil. What for, I wasn't sure, but it looked like a good idea. If I was deficient in anything, it was cooking. The closest I'd ever come was carving slices of a cold roast chicken or cutting up an apple. Now might prove the time to learn.

Beau plopped down a cast-iron skillet on the woodstove and looked at me over his shoulder. "I can make us some biscuits, I reckon."

That sounded pretty good to me. I rummaged through the sacks from Molly and Eddie. We had three oranges, two apples, the remnants of jerky, and some very stale bread. There was also a small sack of cornmeal, and one of beans— hard little things. I didn't know how to deal with those. I showed Beau, and he promptly dumped them into the boiling water with pieces of an onion he'd found. *Well, all right then,* I thought. *Maybe the guy can cook.* I put the eggs in a bowl and sat down in the other wooden chair.

I watched him mix flour, sugar, and water and make little cakes out of the resultant mess, placing them into the skillet.

"We can start with these. Them beans'll take some time."

Starting with anything warm sounded like heaven to me. I took off my boots and sighed with pleasure. The niggling dread that had been hovering over me for days finally moved to the back of my mind. Smoke from a stovepipe was one thing, especially after dark, while an open fire was another. We needed to get warm, eat, sleep, and heal both our minds and Beau's body. Tomorrow we'd figure things out. Tonight was for us.

I set the whiskey bottle on the table, and Beau looked over from where he was frying his biscuits. He grinned, the bandage askew on his head and a shock of corn-colored hair falling across his brow.

"Hell yes, mister."

I smiled a little. "Name's Charlie. Charlie Birdsong. Nice to meet you, Beau."

I figured he'd told me some of the truth, along with some whopping lies. I could match him there in spades. We might get on. I planned to sleep with my guns anyway.

* * *

THE COMBINATION OF WARMTH, hot food, and sheer exhaustion was a potent sleep-inducing elixir, and I woke up in the morning on the unfortunate farmer's rustling mattress in the same position I'd started in. I looked over and saw Beau curled up in blankets beside the woodstove, still sound asleep.

I crept around him, carrying my boots out onto the porch, and sat down on the side of the porch to lace up my boots. It was another sunny day, clouds scudding through a blue sky, and quiet as could be. As far as I could see, there was no sign of life or, more importantly, pursuit. I took deep breaths of the fresh air, relieved to be out of the stagnant cabin, which was still faintly redolent of the poor dead farmer and his wife, in spite of our cooking the night before. I stopped myself from glancing their way and instead made for the shed to see Rufus.

He snorted at my approach and pranced a bit, and I went into the corral and put my arms around his neck. The mule looked better but kept his distance at the far side. I stood there, my cheek against the coarse hair of Rufus's neck and the wonderful familiar smell of horse that reminded me of home. For some reason, I began to cry. Great, grinding, soul-wrenching sobs came out of me, and the horse stood very still, as though he knew I needed him for release and solace.

Once the dam I'd so carefully constructed broke, I couldn't seem to stop. I cried for dreams shattered, promises unfulfilled, for disappointment, and for my own naiveté, pride, and impulsive temper, which had landed me here in this place at this moment. For pain, hurt, anger, and innocence lost to violence. I even shed a tear for poor, stupid Duane Olson. It hadn't had to end like that for him, if only I'd been wiser, or he had been. But that was the last tear, and my remorse only lasted as long as that tear took to fall down my cheek.

Leland had always taught me that we learn from our mistakes, not our successes, and he was right. This particular mistake had almost cost me my life, and it still could, but I was wiser now, along with something else that bothered me a little but had been firmly planted that night in the schoolhouse and was growing like a noxious weed.

Ruthlessness.

The wind was cold, drying the tears on my cheeks. Rufus chuffed, and I turned my head. Beau stood on the porch, watching me. I wasn't sure how long he'd been there, but it didn't really matter to me in my newfound clarity. If I could trust him, fine. If not, well, that would be unfortunate.

"Mornin', Mr. Birdsong."

"Morning to you, Beau. You got any ideas for breakfast?"

He grinned and went back inside the cabin. I threw out some hay and followed him in. He mixed up more biscuits, which weren't half bad, and scrambled the eggs I'd brought in the night before. We ate at the table, and, when we finished, I sat back and took a good look at him. He was pale, and sweat beaded his forehead.

"How you feeling, Beau?"

He smiled wanly. "I'm all right. Just a little dizzy is all. Maybe if I slept some."

With that, he toppled off the chair onto the floor. I pulled him over to the bedstead and got him on it, lifting his legs last. He breathed shallowly, but he was breathing. I covered him with the quilts on the bed. I wasn't sure what to do. This seemed like more than the graze on his head, but I was no doctor. I didn't need this, not when I was in a hurry to get further east. I cleaned up the pan and dishes, went back to the bed, and stood over him.

Maybe I hadn't looked close enough in the dark. I pulled back the quilts and unbuttoned his shirt, exposing the same bruises and minor cuts I'd noticed before. I pushed him over to get a better look at his back and gasped. On his lower back, a stab wound, oozing pus, gaped open. *Christ Jesus.*

You can do this, I told myself as I put a pan of water on to boil. They always did that when cleaning a wound, or was that childbirth? I didn't know. Still, hot water wouldn't hurt. I found an old shirt in a trunk at the foot of the bed, tore it into strips, and made a rag with the rest.

Waiting for the water to boil, I tried to remember the Indian remedies Matthias had used now and then around the farm, but all I could recall was moss, and there wasn't any of that around. I rummaged through the cupboards and drawers and found a needle and thread. When steam rose from the pot, I dipped a knife in and went to work. I scraped out the wound, cleaned it using hot water and a rag, and dribbled whiskey on it. Beau moaned throughout my ministrations, so, before I started to stitch, I gave him a healthy slug of whiskey, too. I put six stitches through the skin on the sides of the cut and drew it closed. He yelped but let me do it. After I wrapped the bandages around him, he fell back asleep, thankfully. We weren't going anywhere this day or those clumsy stitches would rip right back open. I covered him with a quilt and went out to the porch.

It was cold. Clear and sunny, but who knew how long that would last? I put an old sheet over the bodies, as the ground was too hard to dig a grave, and silently asked their forgiveness. Rufus and the mule were getting along in the small corral, and I was sure the horse was enjoying his respite. I looked through the tools hanging in the shed and took some snares, along with an ax. I was still reluctant to try hunting, worried a shot or two would alert someone to our presence. Still, we were nearly out of food. I looked over at the chicken coop.

The ax came in handy. I'd never killed a chicken before, but it was somewhat like field dressing a deer, and, after dunking the bird in a pot of boiling water like I'd seen Hilda do a hundred times at Harrowhill, I spent an hour plucking the damned thing. I went through every cupboard in the kitchen, thoroughly this time, and found old potatoes, turnips, and onions, and put some in a pot with the chicken to boil. There were jars of green beans, tomatoes, and other vegetables as well in a cellar underneath a trapdoor beside the bed. Apparently, murdering bank robbers weren't very interested in looking for provisions, which was good for us.

We weren't going to starve, at least, but I was edgy about staying too long. I tried to put that thought aside since there wasn't much choice, what with Beau in the shape he was. And a day or two of rest wouldn't hurt Rufus or me. I'd thought about leaving him; after all, he wasn't my problem, and he had food and the mule to take him somewhere. Somehow, I couldn't. Ruthless or not, I still had a conscience, and I thought of that old Chinese proverb that said if you save a life, then you're responsible for that life. I'm not sure that's how it went, but it's how it felt to me.

With Beau unconscious still into the afternoon, I warmed more water and took a bath of sorts, washing off the dirt and sweat of the last few days. I bound my hair up securely under the hat and put on another shirt I'd brought along. The cotton felt soft against my clean skin, and I sat at the kitchen table and put my feet up.

"Mr. Birdsong?"

I jerked awake, the chair legs hitting the floor and my boots following a second later. It was near dark, and I peered across the room. "Yeah?"

"That surely does smell good," Beau said from where he lay on the bed. "Is that chicken?"

CHAPTER 13

*J*n the end, we stayed three more days at the farm. My skills with the ax improved, although we both got pretty tired of chicken. Beau's fever broke, and his wound was healing, and I decided we couldn't risk another day of staying in one place. In this case, good things do not necessarily come to those who wait—and we were out of food, anyway. We decided to leave at dawn. I fried the last two chickens. We ate one for dinner, and I packed the other in my saddlebags, considerably lighter than they were. We'd picked the place pretty clean, even packing the last jars of vegetables.

I'd found one of the Shakespeare books I'd ordered for the school in the bottom of Molly's sack, with a note inside: "Goodbye, Miss James. I hope you are safe. I love you. Liam." I stuffed the note in my pocket and went outside so Beau wouldn't see the tear that slid from my eye.

"I love you, too, Liam Clarke," I whispered to the wind. I loved that whole wonderful family, and, without their help, I wouldn't be here. I'd never had a good woman friend before, but Molly Clarke would hold first place in that category forever. I smiled, remembering Thanksgiving and how I'd told them all stories of Harrowhill and the horses, and the legendary Christmas party Leland hosted every year, where it seemed everyone in the county showed up wearing their finery, many staying until morning. Maybe I'd celebrate Christmas this year at Harrowhill, instead of running for my life. It was likely far past the new year already, but I hadn't been keeping track. I took a deep breath and went back inside.

"What you got there?" Beau asked. "I surely would like to read a book myself. Haven't had one around in a long while. The Ridleys weren't readers."

"It's Shakespeare," I said, and I tossed it to him. "You know it?"

He didn't answer but grabbed the book eagerly and opened it, a big smile on his face. "Yessir, I do. My mama read us this and the Bible near every night."

"*Well, well,* I thought. Mr. Beau Durant wasn't quite the ignorant dirt farmer he'd portrayed himself to be. I went back to packing and watched him from the corner of my eye. He was absorbed, reading intently and not moving his lips, as so many poorly educated people did. He had a faint smile on his face.

I'd been watching him closely for a while now. He'd slept a good part of the last two days. Food and rest had done wonders, and he looked much less gaunt, with normal color back in his face. In spite of myself, I had to admit it was a very attractive face, too: square jaw, high cheekbones, and bright-green eyes, now clear and steady. I hoped he hadn't been observing my whiskerless face as closely as I had his but dismissed the thought. The light was dim in here, and he'd not been awake that much. With that thought in mind, I neared the bed.

"Sit up and turn around, Beau," I said. "Let's take a last look at that cut."

He complied, and I unwrapped the makeshift bandage. It was red around the stitches, but they were holding, and there was no infection that I could see. I thought it best to leave it alone, so I rewrapped it with pieces of the last sheet I'd found in the trunk.

"Looks all right. How's it feel?" I stood up, and he turned around quickly, so I did, too.

"It's sore, but not like before." He touched my sleeve. "Thanks. You been kind to me, and I appreciate it. Hadn't been for you, I'd be dead."

I shrugged. "Couldn't leave you out there, could I?"

"Some folks would. Some did."

"Well," I said. "I'm not some folks." I moved away, back to the kitchen area. "You ready to ride tomorrow? I found a saddle for that mule. We might as well take him; he'll just die here if we leave him." Like the chickens would have, sooner or later.

"Sure." He waited a beat. "So, are we partners? Riding together and all?"

I chuckled a little. "Well, we haven't come too far, but I guess so. You have any idea where in hell we are? You been around this territory for a while now."

I sat down at the table, pulling my hat lower, my chin sunk into my collar.

Beau ambled over and sat down across from me. "Last town I was in was Hutchinson. The Ridleys were thinkin' about robbing the general store there, but we rode out. We went east for a day after that." He sat back, rubbing his hand over his chin. "As I recall, there's a town called Newton and another one good size, Florence. If we follow the railroad, we'll find 'em."

"All right," I said. "Any idea how far to Topeka or St. Joseph?" I recalled Topeka was the first large town on the railroad once we'd crossed into Kansas, and St. Joseph was on the border itself. I didn't want to chance buying a ticket in a small town and getting stopped by some local sheriff on the lookout, or a railroad detective. Even though I was disguised as Charlie Birdsong, it wouldn't take much to look closely at my face and match it up to a wanted poster, if such was out there. As much as I wanted the comfort of a train, it could be a nasty trap if anyone recognized me, sitting there mile after mile. I wanted to be closer to the border and surrounded by more people before I got on one.

Beau stared at me. "Topeka and St. Joe are a long ways off, days of ridin'." He looked down, choosing his words carefully. "Pardon me, mister, but you're an odd one, not that I'm complaining. It's not often you run across a man that doesn't know where he's at, or where he's goin', is all."

I wished at that moment I'd never said a word, just gotten on Rufus and ridden blindly east. "Yeah, see, I came west on a train, and I was sick for most of the trip. I'm from Canada, came to do some business in, uh, Medicine Lodge, but ran into some issues, so I decided to call it quits." I knew there were no railroads south of the Atcheson, so that sounded credible. "Just trying to get back to the train and go home. Didn't figure I'd need a map, and that was my mistake." I gave a dry chuckle for credibility, but it sounded phony even to me.

"Hmm," said Beau. He didn't seem convinced.

For the next few minutes the only sound was the wind outside. It was picking up, and I hoped it wouldn't snow before we were away from here. I'd gotten complacent, believing I'd fooled him, and he wasn't a threat to me. That was a mistake, clearly.

"I think you're on the run. I don't mind, but I might could be of some help if you told me the truth." Beau's voice was soft. "For starters, you could take off your hat. I know you're a woman."

There it was.

I thought I'd been so clever. Who wears a hat night and day in a house? Stupid Chastity James, apparently thinking she's pulled the wool over this country boy's eyes. I sighed and took off the hat, which I'd truly come to hate, and my hair fell down around my shoulders. I also took off my heavy coat, as I'd been sweltering in the thing for days with the woodstove burning. I likely stunk like a goat.

"Satisfied?" I said.

Beau smiled in appreciation. "No, but I bet you feel better. You could use a bath, though."

Then he started to laugh, shook his head, and laughed harder. It was infectious, and I couldn't help myself once I caught his eye. I laughed like a hyena, too, neither of us stopping until we were breathless. It felt good—in fact, the best release I've ever experienced. I'd been so tense, so scared for so long, taking off the coat and hat felt like taking off a mask that hid me from the world, shielding and suffocating me at the same time. My hand went to the Colt on my leg, but I didn't think I'd need it, at least not for a while.

I put the whiskey on the table after taking a long pull, and Beau followed my lead.

"You're her, the schoolteacher," he said. "Has to be."

"How could you know that?"

"Me and the Ridleys was in Hutchinson, like I said. News like that travels fast out here. Everybody in town was talking about this crazy Dodge City schoolteacher gutting some guy and how they planned to hang her." He shrugged. "Me, I figured you must've had good reason. Schoolteachers don't just go around killin' people. Then, the day we left Hutchinson, sheriff got a wire sayin' you'd escaped. There's likely wanted posters up by now."

We both took another drink. That wasn't good news.

"You want to tell me what happened?"

"Why not?" I said. "It's an old story, only the outcome changed this time."

So I told him all of it, leaving out Kate and Molly, of course, and that I had any money on me to speak of. It didn't take too long, really, but the whiskey bottle was half empty by the time I finished. I fell silent, the only sound the snap of wood burning in the stove.

Beau reached his hand across the table, motioning with his fingers, and I put mine in his. "You hadn't stopped for me, you'd likely be in Topeka by now, Chastity."

"I know that."

"I owe you, and I pay my debts. I also believe every word you told me." He squeezed my hand, and I looked at him. His face was set, eyes intense. "When I was eight years old, some Union soldiers come by and raped my mama right on our front porch one afternoon. I hid behind some cornstalks like she told me when she saw them comin', 'cause she knew they'd kill me if I did anything else." He angrily wiped a tear from his eye. "She died that day, but it took ten years 'fore it was over. There was nothin' I could do to help her then or ever. I swore if I ever saw those men again, I'd kill them where they stood, but 'course I never have. Still, a man who would do that to any woman deserves killin', and I'm proud you killed the bastard did it to you."

"God, Beau, I'm sorry." I squeezed his hand and gently disengaged from his grip. "Thank you for believing me. You still want to ride with me, now that you know who I am?"

He smiled. "'Course. I've known who you were since the second day. I was just waitin' to see if you'd tell me and not shoot me."

"I thought about it for a second there." I laughed.

He didn't. "I know; I saw your hand on the gun."

We stared at each other for a long second, and then I reached over and kissed his cheek. It startled him, and I wasn't really sure why I did it, only that I wanted to. "We have to trust each other if we're going to go on, Beau. Maybe you should tell me all the truth, too."

He looked down at the table. "I rode with the Ridleys after a while because I kinda liked it. It was excitin', and the money was good, no doubt about that. For the first time in a long time, I had a good horse, a gun, some clothes that fit me, even boots." He stuck his leg up. They were indeed nice boots, all that they'd left him. "I coulda got away a lot of times, but I didn't. You knew that, didn't you?"

I nodded. "What did it really take?"

He gestured around the cabin. "This. That poor damn farmer and his wife. Killin' people for no reason 'cept meanness; I can't abide that. That's not who I am, and I don't ever want to ride with people who'd do that. Them Ridleys are rotten through and through, but I was lazy and took too long to figure that out."

"Well, you learned something, didn't you? Don't tell people what you're going to do; just do it and get on with it. My father says we learn from our mistakes. I did, and I expect now you have, too."

I traced my fingertips over the old pine boards. Then I held out my hand. "So, I got a train to catch. James Beauregard Durant, are we riding out of here together in the morning?"

Beau grinned and shook my hand. "Yes, Chastity James, we are."

As I fell asleep on my delineated half of the bed while Beau snored beside me, I thought about what I'd told him. Just do it and get on with it. I'd taken the bullets out of the rifle, though. I'd learned from my mistakes.

CHAPTER 14

*W*e rode into Newton in a snowstorm. It was a sad little town, shabby in the dusk. Only a few people were out, likely because of the storm. I tied my hair back up under my hat, then went inside the building with a hotel sign on it, secured a room for the night, and got directions to a stable for our mounts. Beau hadn't complained about his, but the mule was about done in. Rufus was happy to see oats, which I paid extra for, and they were both munching contentedly when Beau and I went back to the hotel. There was a restaurant—more like a couple of tables and scattered chairs, but we ordered the beef stew, and it was surprisingly good, especially after days of my amateur chicken butchering and cooking.

We went up to our room, and Beau grinned and raised his eyebrows when I said there was only one. He sure was healing fast.

"It's not love, Beau. It's expediency." I didn't bother to mention it was also about trust, but I think he knew that. Chastity James was a suspicious woman, and she'd earned the right to be.

I'd asked for hot water, and a tin tub had been filled while we ate dinner. I went first, peeling off the clothes I'd worn for some days behind a screen while Beau lit up a cheroot I'd purchased for him in the restaurant. I sank into the warm water with a sigh of bliss, and Beau chuckled on the other side of the screen.

"Feels mighty good, eh?"

"Ahh, God, yes."

I scrubbed my skin with the hotel's rough cloth and soap, and I washed my hair, rinsing it with the ewer of water thoughtfully provided. I wrapped myself in a towel and, for the first time in a while, felt like myself again.

"All yours; sorry for the seconds. We can call down for more, but it'll take a while."

Beau shook his head and tore off his shirt. "I'm fine with damn near anything at this point, Chas." He'd taken to calling me that, and I didn't mind, since I was still Charlie Birdsong to anyone else. He disappeared behind the screen, and I stifled a laugh at the sighs and splashes as I got dressed in the same clothes I'd worn to get here. Maybe tomorrow we'd go shopping for something new, if all went well.

The next morning, we woke up at the same time, in the same bed, and Beau's hand clasped in mine. I quickly removed my hand.

"Mornin', partner." He smiled.

"Morning to you. I'm hungry. I might be hungry for a long time, but at least here somebody else is cooking, and it's edible in comparison to mine."

Downstairs, we ate eggs, bacon, and potatoes as we watched the sun rise over Newton. It didn't improve it much. I asked the waiter/cook where the general store was, and he pointed down the street.

We bought Beau a hat, and both of us new shirts and pants. I could hardly wait to put them on, so I didn't. I changed behind a makeshift curtain at the store, and Beau did the same. Then we stuffed our old clothes into a barrel outside. Next, we went to the gunsmith's. I bought Beau a Colt .45 like mine, along with a belt and holster, and we re-supplied bullets. My money was dwindling rapidly, but I still had enough for a train ticket and then some.

"Good to know we don't have to rob a bank or a stage-coach, Chas."

"Well, not for a while, if everything goes according to plan," I said. "Hopefully we'll get to Topeka before we need to do that."

We left Newton around noon, supplied and rested. Nobody had questioned us or even seemed to notice we were in town. I saw no lawmen or wanted posters, but then, it was a very small town. I traded the mule and fifty dollars for a horse at the livery, and Beau was ecstatic. He immediately named the mare Belle and whispered in her ear. She flicked her ears and seemed to understand every word.

"Chas, I can't thank you enough for this." His grin was thanks enough, and my own grin was just as big as we left town, saddlebags full and hopes high.

* * *

WE CAMPED THAT NIGHT, and, for the first time, I allowed a fire. Beau kept looking around as though he expected bogeymen to be out there in the dark, and I felt close to the same way, but I kept it to myself. Wyatt Earp was the only bogeyman I was worried about, but Beau had a gallery to choose from, not the least of which were the Ridleys. They worried me some as well, but frostbite was a bigger danger than any of them.

We slept uneasily and were up and riding as dawn broke— and we rode hard. Around noon, we passed a caravan of colorful wagons on the road. We waved at the travelers. They were a friendly bunch, waving and laughing as we went by. One wagon was emblazoned with a painted sign that read

Professor DeMonte Traveling Medicine Show, Curiosities, and Theatrical Marvels. I laughed when I read it. Professor DeMonte seemed a man who valued diversity. If one thing didn't work out, there was always another. Good planning.

I wasn't looking forward to another night on the road, so, when we spied some lights south of the railroad, we crossed the tracks and rode into Cottonwood Falls, or so the crooked wooden sign proclaimed. There were no cottonwoods I could see, much less falls. If Newton was small, this place was minis-cule. We tied up our horses outside the lone saloon, which didn't have the dignity of a sign, and went inside. It was a barren place reeking of old beer and something much worse, with only a few tables and chairs. Two men sat quietly at one, and a lone drunk slept at another. Beau and I looked at each other and shrugged.

"Two whiskies," Beau said, and I plunked down two dollars on the grimy bar.

We drank in silence, and, when the saloonkeeper offered another, I shook my head.

"Anyplace around here to spend the night, for us and our horses?"

He jerked his head towards the door. "Livery, around the corner. If he's open."

We took the hint and led our horses down the next street towards a light in the open doorway of a barn.

"Hello," Beau called, and a man in a worn shirt and pants shambled out from the depths of the stable. "We could use a place for our horses, and maybe us, for the night."

The proprietor eyed us suspiciously. "Joe Parsons. That'll be five dollars, and you can sleep in the loft," he said, gesturing to a ladder on the back wall. "Plenty do."

Highway robbery, I thought, but grudgingly handed over the money. We took care of our horses and climbed up the ladder. There was enough hay for a semi-comfortable bed, and we rummaged in the saddlebags for biscuits and jerky, munching stoically as we stared at each other.

"Should've had another whiskey for this," Beau said. Then he laughed softly. "Or three."

I had to agree. "Tomorrow, Emporia. Then, the train. You ever thought of going east, Beau? Harrowhill could use a man like you."

He shrugged. "No, Chas, I never did. But then, my mama always said you need to be open to opportunity when it knocks at your door." He chewed on his jerky. "Seems to me you could be named Opportunity when it comes to me. If I hadn't met up with you, I could still be lyin' on that prairie, food for crows." He reached over and touched my cheek. I tried not to flinch, but he dropped his hand anyway.

"So, yeah. East sounds good." He smiled just before Joe blew out the lantern, and darkness enveloped us like a shroud. We ate the rest of our food, and I heard Beau lie down, sighing as he pulled a blanket over himself. I did just the same.

Morning came with cramped muscles and hunger pains. I brushed off the hay and nudged Beau, gathering up the saddlebags. I stepped down the ladder in the grey light and set to saddling Rufus while Beau followed. We rode out of town without seeing a single soul, even Joe Parsons, our erstwhile host, which was a good sign. The sun broke through the clouds as we rode northeast to Emporia. I'd started to get a bad feeling in Cottonwood Falls, and, the farther we got from that dismal town, the happier I was.

Mid-afternoon, I saw a church steeple in the distance. Hadn't seen one of those in a while, at least not one you could see from a distance. Churches weren't a high priority in Dodge, in height or value. I vaguely remembered Emporia as a pretty little town when I came through on the train, a treed oasis in the dusty prairie. Those trees were bare now, but I could see it was still a pretty little town as we rode closer.

"You been here before?" I said to Beau.

He grinned. "Well, kinda. We robbed a bank here, me and the Ridleys."

I think my mouth fell open a little, and I snapped it shut with an audible click of teeth. "What the hell, Beau?"

He had the grace to look somewhat contrite. "We wore bandannas, Chas. Nobody's gonna recognize me."

I pulled Rufus to a halt. "Goddamnit, Beau, that's not the point. Well, it kind of is, but the real point is, you lied to me."

He pulled the mare around to face me. "I never lied to you. I told you in the beginning I wasn't a good person, and I told you just the other night that I did some jobs with the Ridleys not because I had to, but because I'd come to like it. Don't you beat me with that now, or call me a liar." He was really angry, and so was I, clenching the reins in my hands because I wanted to punch him in the face. "I want to change my ways, Chastity James, and I took up with you in good faith. Do I call you a killer? I could, and you know it. We're both sinners, and we'll both pay for those sins, but not here and not now."

Beau hadn't said that much at one time since the night I dragged him out of the brush, and maybe not even then. He leaned on his saddle horn and stared at me. "If we don't truly start trustin' each other right now, we may as well call this partnership quits."

I stared back at him for a minute and then looked away. I felt a proper ass because he was right, damn him. I didn't trust him. I didn't trust anybody anymore, and I wasn't altogether sure I ever would again. But maybe it was time to try. Having someone to share all this had made it more bearable, and I didn't want to lose that camaraderie.

"I'm sorry, Beau."

"What? Speak up, Chas."

"I said I'm sorry. Don't push it too far. You can't imagine how hard it is for me to say that."

"All right, then." He turned his horse around and shook

his head. "You think I don't know how many times you thought about just shootin' me or leavin' me out there? I ain't stupid."

"Oh, I know that," I said. "But you've grown on me. Hell, I bought you a gun." I held out my hand. "Partners, no matter what?"

He shook it, and we rode on into Emporia, united in necessity, desperation, and something I wasn't ready to define, once again.

It was mid-afternoon, perhaps not the best time for outlaws (because that's what we were) to enter a bustling prairie town. But we looked just like anybody else on the main street, moving among the horses and wagons. People strode briskly on the sidewalks, women with baskets on their arms, men going about their business, stores and restaurants open for trade. This was a town primed with ambition, and it showed in every brick, pillar, and storefront. We passed the county sheriff's office and kept going, walking our horses sedately. As we passed the bank, a substantial red brick building, Beau grinned and nodded his head towards it.

Straight-faced, he said, "I remember the layout. Just in case."

I snorted and tried not to laugh. We watered the horses and tied up outside one of the general stores. Down the street, I saw the train depot. I had an urge to just go buy tickets to Chicago, but we'd need food, whether we were on the train or a horse.

We made our purchases and nonchalantly sauntered out to the horses. That's when I saw the two men who'd been drinking in the saloon the night before. They were standing in front of the sheriff's office, looking up and down the street. Before their eyes could land on us, I grabbed Beau's arm and dragged him back into the store.

"What the hell, Chas?"

"Shush. Look over there. You recognize those two men from the saloon in Cottonwood Falls last night?"

He stumbled into a rack of fabrics, caught himself, and peered out the window. "Yeah, I think I do. How'd they get here so fast?"

"We slept. I guess they didn't," I said. "I have a very bad feeling about those two."

As though I'd predicted it with my words, a man in a black hat joined them in front of the sheriff's office, and my heart sank like a stone.

"Christ Jesus," I said. "That's Wyatt Earp. He's after me, Beau. Only reason he'd be here."

Beau's hand on my arm steadied me, and I looked up into his clear, green eyes. "Chas, it's going to be all right. He hasn't seen us yet. We got to think this through."

The proprietor was eyeing us, seeing as we'd just left the store and had dodged back in. I managed a smile and sauntered back to the counter. "We were thinking maybe some of that honey you mentioned earlier would be a good addition," I said.

"It surely would," he beamed. When he went back to the storeroom to get a jar, I grabbed Beau's arm.

"Could you get the horses and take them around back?" I said. "I know he'll recognize me, hat or no. He's smart."

Beau snorted. "I ain't seen one of these lawmen that's much, so far. He won't notice you, Chas."

"Trust me, this one will." I pulled a black hat off the shelf and exchanged it for the white one on his head. "Just pray the others don't recognize you."

Beau shrugged and adjusted the hat. "They aren't after me, are they?"

Before the proprietor returned with the jar of honey in his hand, I dodged out the back, hiding behind the door. Beau went out the front door before the man noticed the hat on his head wasn't the one he'd come in with.

It didn't do us any good. Just as I saw Beau coming around the building with the horses, I was confronted by Wyatt Earp, his gun drawn, in the alley behind the general store. Beau's assessment, as I already knew, was way off the mark.

"Chastity James, put up your hands. Your running days are over." His Colt was pointed right at me. Was it "dead or alive" by now? It wasn't a pleasant thought.

I raised my hands, but before I could even blink, the marshal went down like a felled tree, gun still in his hand, hat skittering across the muddy snow. Beau grinned and held up his hands, palms out. Then I saw the horseshoe beside Earp's head.

I knelt down beside the marshal. "Christ Jesus, I hope you haven't killed him." I felt for a pulse, and there it was, strong and steady, although there was already a good-size lump on the side of his head. Looked to me like he'd survive. I was becoming fairly expert at assessing injuries. I vaulted into the saddle, and we came out onto the main street to find the two men from the saloon standing there, brandishing guns as well. Beau shot one in the leg, and I saw him go down. The other man foolishly fired off shots, missing us as we rode through town, dodging wagons, pedestrians, and other riders.

Once we were in the open, we galloped like a team of devils was behind us, and for all I knew, they were, even if a couple of their number were down for the moment. After half an hour, Beau pulled up and surveyed the road behind us.

"We have to find a place to hole up. There's nobody coming now, but they will be. We can't keep up this pace, and they'll have fresh horses."

I surveyed the landscape ahead of us. It was pretty bleak —prairie and rock hills rising haphazardly here and there, none of it looking likely for a hideout.

"I agree, but where?"

"Hell, Chas, I don't know," he said. "Just keep on the lookout for anything, all right?"

"Of course," I said, and we rode on, a mite slower, a pace at which we could talk a bit. "That was some fancy shooting back there, partner. Hope you didn't kill anybody, with a horseshoe or a bullet."

Beau shrugged. "There was nothin' else to do, either time. They'll be fine, leastways I hope so." He caught my eye. "You've got me in it now, Chas."

"I know," I said. "You could've left me back there, and I'm grateful."

"I will never leave you to somethin' like that," he said, his voice low. He pulled his hat brim down against the wind but not before I saw his eyes, intensely staring into mine. He turned his head, and the wind carried away his words. "Or nothin' else."

I almost missed the last part.

CHAPTER 15

*I*t got dark quickly this time of year, especially out on the prairie, and we hadn't found anywhere defensible or hidden enough to stop. We rode on into the full dark for a few miles until we saw the glow of a campfire, maybe more than one. We stopped beyond the circle of firelight and peered ahead. Wagons were pulled into a circle, and I recognized the traveling medicine show we'd seen before. I heard laughter and someone playing a guitar, singing "Greensleeves," and another voice joined in, harmonizing. The smell of roasting meat wafted through the camp, and my stomach growled.

I looked over at Beau. "They travel fast. I guess they didn't stop anywhere, even Emporia. What do you think? Should we go in?"

"They seem harmless enough," he said. "Besides, it smells mighty good."

"Oh, it is," said a deep voice very close by. "Stolen chickens always taste the best."

A tall, bearded man materialized beside Rufus's head, white teeth gleaming in his wide smile. "Come join us, travelers."

I glanced at Beau. Our choices were limited, but they seemed friendly enough, and, besides, I was hungry. We walked slowly into the campsite, following the bearded man. An interesting group of people wandered around in front of the painted wagons: some perched on stairs that folded down from the doors of their caravans; others who looked to be rehearsing lines of a play—*Macbeth*, if I wasn't mistaken; even a woman in a turban-style head wrap, shuffling cards, her sharp black eyes intent on us. Gypsies, I thought, but that wasn't all. A tall man in a top hat strode forward, lifted the hat, and bowed briefly, holding out his hand in an elegant gesture.

"Good evening and welcome to our humble camp, friends. Professor Julius DeMonte, at your service." His smile was warm, and his accent was very proper English. "Please, join us for dinner. We always have enough for guests." He gestured with the silver-handled cane in his left hand.

"Good evening to you, sir, and thank you," I said, shaking his hand. "Charlie Birdsong, and this is my partner, Beau Durant."

DeMonte shook Beau's hand as well and led us to a couple of empty stools on the other side of the fire. I had hardly settled my saddle-sore behind onto the stool when a pretty young woman smilingly handed me a tin plate of roast chicken and potatoes, and an identical one for Beau, before she skipped off into the shadows. We applied ourselves to the task at hand, and, within minutes, the food was a pleasant memory. I set the plate on the ground and took a good look around.

The wagons were painted in bright colored designs that ranged all over the map of art and occult symbols, from Egyptian symbols to spirals, eyes, and murals that looked like Shakespearean characters in scenes from *Julius Caesar* to *Romeo and Juliet*. I'd seen at least ten people, and likely more were inside a wagon or two. We had been thoroughly observed since we arrived, but discreetly so. Professor DeMonte sat down beside us.

"Thank you so much. The food was delicious and much appreciated," I said. "This is an amazing caravan you've got here. What exactly do you all do? Plays, music, fortune-telling, medicine?"

He chuckled. "Exactly that. We are entertainers, Mr. Birdsong. We do it all, bringing joy and enlightenment to the denizens of the frontier, especially in the small towns that are eager for distraction and a small sip of sophistication, elements of the cities many of them have left behind. We supply thrills, drama, comedy, dancing, music, even medicine, not to mention providing haven for those who are not always deemed suitable for polite society."

I smiled. "For only a slight fee, of course." I was beginning to understand the professor a little.

At this, he threw back his head and laughed. "You are an astute observer, Mr. Birdsong. I suspected as much the moment I saw you." He was a handsome man, his mane of long, white hair carefully tended, his clothing fashionable, if a bit travel worn. In fact, that was true of most of the people I'd seen here so far. But then, attractiveness was a necessity in a troupe of traveling players, along with charm and guile, and this group was well-endowed with all those attributes.

Beau hadn't said a word, but I knew he was assessing everything around us just as carefully as I had and was drawing his own conclusions.

I stood up and stretched. "I'm surprised you all weren't performing in Emporia this evening, Professor. Not on your itinerary?"

"We had to change our schedule, Mr. Birdsong. Saving our vitality for Topeka, which will be a three-night engagement for us." He shrugged. "Contingencies arose."

I wondered what had gone wrong in Emporia—but not for long.

144

He gazed at me, all traces of mirth gone from his expression. "It looks as though things didn't go as planned for you and your companion in Emporia either. Is there anything you'd like to unburden yourself of?"

"Not that I can think of, Professor."

He moved so quickly, I had no time to even reach for the Colt as he knocked my hat off with his cane. My hair tumbled down onto my shoulders, and Beau shot up off his stool like a jack-in-the-box, but a dark-haired man I hadn't seen before grabbed his arms from behind and sat him back down.

"Let us not be foolish, people," Julius DeMonte said. "We have things to discuss, and they cannot be tainted with violence of any sort." He bowed to me. "I apologize for the rudeness of my gesture, but sometimes I find it best to dispense with polite chitchat and arrive at the point, Chastity James."

Professor DeMonte was a well-informed man. I guess those wanted posters were definitely up. I glared at him, and he smiled, shaking his head.

"Don't be alarmed, Miss James. This entire debacle could have been avoided for both of us, but for Emporia, that pathetic little town trying to live up to its Grecian namesake. We have the same problem, I think, and its name is Wyatt Earp, a voraciously enthusiastic but not terribly bright lawman."

I couldn't help but smile, in spite of the circumstances. "He is that, all right."

"Indeed," said Julius DeMonte. "You see, Mr. Earp and I have a history, and he is eager to see me 'brought to justice,' as he terms it. A minor infraction in Dodge City involving what he deems fraud and public injury, which I rightly qualify as stupidity and loutish unreasonableness, but I am on the distaff side of the law, according to Mr. Earp." He waved his hand, dismissing Earp and his opinions. "Unfortunately, as we came to Emporia yesterday, so did the train from Dodge City, and since I never enter a town without sending an advance party to assess the mood and general circumstances, they were lucky enough to observe Mr. Earp disembark from that train."

Here he stopped and peered at me. "It seems he was on a mission to arrest a nefarious murderer and had been alerted to her possible presence, which my agent discovered in a conversation with two gentlemen outside the sheriff's office who were only too delighted to show them a wanted poster depicting this depraved woman. Since the local sheriff was in a zealous fervor and Emporia's a prim and proper, rather low-money place for us, we moved on quickly toward Topeka, where I have friends."

I looked about, and a quiet and curious crowd had gathered, sitting around the fire and listening to this tale. DeMonte pulled the poster from his pocket, unfolded it, and handed it to me.

"Well," I said. "That's a terrible likeness. I look like a deranged princess out of a fairy tale, or perhaps the ogre." I handed it back to him, and he threw it onto the fire, where it disintegrated into ash.

Julius DeMonte cocked his head, his eyes bright. "Would you care to enlighten us? We do love a good story. Tales of murder and revenge are our favorite fare, our stock in trade, so to speak." Murmurs of agreement came from the assembled players. "And what of your knight errant, the handsome Mr. Durant? He plays a part here we are eager to hear as well."

"It's hardly *Hamlet*," I said, "and I am loath to bore you."

He laughed, and more than a few chuckles rippled through our audience. "Oh, I assure you, we are not easily bored. Please proceed."

In for a penny, in for a pound once again, I thought. There wasn't a lot of choice, and lying was pointless. They were either going to help us or turn us in. I launched into my tale of an eager but naïve schoolmarm whose life had gone awry, eliciting a gasp or two when I recounted the night of Olson's killing, whether for my abused person or Olson's worthless life, I didn't know, but I hoped the former. Again, I left out Kate and Molly's names. When I got to where I found Beau, I glanced at him.

"You want to tell your part?"

He shrugged. "You mean how I got to be Sancho Panza, *mi capitan?*"

Julius DeMonte chuckled, and I barely stopped my jaw from dropping. The country boy had surprised me once again, and I felt a little curl of warmth that started in my belly and led to a flush on my cheeks. I was grateful for the flickering firelight because I could feel Julius's eyes on me.

Beau's story seemed to enthrall our audience as well, and when he told them of knocking Earp unconscious in the alley as he tried to take me into custody, nearly everyone laughed. "I didn't mean to hit him so hard, but that horseshoe was all I had to hand. Chas said he'd likely be fine, so we hightailed outta there."

Beau pushed his hat further back on his head and surveyed the group around the fire, including DeMonte. "Here's the thing, folks. Since we've been so entertaining for y'all, perhaps now we're entitled to some enlightenment, too. Are we ridin' out of here tonight, you turnin' us in, or are we auditionin' for a job?"

Bravo, I thought. My concerns exactly, and I couldn't have said it better. All eyes turned to Julius.

The man stood up and took off his top hat with a flourish and a bow. "My dear young people, I commend you both for your honesty as well as your style. You have the makings of fine careers treading the boards." He put his hands behind his back and waited a long beat before continuing, quite an actor himself.

"We knew you were coming. Mama Rosa saw it in the cards, so we talked it over before you arrived. We are short of hands at the moment, with three of our group having left for Deadwood, so we can use your assistance. What we needed was to see you and hear your stories, and that we have done. Frankly, I was curious to meet the schoolteacher who so forcefully took justice into her own hands, which I rather admire. From the lurid stories, I was expecting Lady Macbeth, but, instead, I see Rosalind. I would be honored to help you.

"For your part," and here he bent down to closely face Beau and me, "you must decide whether to continue to make a run for it, with the wily and now revengeful Mr. Earp on your trail, along with whatever minions he may gather to him in his quest, or—and here he flung out his hands—"you may join us and remain incognito, hidden from the prying eyes and hands of the authorities until we reach a destination that is safer for you both. Your choice, as it always has been, my dears."

Well, I thought, *Act III begins with a dramatic flourish.* I glanced at Beau, and he jerked his head toward the wagons and stood up.

"Thank you for your offer," I said. "We need a few minutes to talk this over. It is an unexpected turn of events."

We strode over to the backside of one of the wagons where the horses were tethered, and Rufus snorted as we approached. It was very cold away from the warmth of the fire, and I shoved my hands in my pockets while Beau held his in front of his mouth and blew on them.

"I don't trust that man a lick," he said. "He'd sell his sister to a fancy man for a dollar. 'Course, I don't relish outrunnin' Wyatt Earp much, either, and them wagons look pretty cozy."

I snorted. "You can tone down that cornpone, Sancho. Kind of gave yourself away back there."

It was dark, but not dark enough I couldn't see his grin. "Cain't hardly help myself no more, Miss Chastity."

I swatted him on the arm. "You are a natural-born liar,

but we'll get into that later. What do you want to do, seriously?"

"I think we should stay for a bit. Keep our guns on, much as we can, and our eyes open, because there's a reward for you, and there'll be one soon for me, the way things are progressin'."

I agreed. "My thoughts, too. For all his talk about taking in those who don't abide by society's laws, I agree with you. He's no stranger to double-dealing and intrigue, but he's a paradox, with the manner and voice of a well-born Englishman. I'm still wondering about that 'Mama Rosa saw it in the card's crap. More like he just figured on the odds of us showing up and posted a sneaky sentry. After all, it had to be either us or a posse, so he had it covered either way."

"Yep. So let's throw in, Chas. At the very least, I hope we'll get one good night's sleep out of it."

We walked back to the fire, now blazing again with some new wood. Nobody seemed terribly interested in us—even Julius. He sat with a couple of very pretty women, laughing at something one of them had said, a tumbler of what looked like whiskey in his right hand and his other arm around the woman in his lap.

"Can we have one of those?" I said, pointing towards his glass.

"Why, of course, my dear." He gestured to one of the women, and she produced two more glasses from a box beside her, pouring and handing one to me as well as Beau, along with a charming smile. Well prepared.

I took a sip. It was good whiskey, and I was developing a taste for it. I smiled. "We're in."

Julius smiled, too. "Excellent. I was hoping very much you'd say that, Miss James. We took the liberty of preparing a wagon for you both, one recently vacated, as I mentioned." He gestured towards a wagon with a starburst painted on its side. "I think you'll find it comfortable, even with the dastardly temperatures out here this time of year." He sighed. "We're a bit late this season, but we persevere, in travail and turmoil, as did the Bard."

"Thank you, sir," Beau said and doffed his hat. Julius clearly loved that and held up his glass for a toast. We all clinked our glasses and downed our whiskey.

"We shall see you in the morn, my darlings," he said. "Breakfast at dawn, then rehearsals, if it doesn't snow." He sniffed the air, peering up at the sky littered with stars. "I think conditions are favorable. Good evening to you."

He turned back to the woman on his lap, nestling his lips on her neck. We knew a cue when we saw one and walked over to our new temporary home, retrieving our saddlebags and blankets. I opened the door and couldn't stifle my gasp of amazement.

Pale-blue silk panels glimmered in soft folds against the wooden slats, and a lantern burned on a small table. Tussocks sat beside it, upholstered in more blue silk, and a bed was made up, its pristine-white down comforters rising fluffily beside the pillows at its head. Pegs on the wall beside the rounded door were neatly made for our clothes, and a glowing Oriental rug covered the floor.

I took off my coat, hanging it on one of the pegs, and hung my gunbelt with it. I almost hated to dive into that bed, given my undoubtedly pungent state, but weariness took over. Beau followed, but kept his gun with him. He looked at me, and the shadows played over his face.

"This is somethin' I've never seen before," he said, a smile twitching at the corners of his mouth, "but I like it."

"Me, too," I said as I sprawled across the featherbed. "These people know how to travel, that's certain."

It didn't take him long to lie down beside me. "I'll say, Chas." He propped his head on an elbow. "What in hell have we gotten ourselves into?"

I laughed softly. "At the moment, I don't care. As for you, no funny business."

"I'm so tired you could be the queen of Egypt and I wouldn't care none," he said and rolled himself under the comforter. "Night, Chas."

It couldn't have been more than a minute before I heard his snores. Mine, I was sure, would not be far behind. My knight errant and I were done for the night. I blew out the lantern.

Finale.

CHAPTER 16

"*E*n garde!"

I shot up from beneath the down comforters, and Beau wasn't far behind, blinking in the pale dawn light from the small window in the door of the wagon.

"No, no, Tybalt strikes the first blow in our scenario. I appreciate your warning, but it's not in the scene, as you know. Ramon, two steps back, and Josef, you will attack. Begin again." I recognized Julius's voice.

"Tybalt, you rat-catcher, will you walk?" A man's voice.

Then another. "I am for you."

A clashing of metal, again and again and again. My ears were ringing.

"I am hurt!"

"Excellent, excellent, gentlemen. This is how it will be played. Practice, practice." Julius's voice faded, but the sound of swords went on.

"*Romeo and Juliet* is not what I thought I'd hear this mornin'," groused Beau as he fell back down on the pillows. "Especially not so early."

Neither did I. I sank back down, too. "Which begs the

question, Sancho. What sort of Louisiana farm boy would know that?"

There was a muffled snort from the other side of the bed. "It was what you Northerners would call a plantation, I s'pose, up the river from New Orleans, Creole country. My grand-daddy named it River Dell. It's gone now."

I thought about that for a minute. He was such a liar, but something about the tone of his voice rang true. I put my hand on his back, and he turned around, his face inches from mine.

"I'm sorry, Chas. I've never seen the point of tellin' people about what my family used to be before the war. Since I was fifteen, that's all been nothin' but a memory. My mama kept up my education as best she could, but we were rattlin' around in that big old house with hardly any furniture left. We came to care more about what we were eatin' for dinner than what we read." He smiled ruefully. "We even burned the family Bible in the drawin' room one winter night just to keep warm. The war shamed people like us, and we all kept to ourselves. When Mama died, I let 'em take it. We'd let out most of the fields, and what horses they left us had to be sold, so there wasn't much left anyway."

"I'm sorry," I murmured. "To have your whole life taken from you—I can't imagine what that'd be like."

"Hope you never have to," Beau said. "Yeah, we owned slaves, just like everybody else, couple hundred of 'em, and it never seemed right to me, growing up. My daddy treated 'em well, but that wasn't the point. People shouldn't own other people, and I came to see that maybe what happened to my family and a lot of others like them was justice in a horrible way."

"Still," I said. "That wasn't your doing."

Beau put his hand on my shoulder. "But it would have been, eventually, except for the war. I guess I would've had choices, and maybe I'd have made the right one, but not knowin' for sure doesn't bring me peace." He stared into my eyes.

My hand caressed his cheek. "You would have. I'm sure of it." I kissed him, and he groaned, kissing me back. It was a good thing we had all our clothes on, including a gun belt, because this wasn't anything I'd ever planned on, not that my plans had been going all so well lately. I put my hand on Beau's chest and pushed him away.

"We can't do this," I said. "I'm not sure where that came from."

"I am," he grinned. "From the first minute I saw you."

I sat up, smiling. "That's nice to hear, Mr. Durant, but we're in a bit of a situation here, and we need to keep our wits about us, and this isn't the best way to go about it."

Beau laughed, making a show of adjusting his clothing. "You really are a schoolteacher, aren't you, Chas?"

"Well," I said, "not anymore."

* * *

BREAKFAST WAS a substantial meal at the traveling show. Eggs, likely from the same source as last evening's purloined chickens, with bacon and spiced peaches, again likely stolen from some goodwife's winter store, were in abundance. The coffee was strong and woke us up so we could enjoy the repast. The troupe all flowed out from their practice grounds and wagons and joined us around the fire, clearly started a good hour before we emerged. In the morning light, they were an eclectic group—some stage actors, a few gypsies, and some like us, a mixture of people who had thrown their fortunes in together. That Julius was the ringmaster of this particular circus was evident from the deference he was given by everyone, and we were no exception.

"So, *Romeo and Juliet?*" I said, after a mouthful of bacon went down. "Kansas likes tragic love?"

"Doesn't everyone?" Julius laughed. "We give them tragedy, comedy, love, and the mystique to keep on with their bleak little lives." He was nothing if not sarcastic. A man after my own heart.

"What else?"

Julius sipped his coffee. "My miracle cure, of course. Destinies foretold by Mama Rosa." He nodded to the turbaned woman of the night before, this morning her hair cascading down her back, her black eyes just as intense. "A few tunes, some dancing …"

He gestured toward the two women he'd been drinking with the night before. "Juggling and acrobats, of course." He pointed to a couple of agile young men and added, "Plenty to keep them off balance."

I wasn't sure what he meant by that, but I was sure we'd find out in good time. "So what roles will we fill for you?"

"I've given that some thought, my dear," Julius said. "Since we're doing *Romeo and Juliet* in Topeka, you would be perfect for Juliet, but that simply won't do, since you're incognito, of course." He smiled. "Anyone as lovely as you would be noticed and remembered, and we can't have that. I'm casting you as the nurse. Wimples do wonders."

"Always my dream," I said, finishing my eggs. "What about Beau?"

"Pretty as he is," Julius smiled, "he'll be my Juliet. We have wigs. Excellent camouflage."

I heard Beau choke on something, and Julius laughed. "I'm joshing, young man. You'll be Mercutio, of course. That was always Ramon's role. We'll darken your hair and face, and you'll look just like a Rom, fit right in."

"What makes you think we can learn all those lines so fast?"

Julius sighed. "Because I'm sure you're both familiar with them. Just takes a little refreshment, but you'll have to apply yourself in the next two days. Besides, I adapt all the plays to suit our needs, and there aren't that many lines when I get done. The attention spans of our audiences out here aren't the same as in London, I assure you."

I rolled my eyes and glanced at Beau, who shrugged. There was little point in arguing with our benefactor, and his disguise suggestions were good. I finished my coffee and enjoyed the sunshine that took the edge off the frosty morning. We'd been fortunate so far with the weather. I'd heard stories of the famous plains blizzards when I was in Dodge City, but the two snowstorms so far had been manageable and the temperatures, relatively mild.

As though in response to my complacent thoughts, Mama Rosa held up the cards she'd been studying and made an announcement. "Storm is coming. We must go."

Julius didn't miss a beat. "People, pack it up. I want us on the move in twenty minutes." He threw the rest of his coffee onto the fire.

It was truly amazing, the efficiency this group had. Canvas awnings furled; fires doused; cooking pots cleaned and stowed; the stage levered up onto the side of the long wagon; horses harnessed, saddled, or tied; and in less than Julius's allotted time frame, we were headed north toward Topeka, in an orderly fashion.

Beau and I sat on the seat of our temporary home, pulled by two large draft horses who seemed up to the job, while Rufus and Belle trotted alongside, tied to the rails. I held the reins for now, and we'd trade off later.

"You think we'll make Topeka by nightfall?" I asked. He had a much better idea where we were than I did.

"We could," Beau said. "If it was just the two of us riding, sure. But we've got quite a procession here." He looked around. "Have to see how fast they go. It's less than thirty miles, I think."

"I wonder if she's right about a storm." The sky was a

bright blue, a few wispy clouds high overhead. "Sure doesn't look like it."

"Don't be fooled. The weather here changes fast," Beau said. "Besides, she's spooky enough that I believe her. She's like a gris-gris woman, and you don't mess with them."

I nudged him with my elbow. "Well, well, I had no idea you put such stock in the supernatural. Seen any ghosts lately?"

He snorted and elbowed me back. "Keep it up, Chas. You'll be changin' your know-it-all attitude pretty quick, I bet."

We plodded on for another couple of hours before Julius called a rest break for the horses. I jumped down and went over to his wagon, where he stood conferring with a couple of the gypsy men. They nodded, quickly took a couple of fresh horses, and rode off to the north, Julius watching them go.

"Where are they going?" I said, and Julius whirled around.

"Ah, Miss James," he said. "As I mentioned, I always send someone ahead to a destination. We do business with a partic-ular boardinghouse in Topeka, Mrs. Baxter's. She is expecting us, but not precisely sure of the date, so it's wise to prepare her for our arrival." He smiled. "She stocks up on food, bathing tubs, and items of that sort. She's also got a very large barn and yard for the wagons. You'll be happy with the accommo-dations, I assure you."

"I'm impressed with your organization, Julius," I said. "Will we be there before dark, do you think?" I looked up at the sky, still clear, but the wind was picking up a little.

"Yes. Before the storm." He lifted an eyebrow. "Don't believe Mama Rosa, do you?"

"Well, no, not really," I said, a little apologetically. Julius just stared at me and wrapped his black scarf higher around his neck.

He smiled. "You will."

We set off again within minutes. After a few miles, I crawled into the back of the wagon and rifled around in our saddlebags for food. It seemed to be getting colder, so I found a heavy blanket and wrapped it around Beau, who smiled gratefully. I took the reins so he could eat the cheese and apples I'd brought. Sitting on a wagon seat was a lot colder than riding a horse, I discovered, and when he took the reins back, I went inside and wrapped one of the comforters around my shoulders. In spite of the jolting of the wheels, I began to relax. I needed to think about my situation and the people I was with, rather than reacting and careering from one debacle to another. Instead of remaining the lone fugitive, I had entangled myself, first with Beau, and now this troupe of players or whatever they really were.

My disposition had never been typical of my sex, timid or unassuming, but since that night in Dodge, I wasn't just assertive but so aggressive some of the words that flew out of my mouth startled even me. On the physical side of things, it was equally so. My first experience with sex had been with Matthias's nephew one summer night when I was sixteen, and although I thoroughly enjoyed myself, neither circumstance nor a likely candidate had caused me to repeat it. That night in Dodge was as unlike the first time as night was from day. I had feared I would be disgusted with physical love forever after that, but whether my pragmatic nature had taken over or the rustic charms of Mr. Durant had enticed me, I wasn't sure. There was a gentleness to Beau, and an attraction that started a warming sensation in my stomach and flowed like molten gold through my veins. It began at the farmhouse and had only intensified, but I knew it wasn't wise to give in to it under the circumstances.

As for Julius DeMonte and this motley group of players, we seemed to have fallen into a lucky and comforting situation here, but things that seemed too good to be true were usually just that. I sighed and snuggled into the comforter. Everything was strange, and the more I pondered it all, the heavier my eyelids seemed to be.

I jerked awake when a particularly large rut lifted the caravan underneath me and my hipbones hit the wagon bed. I threw off the comforter. How long had I slept? I poked my head through the curtains and scrambled into the seat beside Beau. The sky was blue no longer, and a close ceiling of dark clouds hung low. The blanket had fallen off his shoulder, and I tucked it around him, my leg warming his cold one.

He turned and smiled stiffly at me. "Storm comin', Chas. Told you."

I took the reins from his frozen hands. "Go back there and get warmed up. I got this."

He didn't argue, climbing through the curtains without a word. I gazed around at the accompanying wagons. Nobody looked happy. Josef rode by on his horse, circling his hand at me to pick up the pace, as I saw him do with all the other drivers. The horses were tired, but we complied, following Julius, who was in the lead and lengthening it as snowflakes the size of silver dollars began to fall softly, swirling in the wind.

The lights of Topeka were a beacon urging us onward, even though we were miles out and the snow thickening as we went. Mama Rosa had definitely been right, and I was fervently glad we weren't out there on horseback, looking to camp somewhere. I heard Beau snoring even with the creak of harness and the wind, which was blowing at a good clip. My face was frozen, snow sticking to my eyelashes as we hit the edge of town. Two- and three-story buildings loomed ahead, and I could see Topeka was a city, not just some prairie village —much bigger than what I'd glimpsed from the train before.

Even with the snow starting, the streets were busy with people shopping and going in and out of restaurants and hotels, and plenty of wagons and horses were churning the muddy thoroughfares. We plodded on, finally pulling into a property with a large, three-story house blazing with lights, behind which were three large barns, more than big enough to house the wagons and our horses.

We made short work of unharnessing and caring for the horses, and soon the entire troupe followed Julius into the house. Apparently no one stayed out in the cold caravans when in Topeka, and the welcoming warmth in the large front hall was a delight.

"Julius, you old rogue," cried a smiling, pink-cheeked woman, her coppery curls bouncing from the top of her head to her shoulders. "Give us a kiss." She threw her arms around him, and he complied with gusto to her order, picking her up and whirling her around, her yellow taffeta skirts nearly over-whelming them both.

"Nell, I've missed you," he said. "We've come through hell just to get to you, my dear."

She grinned and rolled her eyes. "I don't doubt it, but it's my house you're lusting after, not just me. You're late, and sleeping in those damn wagons this time of year, I swear, you'll all die of pneumonia. Speaking of which, get on in here, all of you, and get warmed up." She hustled us into a large front room with a blazing fire in the massive stone fire-place. "Shoes can go on the drying racks to the left of the fire; coats on the hooks in the hallway. You know the routine." Everyone began taking off their coats and shoes and edging close to the fire.

Nell caught sight of me and Beau. "Newbies, are you?" She put her hands on her plump hips and appraised us. "Julius, where'd you find these two pretties? Brother and sister, are you?"

I hadn't thought about it before, but with our light-blond hair and slim builds, we could pass for family—and what good cover that could be. "Yes," I said quickly, nudging Beau's foot. "Charity Birdsong, and this is my brother, Beau."

Julius was watching us from his perch on the couch, a sly smile on his mouth. He caught my eye and nodded. "And, I must say, Nell, we are more than happy to have the Birdsongs with us, aren't we, everyone? They'll be joining us on stage for the first time here in Topeka. Very quick on their feet, they are, and two more promising aspiring young actors I've never seen." He actually clapped, and the others did, too, more than a couple with knowing smirks. But the message was heard and received: that our true identities would not be revealed to Nell Baxter or anyone else, and there was likely good reason for it. I was sure we were not the first fugitives who had found their way into Julius's care. It was a mutual aid society, and everyone looked out for everyone else in this troupe.

Supper followed in a big dining room, all of us at the long table, and it was a raucous affair. It gave us an opportunity to observe our new colleagues, a lively bunch. The Acaro family, two brothers and two sisters, were acrobats, jugglers, and actors as well—Josef, Daniel, Maria, and Elena, all in their twenties with flashing eyes and curling, dark hair, Romany to the core; Mama Rosa and her apprentice, a fey, beautiful child named Angel whose gender I couldn't ascertain; Ramon, Mama Rosa's son, a charming and handsome actor; two sisters, Merry and Ellen St. John, actresses and dancers and Julius's companions of the night before; James Harper, a burly, genial man who did anything that needed doing, and Sean McKean, an Irishman who called himself a roustabout, but Julius said he'd made a great Henry V last year. A merry crew, they treated us as though they'd known us forever, and within minutes, Beau and I felt comfortable.

Nell Baxter set quite a table. Simple food, but wonderfully prepared. We feasted on a thick vegetable soup, baked ham, au gratin potatoes that Delmonico's would envy, and fresh-baked bread. It was undeniably one of the best meals I've ever eaten, spiced with hunger and hard work, the best enhancers. When Nell brought out peach pies, the entire company groaned and polished them off.

"Nell, this was marvelous," I said. "Thank you so much. I

haven't eaten this well for a long time." We sat back in our chairs like fattened hogs. Nell pulled back the curtains, and the world outside was a blur of swirling white against the dark night. Topeka was under siege, and I wondered what tomorrow would bring. I hoped Nell had quite a store in her pantry, but I had a feeling she wasn't new at this.

We trooped back into the front parlor, and in groups of three, made for the bathing room she'd set up, with Sean and James helping to fill and refill the tubs.

I sat down next to Julius. "Once again, my thanks. When I think we could be out there in this, or trying to find a hotel room here, I cringe."

He patted my arm. "No thanks necessary, my dear. We take care of our own, and you and Beau are now our own." He smiled at me like a benevolent father.

"This house is marvelous, and the food," I sighed. "Do you always stay here?"

"Of course," Julius said. "After all, I own the place."

"What?" He was full of surprises, this one.

"Nell's my wife, Chastity," he grinned. "She's a jewel, that one, puts up with me being on the road a lot."

I was truly surprised. Who was this man? A lot more than a traveling showman, that was certain. I couldn't wait to have a further conversation, but just as I opened my mouth, Maria and Elena beckoned to me.

"Come on, bath's ready."

Nothing was going to keep me from that. I smiled at Julius and followed the sisters to the bath. Heaven was down the hall, and questions would have to wait.

CHAPTER 17

"Something smells real good."

Beau's whisper in my ear woke me, and I turned over onto my stomach and sniffed. He was right. It was very quiet in our room, as though we were covered in a quilt that masked all outside sound. I reached over and pulled back the curtain. Everything was white, and the wind blew snow against the window. The storm had come, all right.

"Hilda always said men's feelings start in their stomach," I said.

"She was a little off the mark there, Chas," he said, running his thumb up my bare arm. I didn't pull away. He nestled his face in my hair. This was dangerous territory.

"God, you smell even better."

I snorted. "Nice to know I rate higher than sausages." I sat up and went to the window. Blizzard, no question. White drifts were piled up everywhere I could see, against the house and the barn doors, and I couldn't see any delineation for streets or other buildings farther out there. I'd never doubt Mama Rosa again.

Beau's arms encircled my waist, and I stood as still as a stone, despite my inclination to turn around.

"We need to get dressed and get downstairs," I said.

We stood there for maybe a minute before he moved away. I could hear him pulling on his clothes and boots. The door shut softly behind him, and I hastily threw on my own clothes. After brushing my hair back and tying it with a leather thong, I followed him downstairs.

Some of the troupe were in the dining room, where platters of pancakes, eggs, and sausages sat on the table, along with pots of coffee. Beau was pouring maple syrup on a mound of pancakes, flanked by the Acaro brothers, who were schooling him on sword craft, waving their forks around to demonstrate. I sat beside Ramon, who graciously poured me a cup of coffee.

"Morning, uh, Charity," he said, grinning. "Sleep well?"

"I did," I said. "And you?"

"As though I was in my mama's arms," he assured me, casting an eye at Maria Acaro, who gave him a sly smile. *Always good to know where the wind blows,* I thought. Beau helped himself to the platters full of eggs and sausages, and I did the same. The St. John sisters came in, looking lovely, as always, and sat beside me.

"Morning, Charity," Merry chirped, and Elena nodded. They had a tendency to speak as one, I'd noticed.

"Morning to you, ladies," I said and took a mouthful of the eggs, which were delicious, scrambled with herbs and cheese. *I'll have to tell Hilda,* I thought, and for a moment, I fervently hoped I would be able to do just that.

Mama Rosa and Angel entered the room, sitting on the other side of the table by themselves. I was pretty sure Angel was a teenage girl, but I wouldn't have placed bets on it. Her pale hair hung over her perfect face, but when she lifted her chin and met my eyes, she smiled, and I no longer had any doubt. Besides, there was no Adam's apple in that swanlike neck. Juliet looked at me through those sky-blue eyes, no question in my mind.

Everyone else drifted in, and, finally, Julius and Nell, arm in arm, sat down. For a time, we all applied ourselves to the delicious food, with occasional comments about the storm that raged about us. I gathered we had two rehearsal days instead of one, due to the weather, and even that was to be determined, as we could all see the whiteness outside the windows.

Everyone shot to attention as Julius stood up and clinked a knife on his coffee cup. "So, my darlings. We will be at the Crawford Opera House for three nights, since our arrival and notice of *Romeo and Juliet* had advance word. We are sold out for the entire run. Even Governor Anthony will attend. We have two days of rehearsal, weather permitting, and, in two nights, Topeka will be mesmerized, as always."

Everybody applauded, even me. Julius then went over the nightly schedule. We would open with music, songs, and dancing, alternating with French, Spanish, and even American tunes. Then Mama Rosa and her assistants, Ramon and Angel, would come on with magic, sleight of hand, and—here Julius winked—"her usual uncanny glimpses into the future." Next, some chosen soliloquies, followed by the Acaro family with acrobatic feats and flaming torches before the primary attraction: Julius's adaptation of *Romeo and Juliet*. Everyone began to scatter to rehearse their various parts. It seemed they'd done this routine before.

Sounded like quite the ambitious agenda to me, but no one seemed daunted in the least. I was impressed, and I hoped we wouldn't disappoint. As though reading my mind, Julius crooked a finger at me and wagged it to include Beau.

"You two, come with me." We dutifully followed him upstairs to our room, where we all sat on the bed, and he handed us two tattered copies of a highly redacted *Romeo and Juliet*.

"Since nobody's going anywhere today"—he glanced pointedly at the window where the open curtains showed nothing but white—"fortunately we have time for you to learn your lines. Nurse and Mercutio. In my version, Mercutio doesn't have too many lines, but the sword fight— Well, that's the crowd pleaser every time, trust me." He grinned wolfishly. "Beau's going to be a natural at that, I think. After luncheon, Maria will meet you in the kitchen for your transformation. Your own mothers won't recognize you after that. *Au revoir,* darlings."

He shut the door, and we looked at each other, the pages in our hands. Both our mothers were long gone, but I hadn't bothered to point that out.

"Christ Jesus," I said. "What a price we pay, eh?"

"Come on, Chas," Beau laughed. "We could have frozen our asses off out there, so, whatever this man wants, it's a small price to pay, far as I'm concerned. I can figure out how to wield a sword for room and board like this any day." He stood up and feinted as though he'd drawn a sword and pointed his arm at my throat. "Might could be fun."

I snorted and waved the script pages at him. "Mercutio, you have work to do."

* * *

By NOON, we were seriously bored with our scripts. We were quick studies. Beau was smiling slyly at me, and that spelled trouble. As his hand touched my waist, I vaulted off the bed.

"I'm hungry, how about you?"

A long sigh. "Yeah, I could eat." I heard his boots hit the floor, but I was already out the door and down the hallway.

A large tureen of soup sat on the table in the dining room, surrounded by platters of bread with butter, jam, and honey. Sean McKean and the Acaros were already there, spooning in soup, and it looked as though they hadn't been first. We joined them, and the soup was delicious, as expected. It was still snowing. It didn't stop me from polishing off two bowls of soup.

Maria stood up and jerked her chin at Beau and me. "Kitchen, my friends. We've work to do."

She sat Beau down first in a wooden chair and proceeded to slather brown stuff all over his hair, and then his face, neck, and hands. When she was done, she told him to wait nearby and sat me down in the same chair.

"First, we cut, yes?"

"What?"

"Julius says." She tied a kitchen towel around my neck and brandished her scissors. I watched my long, blonde hair fall in substantial chunks to the floor. For the first few seconds, I was in shock. Then I realized I should've hacked it off long before now.

"Don't worry; will be fine, Charity. You are beautiful. Hair just hair."

When she finished cutting, my hair fell to just below my ears. Then she proceeded to douse it with the same brown dye she'd used on Beau, including my neck, face, and hands, just like him.

"You will be proper Romany now," Maria laughed. "Wait an hour, and we wash off."

Later, I stood in front of the mirror in our bedroom, not recognizing myself. Beau stood beside me, wearing the same bemused expression.

"Christ Jesus," I said. "Who the hell am I?" I was still Chastity James, but a different woman altogether.

Beau laughed. "We are Romany, Chas, just like Maria said." He ran his hands through his dark hair, his green eyes bright against his darkened skin. "I kinda like it."

He moved his hands to my head, ruffling the short, dark curls. "Those big blue eyes and that olive skin ... hmm ... reminds me of a Cajun girl I used to know."

I pivoted sideways and put my hands on his shoulders. "Cajun girl, eh? I never want to hear about her again." I kissed him soundly. "We're Romany now, pal."

He growled deep in his throat. "I'm not your pal," he said, kissing me back as we fell onto the bed. Maybe it was the transformation in how we looked, but, whatever it was, two hours later we sat up naked in our rumpled sheets and stared at each other.

"Goddamn."

"My thoughts exactly, knight errant." I climbed on top of him. "Must be the gypsy blood." Or something. Whatever it was, I wanted more of it, and so did Beau.

A tap on the door roused us. The room was completely dark.

"Dinner's on in ten." Sounded like Ramon, but I wasn't sure. The soft chuckle could've been anybody as the footsteps faded down the hall.

When we entered the dining room, conversation stopped, and all eyes turned to us. James Harper was the first to clap. We bowed and took our seats.

"Look at you, my little fugitives. You have become one with us." Julius raised his wineglass. "Bravo, my dears."

Burgundy splashed into crystal glasses, and we even toasted ourselves. We were accepted with no conditions, and it felt good.

The evening passed in a blur of good food and wine, which seemed endless. The snow had stopped that afternoon, and Topeka was digging itself out. We were all gathered in the parlor, and, around nine, Julius stood up from the couch he shared with Nell and raised his hand.

"Tomorrow, last rehearsals, together, including my sword fighters. We'll be in the barn with the charcoal burners to warm us, and then, by six, at the Opera House for opening night. You'll all be magnificent, as usual. For now, for we start at seven, light or no, and you need your rest: off with you!"

The master had spoken. Off we went.

* * *

"Does it hurt a lot?"

Beau grimaced. "Not so bad. It's the flat of the blade, after all. The tip, now, that may be a different story."

"I daresay." I rubbed the liniment Nell had given me onto his shoulders and arms. He'd been practicing the sword fight between Mercutio and Tybalt all morning and had taken the killing blow once too often.

"Ah, the price we pay for theater," I said. "Julius is a hard taskmaster."

Beau cast his eyes at me. "I guess, but it beats sleepin' rough."

I couldn't argue with that. I'd been rehearsing all day myself, and, while I hadn't taken any sword hits, I'd been schooled by Angel, who turned out to be a very sarcastic fifteen-year-old girl. She was a Juliet for the ages, that one. I could only imagine where Julius had found her. Likely a tragic story, but one I was reluctant to listen to, which was just as well, as she wasn't forthcoming. I was coming to see that our leader was even more unusual than I'd thought in the beginning.

I put the cap back on the liniment; it made my eyes water. I hoped it was effective, and, from the way Beau rolled his shoulders, it seemed to be. God knows what Mama Rosa had put in it—likely opium or some magical concoction. She was another one whose former life I could only guess at. Julius had a way of bringing people together, that was for certain.

Late in the afternoon, Nell served up more soup, following Julius's admonition that people don't perform well after a large meal. We packed up two caravans with costumes, makeup, accoutrements, and people and plowed our way through the streets to the Crawford Opera House, where Sean McKean and Harper had been working on sets all day. The entrances to the Opera House had been shoveled out, creating paths for us and the audience, and we entered the cavernous space and looked around.

Quite impressive for a Kansas theater, I thought, but then I'd never seen one to compare it with, so I ignored my Eastern prejudices and vowed to have an open mind. I'd had a lot of surprises in the last few months. Rows of seats, rising in tiers, made up the center and both sides of the audience area, with a balcony that could seat at least a hundred, and eight raised boxes on each side. The place would easily hold three hundred. Topeka liked its theater.

The stage was large, with two sets of curtains—one, a deep-claret velvet fringed with heavy, gold tassels; and, behind it, a filmy, cream muslin—each pulled with an elaborate set of ropes from both sides of the stage. Sets for Juliet's balcony, a street scene, and the church with a tomb were in place, each to be lit in its time. Footlights, border lights for each scene, and wing lights were set up. A technician from the Opera House was working the gas table to control the lights, chatting with Sean and making notes on the script, along with a sheet of the different acts for the night. The cold, echoing theater would be warm soon enough. Gaslights brought up the temperature like burning bonfires. The Crawford was a modern opera house, on a par with Boston or New York. I was impressed.

Backstage, we set up our dressing rooms in a warren of boxlike areas behind the backdrop and drop curtain, our fingers soon growing stiff with cold as we dressed and applied makeup. No one complained, knowing the heat from the lights would soon raise the temperature. I shared a room with the Acaro sisters and Merry and Ellen St. John. Maria pulled my hair back and put on the nurse's wimple and veil, the only makeup a liner on my eyes to make them stand out. Then she delicately penciled age lines onto my face, as though drawing a charcoal portrait. When she finished, I gazed into the mirror and saw an Italian woman in her fifties. Even Leland wouldn't have recognized me.

I sat and watched the others do their magic. All were pretty girls to start with, but by the time they were finished with their makeup, hair, and costumes, they were like beautiful fantasy creatures come to life.

Maria and Elena Acaro wore tight fitting one-piece outfits that covered them from neck to ankle like a second skin, one a glittery red and the other blue. A silky tutu-like skirt hung from their waists to mid-thigh—modesty for the audience's benefit, but short enough to not interfere with their acrobatics. Their dark hair was pulled back into tight buns, a spray of glittery feathers pinned atop each. Their faces were arresting, eyes like feral cats and rouge on their cheeks and lips.

Maria posed before me. "Rrowrr," she purred, and we all laughed as she pirouetted away.

The St. John sisters were dazzling in rows of striped, purple and yellow ruffles, the necklines low, with striped black and white stockings winding sinuously up their lovely legs, which would be bared in a French cancan, among other dances. Their hair fell in long ringlets down their backs and over their shoulders; their faces were made up similar to the Acaros. I felt a frump beside them all, but grateful for my disguise as a dowdy nun.

Finished with our preparations, we joined the rest of the performers for a shortened dress rehearsal on the main stage. If I thought the women had been transformed, the men had accomplished the same magic.

Stunningly handsome, Ramon was dressed as Romeo in a medieval doublet and hose, but his looks were eclipsed by his virtuoso guitar playing. And when Elena St. John opened her mouth, I was stunned by the beauty of her voice and the plaintive Spanish ballad she sang. Her sister joined her, as did Josef Acaro with another guitar, for a spate of flamenco dancing, more songs, which Julius cut short, then ending with a French cancan featuring the St. John sisters with Sean McKean playing an Irish bodhran drum. Somehow it all worked, fantastically so.

We bypassed Mama Rosa's act and the Acaros' acrobatics

and went straight to *Romeo and Juliet*. I stumbled on a few lines, while Beau was a magnificent Mercutio, fighting and dying right on cue. Angel was ethereal as Juliet, her high-waisted, white gown flowing as did her lovely, blonde hair.

Julius seemed content. He was dressed in long, black robes, his white hair gleaming on his shoulders, eyes lined like the rest of us, doing duty as master of the troupe, Friar, and Chorus, filling in all the blanks in his version of *Romeo and Juliet*.

"Excellent work, people, as usual," he said. "It's going to be a great performance. You all fill me with pride." I sure hoped he was right.

"Go, relax, and breathe. It's an hour yet to curtain time." He flourished his robes and disappeared into the wings.

We dispersed according to his directive, and I sidled toward stage left, not really sure what to do. My stomach was growling, but I guess that was better than having it too full. A strong arm wound itself around my waist and pulled me close.

"Nurse, can you give me some help?"

I resisted the urge to stomp on his slippered foot.

"Unhand me, Mercutio, before I call Tybalt," I said and turned to face him, backing up a few steps. Resplendent in a midnight-blue doublet chased with silver, his legs encased in tights, he was the epitome of a Renaissance man. "Aren't you magnificent? A true gentleman of Verona."

He swept off his cap and bowed. *"Très bon, madame infir-mière."* He sidestepped, laughing, before I made good on the stomping.

"It's Italy, dolt, not France," I said, grinning in spite of myself.

"I know that, nurse, but I don't know Italian, so you'll have to make do," he said and scooped me up, wimple and all, into the recess behind the curtain ropes. "So will I, considerin' you look about eighty years old."

He grabbed my hand before it could connect and kissed

me, still laughing at first, but we sped past that in a hurry. I'm not sure where either of us got our skills, but we were fast learners at kissing and everything else. We'd proven that.

"I believe it was Julius Caesar who never let his warriors fall victim to temptation on the eve of a battle," Julius intoned somberly, close to our heads. "Or maybe I heard that from a Sioux chief; I can't recall now. Either way, unhand the nurse, Mercutio. We go on in thirty minutes. Panting is not in the script."

He strolled away, shaking his head as we broke apart, giggling like schoolchildren, and made for our separate dressing rooms.

Showtime was nigh.

The theater was full, even with the snow. Topeka had a thirst for entertainment. When Julius stepped on stage, alone, in front of the drawn velvet curtain, it was so quiet it seemed the entire audience held its collective breath. He looked like a king, regal and commanding, white hair flowing over his shoulders, his black robes trailing the floor, an ermine cape thrown over his wide shoulders.

"Ladies and gentlemen, it is my great pleasure to bring the DeMonte Theatrical Troupe once again to Topeka, gracing the stage of the magnificent Crawford Opera House, and to you, our gracious and devoted audience." He bowed to them, and applause erupted like a bonfire.

"Tonight we bring you the best of Europe and, of course, the perfection of William Shakespeare, with the supreme romantic tragedy *Romeo and Juliet* as our main event. We endeavor to give you the very embodiment of the Bard, as well as songs, dances, music, and enchantment that will remain in your memories for many years to come."

He bowed again, his hands out flung like a great bird of prey within the folds of his robes. "Without further ado, the stars of the Venice Opera."

He disappeared stage right as the curtains opened upon

Ramon and Elena, and the evening's entertainment began with the sound of Ramon's guitar, no mean enchantment on its own.

To say the performance was perfect was fairly close, if you discounted my feeble acting, but at least I remembered my lines, and Angel more than made up for me with her mesmerizing Juliet, while the hypnotic Julius as narrator filled in all the gaps in our sparse cast. The Acaros, Ramon, and the St. John sisters were truly wonderful, and Mama Rosa stunned our audience with her eerie abilities. She had a booth set up in the lobby and was doing a brisk business long after the curtains had come down, making appointments for the next few days as well.

We rode back to Nell's tired, satisfied, and happy with our efforts. That good woman had laid out a feast for us: sandwiches of ham, beef, and turkey, along with cheese and fruit and plenty of wine and beer.

By midnight, we all staggered off to our respective beds. As we undressed, I turned to Beau.

"This is no amateur carnival we've associated ourselves with," I said. "These people are professionals who've graced stages all over the world. What are they doing wandering around the frontier, I wonder?"

Beau agreed. "I was thinkin' the same, Chas. 'Course, I don't have your experience, your bein' from the East and all, but still."

I lay back on the pillows, playing with the ribbons on my soft, cotton nightgown, a gift from our incomparable hostess, Nell. "Seriously, Beau. Who the hell is Julius DeMonte?"

He sighed, his eyelids closing. "I don't know, Chas, I'm thinkin' maybe God? I'm sure you'll figure it out if you set your mind to it."

He began to snore softly, and I blew out the light.

CHAPTER 18

$\mathcal{I}$ opened my eyes. It was still dark, but with a ghostly glow beyond the thin curtains. Dawn wasn't far away. Beau snored softly, still sound asleep. I slipped out of bed and dressed in my old flannel shirt and pants, carrying my boots and socks as I made my way down the stairs and into the kitchen, following the smell of fresh-brewed coffee.

Julius DeMonte sat at the wooden table, sipping coffee, and smiled as I entered. I set my boots and socks down at a chair by the table and poured a cup for myself before sitting down beside him.

"Morning," I whispered, not really sure why. It seemed right because no one else was awake. I took a sip of coffee and applied myself to my footgear. Julius watched and didn't say a word.

Finished, I sat back and downed the rest of my coffee, then refilled it from the pot on the stove.

"Who are you, Julius?"

He got up and refilled his own cup.

"A wanderer, a fixer, a seeker," he said, smiling gently. "Many things, my dear. I've been waiting for you to ask because I knew you would. You've clearly always been a curious girl."

Mystified, I stared at him. "How would you know?"

He gestured at the table and chairs, and we sat back down. "Therein lies a tale, and you shall have it, Chastity James. Many years ago, I came to a place called Harrowhill and bought a horse." He peered at me over the rim of his cup. "You were perhaps six years old, running through the stables like a whirlwind, darting here and there, straw in your hair. The horses loved you, and your father knew you would come to no harm.

"I met Leland James at my father's estate in Cornwall when we were both young men; his father had come there to buy a horse from mine. We kept in touch, and when I came to America, before setting out for the West, I stayed at Harrowhill and left on one of the offspring of that same horse. Life takes many turns, and I've never returned to the East Coast—or England, either, for that matter. I doubt I ever will."

"Well," I said. "How peculiar. What were the odds of us meeting again, I wonder?" I was surprised and, honestly, suspicious.

Julius chuckled. "High, very high indeed. But then, as I said, life takes many turns. When I learned of your notoriety, I knew it was unlikely there was another young woman from the East named Chastity James, and I hoped our paths would cross. To be honest, I did everything I could to ensure they did. Your Beau certainly helped out by putting Mr. Earp out of commission for a bit, and we got lucky."

I sipped my coffee. "Why not mention this in the first place?"

Julius leaned back in his chair. "Truthfully, because I'm a bit of a gamesman and because there really hasn't been time. I was curious myself, to see just what sort of a woman the little wild girl had grown into, and I've not been disappointed.

You're a survivor, my dear, just like me, and like most of the people here who've needed a helping hand when circumstances put them in a position they'd never prepared for. I apologize for the delay, but trust goes both ways."

He reached over and touched my arm. "I do trust you, and I hope you trust me, Chastity. You and Beau are under my protection for as long as it's needed. I wanted to wire your father and let him know, but I think it's too dangerous just now. Best to just get you both away as soon as we can."

I agreed with him there. Although my head was whirling with unanswered questions, I felt the tension slide from my shoulders. Julius was an odd one, but I knew instinctively I could trust him, even if he hadn't been as forthcoming as I would've wished. Then again, in his place, perhaps I would have done the same. I put my hand on his arm and pressed it.

"Thank you, once again," I said, smiling. "How did you ever come to be in Topeka, Kansas? And, while it's a nice one, is Julius DeMonte even your real name?"

"We need more coffee," he said and poured us some. He rummaged around in the pantry and came out with an assortment of pastries, which he brought to the table. I picked one up and took a bite. Almond paste and sugar exploded on my tongue. Delightful. He watched me and smiled.

"Julius is my real name, but the family name is Cargill. My father is the Duke of Sandbrooke and I am his fourth son." He bit into a pastry himself and chewed reflectively. "Fourth sons are a trial, and I believe I've succeeded in being one of the most notorious ones. How it works: the first son inherits; the second goes into the military; the third, poor sod, the clergy; and if there's a fourth—like me—well, there's no good future. I gambled, whored, drank, and finally ended up on the London stage, in one frothing scandal after another." He licked his fingers. "After it was rumored a member of the royal family was pregnant with my child, my father would have done just about anything to get rid of me."

He laughed. "Short of being buried in the apple orchard, which was my eldest brother's suggestion, I took them up on their generous offer of a tremendous amount of money to go to America, disappear, and never return. I've not regretted it."

Fascinated, I blurted out, "Was it your child?"

Julius laughed. "A gentleman never kisses and tells, darling." He held out the plate. "Have another."

I did. "So, from a castle to a traveling theater troupe?"

"A shortened version. Long ones can be so boring, as I'm sure you agree. The first couple of years here, I was very foolish and lost a lot of money. Luckily, I came with a rather large amount of it. I finally came to my senses and went back to the stage. The short of it is, I saw a need, or opportunity, to bring entertainment and theater farther than New York, and I'd always been in love with gypsy caravans, and gypsies themselves. When people look for others of a like mind and passion, it is quite amazing how they seem to find one another. Then, I found that those who are wandering or need help are drawn to others who have been there themselves.

"I think people are more important than rules, society, or laws, to be blunt. Sometimes people need a champion, if you will, or just someone who cares. I'd been a taker, without thought for anyone but myself, and I have come to find, over the years, I much prefer being a giver."

He stood up and opened his arms. "So there you have it, my dear. I trust it was an entertaining breakfast?"

I didn't say a word. I rose from my chair and put my arms around Julius's waist, my head on his shoulder. He closed his arms around me, and I pressed my face into his velvet jacket. A few tears fell, and I felt as though it were Leland comforting and holding me, and, oddly enough, it almost was.

* * *

BEAU WAS SITTING on the side of the bed when I came back upstairs. He took one look at my blotchy face and pulled me down beside him. I was an ugly crier.

"What's wrong, Chas?"

I recounted everything Julius had told me, and he listened, raising his eyebrows now and then. He hugged me, and the tears threatened to come again, but I took a few deep breaths. This was no time to fall apart. Besides, things were going very well, considering.

"You believe him?" he said.

"Yes, without question."

"Well, that's good enough for me," he said. "I like him a lot myself."

The rest of the day passed in a little rehearsal time, lunch, fooling around with the rest of the players. Julius was out most of the day, doing whatever business he did. Mama Rosa was receiving clients in a small study off the entry hall—mostly veiled ladies and an occasional man, hat pulled down, but it was all terribly discreet. We avoided the customers, giving them space to come and go.

Another light dinner and to the theater we went. All our things were already there, and we trooped off to the dressing rooms, a repeat of last night, except there was no dress rehearsal. Tonight the governor and his wife were attending, and the theater was just as full as it had been on opening night. By the time Julius gave his opening speech, I felt like an old hand at this business. I gave Beau a pat on his velvet-covered rear and danced off for my opening scene. Everyone was in a good mood, much more relaxed than the night before. This was likely how things went in the acting business, I figured.

The play was going well, Angel ethereal as Juliet. Wimple in place, I hadn't muffed a single line tonight. We were doing the last scene in Act III. Alas, poor Juliet.

"Romeo is banished; and all the world to nothing that he

dares ne'er come back …" I said, when a shot rang out, and the theater erupted in shrieks. People jumped out of their seats, some going for the floor.

"Christ Jesus," I said, diving for the floor myself, pulling Angel down next to me. As we lay there, the house lights came up, and all the stage lights went down. I peered up at the audience, and there was Wyatt Earp, brandishing a pistol, two men in suits with guns beside him, all standing in the center aisle.

"Everyone stay calm, please. My apologies, but I needed to get your attention," he said. "We are law enforcement. There is a dangerous fugitive in your midst."

He strode down the aisle, people backing away from him as he went, and stalked onto the stage via the short stairs from the theater floor.

"Chastity James, I'm arresting you for the murder of Duane Olson," he announced, grabbing poor Angel's arm and pulling her to her feet. "You are in the custody of the Dodge City marshal's office of Ford County."

Angel's long, blonde hair obscured most of her face, and she sagged as he began to pull her away, her long gown trailing across the boards. I kept my head down, not daring to look up.

Julius burst onto the stage like an avenging angel, black robes flying around him. "Unhand that girl!" he roared in full stage voice. "This is outrageous."

Earp whirled around to face him, still holding Angel's arm. "You! I expected someone like you to be hiding a criminal, DeMonte."

"Save your insults for some miscreant you can bully, Marshal," Julius sneered. "That girl is my ward, and you will release her this instant."

The entire audience was enraptured with the reality performance, an unexpected bonus, but, before Wyatt Earp could take another step, Governor Anthony and two large gentlemen stepped up to the stage.

"Marshal," the governor's deep voice rang out, nearly as fulsome as Julius's. "I believe there's been a misunderstanding here. Release that young woman immediately. This is outrageous behavior from an officer of the law. I'll have your badge for this. How dare you?"

Earp's stony demeanor actually looked shaken for a moment, but he recovered. "Sir, there's no mistake. This girl" —he shook Angel's arm—"is Chastity James, the escaped murderess from Dodge City. We've tracked her to Topeka and had good information she was hiding with this theatrical troupe, and now we have her."

"No, Mr. Earp, you do not," said the governor, his tone icy. "I've known my good friend Julius DeMonte and his family for years. You will never harass them again, not in my state. Holster that ridiculous weapon, take another look, and then prepare your apologies and resignation before you leave town."

The ensuing silence was so profound, the audible intakes of breath from the hundreds of people watching filled the emptiness.

"Now," said the governor, and the two men beside him took a step forward. Earp holstered his gun and dropped Angel's arm. She shook herself like a dog ridding itself of fleas, pulled her hair back, and glared at him. His eyes widened, and, discernible even in the shadowy light, his face flushed a dark crimson. He had the wrong girl, and he knew it.

"Ma'am, I … I'm so sorry," he stammered. "I was told … and from a distance, I was sure …"

"That's enough." Governor Anthony waved his hand. "Get out. Out of this theater and out of Topeka."

Wyatt Earp turned and left, his men with him. As he walked down the theater aisle like a gauntlet, people whispered and laughed when he passed. Just before he reached the lobby doors, the governor's voice rang out.

"Mr. Earp? I think Charlie Bassett needs to be more careful about the caliber of people he hires. If I were you, I'd make it a point to avoid Topeka the next time you travel away from your little cattle town."

Earp stopped for a few seconds, gathered himself, and walked out, his back ramrod straight.

The governor shook Julius's hand, the audience resumed their seats, and the show went on.

I even remembered all the rest of my lines. So did Angel.

* * *

"Julius, I must apologize to you for allowing this unpleasantness to happen in our capital," Governor Anthony said, raising his glass. "Here's to many more delightful evenings, courtesy of you and your dedicated colleagues, which I guarantee will never again by interrupted by badge-toting ruffians."

We all clinked glasses and drank, and I looked around the table. Beau and I were seated about halfway down the long expanse, as were all the members of the DeMonte troupe. Governor Anthony and his wife, along with a few other worthies whose names I couldn't remember, were interspersed among us as we dug into our after-theater dinner at the governor's mansion.

After the performance, Julius had invited the troupe to dinner at the governor's house, a surprise he had planned, and even with Earp's interruption, the dinner went on, just like the show. Apparently Julius and the governor were close friends, which didn't surprise me in the least. Angel had recovered from her trauma, which, if her spitting invectives at Wyatt Earp and law enforcement in general were any indicator, hadn't affected her in the least.

"Excellent shrimp, nearly as good as New Orleans," Beau said, taking another bite of shrimp bathed in garlic wine sauce. "I think they must pack it in ice and bring it up the river."

I gave him a baleful glance. "Do most Louisiana farm boys eat at Antoine's?" I couldn't resist. I'd never been there myself, but Leland had touted its praises.

He gave me a half smile. "Well, no. But some do," he said and swallowed a mouthful of wine. "Blame my Aunt Tatiane. I was a mere child."

The evening had been stressful, and there was no point in baiting Beau, even though I reveled in it because he'd been such a liar. I gave a little sigh. *Weren't we all, anymore?*

Julius was the best I'd ever seen. I'd talked to him before we left for dinner.

"Did you know Earp was coming?" I'd said.

Julius had smiled his enigmatic smile. "No, but I suspected he might. So did Angel." He'd smoothed his hair. "Anthony is a particular friend, one I've done favors for. I knew I could count on him if anything untoward erupted. Earp is a bit of a rounder, but he takes his job seriously—in fact, much too seriously sometimes. Now neither of us has to worry about him again. That card's been played, and he lost."

"You could have warned me."

"I know, but what's the fun in that?" Julius had laughed. "You're an actress now, Chastity, and I knew you were up to the task. After tomorrow night's performance, however, if the weather holds, I want you and Beau on the next train to Chicago. I need a favor, and afterwards," he'd said, his demeanor sobering, "on to Harrowhill for you."

A clink of silver on glassware brought me back to the moment. Julius stood up, raising his glass, and all eyes focused on him, elegant in his black velvet waistcoat, the embodiment of the aristocrat he truly was.

"A toast to all my troupe. Once again, you have delivered

an amazing evening's entertainment, despite all odds, weather and otherwise. I treasure each and every one of you. Thanks as well to Governor Anthony for this magnificent repast and the favor he has shown us."

We all drank once again, and Beau and I linked gazes. I knew we were thinking the same thing. *Here's to a life on the road as well as the stage,* I thought, *because the road was once again where we were headed.*

PART III

The course of true love never did run smooth.
--Shakespeare, *A Midsummer Night's Dream, Act I*

CHAPTER 19

"*M*a'am?" The elderly woman across the aisle tapped my arm. "Do you usually see people riding outside the train?" She smiled unsteadily, her eyes watery in her sun-worn face. "This is the first time I've been on one, but is that something that's real likely?"

I peered out the window, but I didn't see anyone riding, only blowing snow and late afternoon skies. "Well, I really don't know," I said, "but it would seem rather pointless, wouldn't you think? It's been a long while since the last town, and it's pretty cold out there."

Poor thing, her nerves were getting the best of her. I patted her arm. "I wouldn't worry about it. Maybe you could use a little nap?"

Her smile fell away, and she glared at me. "I'm not so old I'm seeing things, missy," she said. "Maybe you can't see them now, but I know what I saw." She turned away, affronted.

I felt a trickle of unease. She didn't seem so far gone to be seeing things. Only two kinds of people would be riding alongside a train, if indeed anyone was: lawmen or outlaws. Neither of which boded well, especially the former. I looked out the window, and yet another mile passed by uneventfully.

Don't be ridiculous, Chastity, I told myself. *The woman had a dream or something. All is well.*

We'd boarded the train to Chicago yesterday, just another Kansas farm couple, me in my calico bonnet and Beau in his homespun suit and flat-topped hat. We were accompanied by Mama Rosa and Angel, both in nondescript, plain clothing, and Angel with a hood that covered most of her stunning face. The less attention we drew, the better off we were. We had stowed our saddlebags and horse tack in the freight car with Rufus and Belle, bringing them along because, as Julius said, life takes many turns, or maybe we had both learned the hard way to always have another option.

Julius's favor turned out to be ensuring Mama Rosa and Angel arrived without incident at Julius's house on Lakeshore Drive. Angel was losing the sight in her left eye, and Julius had arranged for her to see a well-known specialist. Sitting in the seat facing us, both had dozed off, snug under their blanket. Angel was frightened and apprehensive about her coming appointment. Even though she was a very sophisticated fifteen, she badly needed the comfort of the older woman. Mama Rosa, like a fierce mother hen with her only chick, was determined to be at her side.

The train rolled on through the endless empty prairie, but anything that put distance between me and Dodge City was beautiful to me. After Chicago, we'd catch the train to New York. The thought of seeing Leland and Matthias again soon made me happier than I would've thought possible, and, all in all, I was managing to be fairly optimistic.

Our train car was only about half full of homesteaders, businessmen, and a couple of families with children—no one that looked a lawman or seemed remotely interested in us. Nell had packed us a large basket of food, so we hadn't needed anything but coffee. I avoided venturing into the more private and fancier Pullman carriages, where the prosperous gentry traveled. We certainly didn't want to draw attention to ourselves. Our seats were fairly comfortable, especially when compared to a saddle, but it was cold and we made good use of the wool blanket Nell had insisted we take with us. I leaned my head on Beau's shoulder and drifted off.

My eyes flew open at the screech of brakes, and I lurched forward in my seat as the train slowed abruptly. Beau jerked awake, and the woman across the aisle shook her finger knowingly at me. We continued our slowdown and came to a final halt with a jolt. People were shouting, and children started to cry, likely at the panic of their parents. Mama Rosa and Angel were wide eyed, staring at us in silence. A porter appeared at the front of the car, hat askew and his hands held up, which was odd.

"Everything's all right, folks … a problem with the track ahead." His voice was shaky. "We'll be right as rain and on our way in no time. Just a short delay."

Then a single gunshot reverberated in the closed carriage, and the porter's body pitched forward and landed facedown in the aisle. A woman screamed, and one of the ranchers jumped out of his seat. A bearded man in a long duster stood behind the body and leveled his smoking pistol at the passengers. He wore a patch over one eye.

"Everybody shut up and sit down. You do what we tell you, and you won't end up like him," he said, and he kicked the man's body aside with his boot. Two other men followed behind him, brandishing guns, including a rifle.

Beau slunk down in his seat and pulled his hat lower, grabbing my hand. "It's the goddamn Ridleys, Chas," he whispered. "Don't move or the dumb bastards'll shoot us. I know how they work." He stared at our charges and put a finger to his lips.

Christ Jesus, I thought. *He sure did.* With Beau's darkened skin and hair, I hoped they wouldn't recognize him, but I was terrified they might.

The man with the patch strode down the aisle between the

KATHLEEN MORRIS

seats. "Here's how it's going to work, friends. Y'all throw your weapons of any kind into this bag here, along with any jewelry or money." He motioned behind him to the third man, who held out a burlap sack. "My brother Ed here's going to watch over y'all, and I'll be back in a few minutes."

He went through the door at the end with the other man. Ed held out the sack, and everyone dutifully dumped things into it. When he came to us, Beau kept his eyes downcast and handed me some paper money and a few coins, which I plunked into the sack. I saw no point in handing over the knife that I'd strapped to my calf. Sweet homesteading women didn't carry knives. Mama glared at him and tossed in a bracelet.

He continued down the aisle, ripping a pocket watch off a man in a brown suit and a brooch from a woman, who shrieked in outrage, until he reached the end of the aisle and turned, pointing his gun at us. I could hear screams and a gunshot or two from the other end of the train. Within a few minutes Tom Ridley, for that's surely who he was, and his brother Whitey came back through, dragging behind them a man in a tailored suit and a girl who looked about thirteen. A smartly dressed woman, tears streaming down her cheeks, followed, reaching fruitlessly for the girl. Whitey carried a similar burlap sack, bulging and heavy now.

"Lookee here, Ed. It's our old poker-playing friend, Mr. Richard White. All that money he bragged about having with him back in Kansas City ain't with him now."

Tom Ridley shook Richard White like a recalcitrant dog. "Lyin' to people you've cheated at cards ain't nice, White, especially a well-known Chicago banker who talks big like you. Since you lied about that strongbox you said you carried, we're going to have to go with another plan."

The man was *in extremis*, his face pale, limbs shaking. The girl's face was ghostly pale, bright pink spots on her cheeks as she clung to her father.

"I can get you the money," White stammered. "When we get to Chicago. My father will vouch for me. As much as you want, I swear to God."

Tom Ridley smiled. "Well, you know, Richard, we've had to go to some trouble here"—he looked down at the porter's body and then the burlap bags—"so I don't think we'll be stayin' on the train with you. We're going to do this a little different, now." He leaned into White and half whispered in his ear, but all of us could hear him say, "We're just going to deal with your rich daddy."

Richard White's head exploded in a red mist, spattering the girl's face and dress, and the woman began to shriek like a banshee. Beau gripped my hand so hard I thought it'd break.

Ridley dropped Richard White's body with a look of disgust. He turned to the woman and slapped her hard across the face. The screaming stopped abruptly, and Ridley sat her down on an empty seat.

"Mrs. White, here's how it's going to go. We'll be leaving now, with your daughter." He shoved the girl at his brother, Ed. "Tell John White we'll be in touch shortly and to have $100,000 ready if he wants to see his granddaughter alive again."

She gasped, and he wagged his finger in warning. "Don't start up again. Tell me you understand."

She swallowed and stared at him. "I understand. Please, don't hurt Amelia."

Ridley patted her on the head like a puppy, and she flinched. "She'll be just fine, but your husband was a very bad boy, Mrs. White. I know how rich his father is, and I'm sure he'll be happy to get his granddaughter back, especially when her mother pleads for her return. Don't disappoint me now."

They made their way up the aisle, carrying the bags and girl. As they passed, Ridley leaned down and grabbed the blanket that still covered us, slinging it over his shoulder. "Thanks, ma'am," he said. "Wouldn't want our little princess to get cold, now, would we?" He never even glanced at our faces.

* * *

THE SOUNDS OF THE RIDLEYS' horses died away and so did the frightened silence in the train. Wails, shouting, stomping feet, and not-so-ladylike screams erupted throughout the train. I filled my lungs with relief; I'd been holding my breath as well as Beau's hand. Mama and Angel were as pale as the snow outside, but the red splotches on the older woman's cheeks suggested her volatile temper was about to surface.

"Christ Jesus," I said, turning to Beau. "You rode with those animals?"

He ignored me, got up, and gently put his arm around Mrs. White, who was still sitting, silent as a stone, on the seat Tom Ridley had put her in. Beau guided her over and carefully sat her down beside me, taking off his jacket and putting it around her shoulders. She was in shock, her face pale and eyes staring. I felt a bit like that myself, having just witnessed two men murdered before my eyes, but then one of them hadn't been my husband, and, to be honest, sudden violence and I had become more than passing acquaintances.

For a long minute, even through the chaos around us, she stared into the distance. Finally, she blinked and focused on Beau's face.

"Save my daughter," she said, and the dam broke, sobs engulfing her. I held her while she cried, but her tears subsided much quicker than I thought they would.

"Ma'am, I'm so sorry about your husband," I said, "and your daughter."

"Don't be so sorry about him," she said, her voice low but cutting. "He was a lying scoundrel. Amelia is all I care about." She brushed her hands across her cheeks. She took a good look at us then, taking in our homely clothes, and I could see hope turn to disappointment in her face. "Thank you for your concern, but you can't take on men like that. We'll have to wait for the sheriff."

"Attention, people, attention, please."

The train conductor stood at the front of the car, followed by two other uniformed railroad workers, likely the engineers. Blood trickled down the side of his face, and he blanched when he looked down at the bodies in the aisle, but he plunged on.

"The train tracks have been dynamited," he said. "We can't proceed until a repair crew is sent out from Peoria, and they won't realize we need help until we don't arrive." People finally started listening at the last sentence. "Conserve your food and water." With that, he walked through the car and into the next one without a backwards glance, stepping over the bodies of the porter and Richard White. I guess he wasn't in the corpse retrieval business—or the empathy one either.

Beau turned back to Mrs. White, holding out a piece of paper and a pencil. "Write down your father-in-law's address, please."

She stared at him for a long minute and then wrote on the paper and handed it back. Beau stuffed it in his pocket and whispered something in her ear. He nodded at Mama Rosa and Angel, and the four of us gathered in the back of the car, heads together.

"Ladies," Beau said, his voice low. "I made a promise to Julius, but I need your help. Tell me honestly, Mama, can you find your way safely to Julius's house once the train gets to Chicago?"

Mama Rosa snorted, black eyes snapping. "Of course I can, young man. I'm not decrepit, you know. I've been there many times. Your job was to keep us safe in the event something like just what happened occurred." She put her hands on her hips. "You did that very well. I saw them coming, but it was too late. Now, you have something else to do, and you're wasting time. We'll be fine, and Julius would agree with me. They'll be here in no time and get the tracks repaired. Go do what you can for that poor family. You'll be back with us soon. This I know." She gave Beau a gentle shove. "Go."

I followed Beau through train cars full of upset passengers, no one really noticing us in the chaos, and ended up in the freight car with Rufus and Belle, roped in and distinctly unhappy about it. I sidled in, leaning into Rufus, and rubbed my hands over both of them, whispering in their ears. Beau was rummaging through our saddlebags.

"Beau," I said. "Talk to me. We aren't a posse or Pinkertons who are used to hunting down killers."

He looked up. "I can't see what else to do, Chas, and I feel like I have to do somethin'. There's nobody else even got a horse, 'cept us." His face was grim. "I know what they're like, and that little girl's in big trouble."

"The kind of trouble that farmer's wife had?" I put my hands on his shoulders. "The kind of trouble I've had?"

He nodded. "And likely they'll kill her, too, so I have to try."

I nodded and stepped away, quickly unbuttoning my dress. "Then I guess we better hurry. Hand me that other saddlebag with my pants."

"Oh, no," Beau said. "You're staying right here. This isn't your fight, Chas, and I'm not draggin' you into it. You've been through too much as it is."

He grabbed both my hands away from the buttons, and I tore them out of his grasp.

"You listen to me, James Beauregard Durant, goddamnit. This isn't your fight, either, but if you're going to make it into one, to try and make up for riding with the Ridleys all that time, then it's my fight, too." My voice was rising, but I didn't care. "I've got an investment in your skinny ass, and I plan on seeing it again, which I likely won't if you go chasing off hell for leather with no backup after three men who've already nearly succeeded in killing you once, and they'll be sure to finish the job this time. We take care of each other." I stopped and took a breath. "Now, hand me my fucking pants."

Beau stared at me like my hair was on fire, and it rather felt like it was. Then he pulled me into him roughly, kissing me so hard at first that our teeth clicked together, but we worked through that. He pulled back and chuckled. "You surely do get a head of steam on, Chas. Your vocabulary's gotten more interestin', too."

I sniffed. "Comes from hanging out with outlaws, I suppose."

Within ten minutes, we'd changed clothes, packed the saddlebags, saddled the horses, checked our ammunition, and thrown back the doors. The calico dress and the flat-topped hat were left on the hay-strewn floor, along with the ghosts of a sweet Kansas farm couple. We rode off into the darkening plain, headed northeast, spurred by vengeance. We termed it justice, and maybe it was that, too.

CHAPTER 20

C/e rode hard, but it was full dark by the time we reached Peoria. The Ridleys' tracks were obliterated by all the others once we hit the main street. We stopped at the train depot to tell them of the attack, and then we tied up the horses outside a restaurant/saloon that seemed the busiest. The warmth was welcome, but my cheeks and hands tingled painfully as they rose in temperature. We sat down at a table nearest the door and surveyed the room. We weren't expecting to see the Ridleys, especially with their captive, but maybe they'd not only been through, but had been holed up nearby before hitting the train.

"What can I get you fellas?" The waitress was maybe eighteen, sashaying her hips as she wiped her hands on a stained apron. I'd stuffed my short curls under my hat and was once again Charlie Birdsong, if no one looked too closely. She didn't, charmed by Beau.

"Two coffees," Beau said, smiling at her, "and two ham sandwiches, if you have them."

"Sure do, honey," she grinned. "We'll get you all warmed up. Cold night out there."

She was as good as her word, bringing the coffee first. I

warmed my hands on the cup. "So, honey," I said, taking a sip. "What's next?"

He shot me a baleful look. "Let's see if my new friend has seen our old ones. Unless you got a better idea."

I shrugged. "Sounds good to me."

We wolfed down the sandwiches, and the smiling waitress came back to refill our coffee cups.

"Listen, we were hopin' to meet up with some friends of ours here tonight. You seen three gentlemen, one with an eye patch, come around?" Beau said.

Her smile disappeared, and she eyed us suspiciously. "If you're talking about them Ridleys, they ain't no gentlemen; they're not welcome in here no more, and I mistook you two for decent folk if they're friends of yours."

"Hold on," I said. "They're not exactly friends of ours, and we don't like them any more than you do." I lowered my voice to nearly a whisper and leaned towards her. "They've stolen something valuable, and we aim to get it back. If you can give us any help, we'd appreciate it."

"We weren't sure you good people knew the truth about them," Beau said, his green eyes sincere. "With men like the Ridleys, we can't be too careful."

She put the coffeepot down on the table and sat on an empty chair beside us, studied our faces for a moment, and apparently decided we were trustworthy, or at least more so than the Ridleys.

"See, they been around town for a week or so, and the other night they nearly tore the place up, going after some farmer who didn't like the remarks they was making about his wife, if you get my meaning," she said. "My daddy owns this place, and he run them out of here with a shotgun. Nobody much in town likes them either."

Beau patted her hand. "I surely can understand that, miss. You have any idea where they been stayin'?"

She shrugged. "Not the hotel, I can say that, since my

uncle runs it and won't let to them. I heard someone say they were keeping their horses out at the old Jefferson place, but I can't say for sure. Could be a lot of places, the way this town's growing."

Beau and I exchanged glances. We got directions to the Jefferson place, thanked her, and headed outside, taking along a bag of extra sandwiches.

"She'll be talkin'," he said, swinging into the saddle.

"Let her," I said. "We'll be long gone or dead before anybody listens. Besides, they'll be all busy rescuing the train."

He shrugged, and we spurred our horses north into the wind.

We found a weathered clapboard house and a barn that looked as though it was about to fall down about a mile out of town, just where she'd said the Jefferson place would be. There were no lights on in either of the buildings, but we approached cautiously. Beau opened the door to the house, and we stepped inside. It looked abandoned, but only recently. There were ashes in the fireplace, empty cans of beans and peaches, and a few empty whiskey bottles. It appeared that someone had camped out in the main room, but the others were empty of anything but dust and mice. Forlorn gingham curtains hung crookedly from a rod on a window. *Houses can be as lonely as people when no one cares for them anymore*, I thought.

"How long you think they've been gone?" I said, kicking an empty bean can.

"This mornin'. There's still embers on the bottom of the grate," Beau said. "Let's take a look at the barn."

Some relatively fresh hay was still scattered on the dirt floor of the barn, and muddy foot- and hoofprints had just begun to harden with the cold.

"What do you want to do?" I said. "We could spend the night here and set off early in the morning. I know they've got a head start, but I bet they don't think anybody's trailing them, and they'll probably stop, too."

Beau looked uncertain. "It's the stoppin' that worries me, especially if the girl is contentious. Still, they've had a full day of it, and they can't see no better than we can in the dark. We're likely to have a horse break a leg."

So we went back to the house and built a fire. I dug out a bottle of whiskey from Nell's stash, and we settled in for a few hours. I rested my head on Beau's shoulder, and he slid his arm around me. The apple wood we'd found in the wood box smelled good, dispelling some of the dusty imprint of the old house.

"You ever kill anybody?" I said. I ran my hand over his cheek and rested it on his throat, idly stroking and feeling his pulse under my fingers.

"Not on purpose," he said.

"It's not easy, but, in some ways, it's not hard either. I surprised myself," I said. "I think it all depends who's being killed. From what I can see, the world would be better off without the Ridleys."

"That doesn't mean we should do it," he said. "Judge, jury, and all that. Still, gettin' that girl home is what matters."

"Yes, it is." I turned around and stared close at him. "We agreed, then?"

"On what?"

"We kill them and take the girl. We knew what this was when we got off that train."

"All right," he said.

We came together that night in the empty house like it was the last loving thing we'd ever do on this earth, and maybe it would be. Neither of us had set out to be vigilantes, but you never knew where life would take you, and every day that passed convinced me once again of that.

* * *

Munching on more sandwiches, we were on the road before dawn. Rufus and Belle had enjoyed the leftover hay in the barn and were ready to run. Hot coffee would've made Beau and me more eager to do the same, but compulsion drove us just as well. It had stopped snowing, but it was misty, the fog hanging low among the skeletal trees as we left. If the sun broke through while we rode down the road, I didn't notice.

After a couple of hours, we hadn't met anyone on the road, going or coming. I pulled up and turned to Beau. The mist had dissipated somewhat, but freezing droplets clung to our clothes and hats. I was miserable, and I could tell he wasn't any happier with the conditions.

"How far ahead you think they are?"

"Hard to say. They've got to be headed this way if they intend to ransom her to her grandfather. Whitey seemed to know a lot about the family, so Chicago would be their destination." He shook his head, and I could tell he was worried. "We don't catch up to them before then, it'll be hard to find 'em in a big city like that."

I agreed, and we rode harder, watching for any sign along the road as we went.

A few miles farther, Beau held up his hand and pointed to the east side of the road. Here was a grove of trees, and a clear path had been trampled through the brush. We approached cautiously, hands on our guns, but we needn't have bothered. There was a cold fire and little else. They'd gone on, but not very long ago. Beau dismounted and walked around the campsite. He stooped and picked up something from the ground, dangling it from his finger. A red hair ribbon.

"It's them, all right, and they're not far ahead of us," Beau said. "I don't like this, Chas. We catch them out in the open, we can't get clear shots because one of them has to be riding with the girl." He tucked the ribbon in his pocket.

"I know." It worried me, too, but we had little choice.

Maybe they'd take a break around noon, if we got lucky. We checked our guns and ammunition and rode on.

It couldn't have been more than an hour later that we came upon a woman covered in a blanket, sobbing while she cradled a man's head in her lap as he lay on the cold ground. Household goods, books, and farm tools were strewn around her. We both dismounted. I put my arm gently on her shoulders while Beau pulled away a buckskin jacket from a wound high on the man's shoulder, the blood seeping into the snow.

"Tell me," I said. She turned her face to me, and the bleakness in her eyes saddened me. This was a woman on her last hope.

Her voice was halting. "They come up on us from behind and just shot Michael for no reason. We were on our way to Springfield to his people." Her voice broke, and my arm tightened around her. "They took our wagon, throwing our things out like they meant nothing, and rode away. They laughed while they did it."

She looked up at me. "They had a girl with 'em. She looked scared."

I glanced over at Beau, who was busy binding up the man's wound. He didn't have much to work with, but he was doing the best he could. I sighed, knowing we couldn't leave them here; they'd surely perish. Beau gave the man a drink of whiskey, and he coughed, but then he sat up, staring blankly at us.

"Can you help us?" he asked, his voice thready.

"Yes," Beau sighed and shot me a look. I didn't say a word. We got them onto the horses and, riding double, started down the road again, much slower than before. We came into Joliet mid-afternoon, dropped them both at the local doctor's office, and rode out again before anyone could ask questions. The wife clung to my hand when I left her on the doctor's porch.

"I don't even know your name," she said. "But for me,

you're an angel of mercy. A lot of people wouldn't have stopped—or brought us here. Bless you."

I hugged her, this woman I'd never see again. "We're not most people, ma'am. Only thing I ask," I said as I stared into her eyes, "anybody wants to know what we look like or where we're headed, you can't remember. Can you do that?"

"'Course I can," she said and squeezed my hand. "May God keep you."

Beau came out after carrying her husband inside, and we got back on our tired horses. Chicago wasn't that far away, and we couldn't afford to waste a minute.

Rufus and Belle were not as tired as we thought, now that they were relieved of half their burden. I was not relieved of mine. We had to catch up to the Ridleys before we hit the city. Shooting people on the streets of Chicago wasn't likely to go unnoticed. Even as we rode, the countryside was becoming more populated, more small farms popping up here and there with a faint cluster of lights through the dusk. Still, there was lots of open country, which we needed.

Darkness fell, and we slowed some, not wanting either of the horses to catch a leg. We waited in vain for a moon to rise and guide us under the starlit sky, but it didn't, maybe because of clouds, maybe the wrong time of the month. I hadn't been paying attention to that.

"Chas."

"Yes?"

"If we don't get to them tonight, we've got a problem."

"I know." I'd noticed that our minds had started to think as one, and I smiled in the dark, although he couldn't see me. Beau Durant was a piece of me now, and I liked it.

I saw the glimmer of a fire in the night ahead and pulled up short, just as Beau did the same.

"Could we get this lucky?" he said.

"Probably some tinker or just travelers like us," I said. But still …

We dismounted, leading the horses, and finally tying them to a tree a few hundred yards from the firelight as we crept forward, our boots crunching on the frozen grass, as much as we tried to step lightly.

A wagon stood a ways off from the fire, and four horses munched with little success on the grass. I smelled bacon and then heard a man laugh. Beau tensed, clutching my arm and pulling me down into a crouch beside him.

"It's them," he said.

I didn't dispute him. He'd know.

We were close, but we needed to be aware of where everyone was, especially the girl. We waited, my knees aching in the cold, and crept closer. The skeletal trees and winter-dead bushes offered little cover, and only the dark itself shielded us. I heard more laughter and saw the gleam of a glass bottle in the flames of the fire.

"The wagon was a good idea, Ed, hafta say," one man said. "Them sacks was heavy as hell, and that damn girl, wailin' and carryin' on all the time. I couldn't have stood much more of that, even though we was tradin' off."

"Whitey, I don't think you rode with her more'n five miles, so shut up," another said. Then he stood up, and I could see the black patch over his eye. Tom Ridley. He walked over to the wagon and peered into the bed. Satisfied, he walked back to the fire.

"She sleepin'?" said the man who had to be Whitey. "Maybe we should wake her up and have a little fun? It mighta been only five miles, but I know titties when I feel 'em." He laughed and took another pull on the bottle. "She's more'n old enough."

Apparently Tom disagreed, as he cuffed Whitey on the side of the head, and Ed snickered.

"Sometimes I think you two are even dumber than I thought," Tom Ridley said. "She's a hostage, you stupid bastards. She has to be returned in good condition." His hand scratched at his beard, and he was quiet for a while. " 'Course, I guess that means different things to different people." He grabbed the bottle away from his brother and took a long swig. "She is a nice little piece. Untouched, as they say, which I always like."

I'd heard enough and so had Beau, who nudged me and jerked his head backwards. We crab-walked about twenty yards to a couple of trees and stood up.

"I'll get Whitey first. You good for Ed?" I said, pulling up the Winchester. "Then we both go for Tom?"

His eyes gleamed in the faint light of the fire, and he pulled his Colt from its holster. "Yeah, that'll work. I think we have to go, right now. I need to get closer, though. There's no range on this thing."

He was right, so I waited a few seconds as he went closer. Doubt slithered in, but so did flashes of the farmers and the bodies on the train, and my decision was made. I sighted at Whitey's head and took a deep breath, holding it as I'd been taught until I pulled the trigger. There was a millisecond, and Whitey's head exploded, his stained hat spiraling into the darkness, and the sound of the shot shocking the other two. Ed jumped up, Beau's bullet took him in the chest, and he fell backwards, arms out flung. Tom Ridley was much faster than I'd thought he would be. I sighted on him, and he went for cover behind the wagon as Beau's next shots went wild.

Ridley grabbed the girl and hauled her out of the wagon, running into the dark, holding her body against his. I ran into the light of the fire, Beau ahead of me, shooting.

"Drop the girl, Tom!" he shouted. "You're done."

"Not hardly. That you, Beauregard? Thought you was dead."

Shots, not ours, erupted into the night, and my left arm felt like it'd been hit by a horse, only much, much worse. I felt the blood running down into my hand, and the pain was excruciating. *So this is what it feels like to be gunshot*, I thought, stumbling and dropping the Winchester. I tripped, and my head hit something sharp. I remember seeing Beau lunge toward me, yelling my name, and then a much deeper blackness than that under the stars, which I could see no more.

CHAPTER 21

 hicago

SOMEBODY WAS MOANING, and finally, I realized it was me. Choking on my own bile, I raised my head, my skull coming into contact with something warm and soft.

"Easy," Beau said in my ear. "Not much further."

"What the hell," I said, staring into the darkness, conscious now of the pounding hooves below me and the dull pain in my head and arm.

"You were shot and hit your head," he said. He sounded somewhat irritated, and I tried to turn and look at him. "Lie back, Chas. I got this."

* * *

THE NEXT TIME I raised my head, all I saw was tall brick buildings instead of trees and fields. The horse's hooves pounded in rhythm to the throbbing in my head. People, a lot of people, passed us as we rode along a wide thoroughfare. Wagons, freighters, carriages, even streetcars drove past us as we plodded along, two people on one horse, pulling another. More than a few glances came our way.

"Chicago?" I croaked, sitting up in the saddle, Beau's strong arm around me.

"Sure as hell smells like it," he said laconically and I started to laugh, except it hurt. I glanced at my arm, wrapped in what looked like a plaid flannel shirt, and everything came back in a rush. I'd shot Whitey Ridley, Beau had shot Ed, and apparently Tom had shot me.

"Where's the girl?"

"Hell if I know, Chas. Tom took her and lit out." He peered down at me. "I was a little more concerned with you."

"Well," I said. Not that I wasn't grateful. We went on.

"So where in hell you s'pose Lakeshore Drive is at? I don't see no damn lake."

I blinked owlishly around at the traffic and tall buildings. "Not here, clearly. We need to ask somebody."

Beau grunted and guided Rufus and Belle to the side of the avenue. Mama Rosa had known how to get to Julius's house, and I hadn't thought to ask her for directions or specifics in the chaos of leaving the train. All I knew was it was Number 28. I could only hope they were already there.

Beau dismounted and looked up at me worriedly. "You all right there, Chas? I'll just be a minute. Hold on to the saddle horn."

I nodded, taking his advice, and watched him enter the door of some emporium. That saddle horn kept me upright as I watched the stream of humanity flowing around and washing over me, as I sat like a stone half submerged in a river. A few minutes later Beau came out, shaking his head. He got back up behind me, ignoring Rufus's huffing. The horse had been pretty sure we were heading for some nice hay and a rest.

"Man in the store says head north at the next cross street

and keep goin' until we see water," Beau said. "There'll be a road along there, and we'll follow it to the right house."

"I can ride by myself," I said, although I wasn't entirely sure. I felt bad about Rufus, though.

"Nope." Beau held me around the waist. "You'd likely fall off, and some damn streetcar or whatever the hell those things are would run you over. We ain't got time for that, Chas. You need a doctor."

I nodded and leaned my head back against Beau's chest, but the pains in my arm and head were both throbbing. I was starting to fade, despite the noise and excess of human traffic, something I'd been blissfully happy without for the last few weeks. Beau guided the horses back into the river of traffic, and along we went.

Lakeshore Drive was easy to find in the end and so was Julius's house. The street was muddy, but the houses lining it were outstanding. There were huge crenellated mansions, brick edifices that looked like some of the New York apartment buildings I'd seen, and Victorian monstrosities that rivaled anything I'd seen in Boston. Julius's house was toward the end, with empty spaces between it and the next house. It was modest in comparison: a smaller, tasteful Victorian; three stories with its peaked roof and a round tower; painted grey with accompanying colors of blue and purple; a wraparound porch; and a welcoming drive. The best part of the street, however, was the other side: Lake Michigan itself—so large it could have been the ocean, its clear blue waters lapping against a rocky beach, winter sunlight glinting and sparkling across the waves.

Like refugees from a storm, Beau and I made our way to the front door. Before he could even touch the elaborate iron knocker, the door was flung open. Mama Rosa and a pale man in a black suit urged us inside.

"We need a doctor," Beau said. "Chastity's been shot."

Mama Rosa clucked her tongue and began issuing orders,

and the next half hour passed in a blur. Washed, dressed in a flannel nightgown, and ensconced in a four-poster bed by the time the doctor arrived, I was feeling much better. But it didn't last long. The doctor promptly had me moved downstairs onto a table in what looked like a keeping room and held out a healthy dose of laudanum.

"This will hurt, my dear," he said matter of factly. "Drink it all. You've had a concussion, but your head will feel fine in a day or two. However, that bullet has to come out." He looked professional and brooked no resistance, his eyebrows twitching under piercing, dark eyes. He'd already laid out some wickedly sharp and shiny instruments on a clean white towel and had donned a white apron. I swallowed nervously.

"Christ Jesus," I mumbled. "This sounds bad." I drained the glass, and Beau held my hand and looked at me, nodding in reassurance. Mama Rosa stood beside him and smoothed my hair from my forehead.

"It will be fine," she said and turned to the doctor. "She is very important to Julius, Dr. Hamlin. Your best work is expected, and I know you will not disappoint us."

"Of course," the doctor said, now sounding a little nervous himself.

It was dark when I opened my eyes, a faint glow coming from the pretty rose-patterned lamp on the bedside table. It was enough to see Beau sprawled in a chair beside the bed, snoring softly. There was a bulky bandage on my arm. My mouth felt as though I'd been chewing cotton balls, and I grasped the glass of water on the table like it was manna from heaven, draining the glass, then falling back onto the pillows. If this is what laudanum does to you, how can people become addicted to the stuff? With that thought, I slept again.

Something smelled really good. I opened my eyes, morning light streaming through the big windows, glittering off the lake. Beau was back, along with Mama Rosa, carrying a tray. Beau propped me up on pillows, and Mama put the tray on my lap, whisking off the cover. I was ravenously hungry, and I quickly devoured bacon, eggs, and strawberries. I downed a frosted glass of juice that tasted like oranges and something undefinable but tangy while the two of them watched wordlessly. Feeling like an ungrateful brat, I leaned back, sated with food but hungry for information.

"How you feelin'?" Beau said. He sat on the edge of the bed, and Mama Rosa perched in the chair I'd seen Beau sleeping in the night before.

My arm hurt, but my head was clear. "Not too bad," I said. "I don't remember much about what the doctor did."

"He took out the bullet, put in a couple stitches, and said he'd be back today later to check on you," Beau said, leaning over to kiss my cheek. "He says it looks good, but you gave me one hell of a scare, Chastity."

Mama Rosa pushed Beau away and took my hand, silently perusing my palm. She shrugged and turned my hand over, patting it, and then put her hand on my forehead, staring into my eyes. Seemingly satisfied, she stepped back.

I threw off the bedcovers and stood up, quickly sitting back down as dizziness nearly overwhelmed me. Beau grabbed my shoulder, but I pushed him away. "It'll pass. I need to get up."

I took tentative steps over to the window, growing stronger with each step. Mama Rosa smiled, nodding her head, then turned and left the room. I padded back to Beau, and he enveloped me in his arms, the best comfort there was.

"Thank you," I said, the words muffled on his chest. "Turnabout's fair play."

"Hmmph," he said and picked me up, laying me back on the bed. "You need to rest."

"No, I need to find Tom Ridley," I said. "Then I'll be feeling just fine."

He laughed. "No, I need to find Tom Ridley," he said.

"You, on the other hand, are staying right in this bed for at least another day."

I stared at him. "Only way I'm staying in this bed for any time at all is if you get into it with me. It's my arm that's shot, not the rest of me."

He stared at me, a smile playing at the side of his mouth. "Mama Rosa will have my hide." He ran his hand underneath my nightgown, and I shivered. Right now, Beau Durant was all I wanted and the one thing that would really make me feel better. We'd work out the rest of the day after starting it properly.

"I think Mama Rosa knows exactly what we're up to," I said. "Whatever she put in that juice, it's working."

Turned out, I didn't notice the pain in my arm at all for a while.

BEAU PULLED ON HIS BOOTS. "Henley and I are headed for John White's house. Find out if Ridley's contacted him yet." He stood up and pushed his hair out of his eyes. I grabbed his arm.

"I'm going."

"The hell you say, Chas. You're not up to that yet," he said. "Once we talk to him, I'll be back, and we can figure out what to do."

I pulled my nightgown over my head and gently shoved him out of the way. "Where's my clothes?"

My arm hurt, but that wasn't going away soon. The rest of me felt just fine, and I couldn't loll around in bed for a day when a girl's life was at stake. We'd already lost a day, and God knows what Tom Ridley had managed in that time. Beau shook his head but handed me my shirt and pants, freshly laundered by somebody in Julius's well-staffed house. He sat scowling while I washed and dressed.

"I oughta go get that doctor and have him give you some

more laudanum," he said. "You are the most stubborn woman I ever met."

"That may be, but I'm going with you," I said, cinching my belt. "Who's Henley, anyway?"

"Julius's butler," Beau said. "Although I think he's a lot more'n a butler. We talked a lot last night, and he's pretty well-informed and … well, you'll see." He grinned and handed me my hat. "Want me to carry you downstairs?"

Henley was indeed more than a butler. The man in the black suit I'd briefly seen yesterday when we arrived stood in the entry hall as we descended the stairs. Now he was still wearing a rather elegant black suit but also a stylish hat, and I could see the handle of a gun in a shoulder holster under his jacket. He smiled and took my hand.

"Miss James, I'm delighted to see you're feeling better," he said, "but are you certain you wouldn't like to rest while we handle this?"

"Mr. Henley, I truly believe I can be of some assistance. Besides, Mr. Durant and I are in this together, and we intend to finish it together."

He smiled. "Your friend here assured me you would feel that way. I might suggest, however, that you could be more persuasive if you were attired in a manner more befitting your sex and social position?" He glanced briefly at my pants and boots.

I laughed ruefully. "You may well be right, Mr. Henley. But perhaps Mr. Durant has neglected to mention that I'm a wanted woman?"

He shrugged. "This is Chicago, Miss James. I hardly think the Kansas authorities' reach extends here. Besides, our police have more paramount concerns."

He may have been right; I didn't know. I did know, however, that I wasn't willing to take a chance on it. I'd dress like a woman when I felt comfortable doing so. We couldn't afford to take a chance on me getting arrested when the White girl's life depended on us, no matter what some know-it-all butler thought.

"Well, I don't," I said. "We made somebody a promise, and we intend to deliver on it. Just so you know, Henley, my name is Charlie Birdsong for now." I stuffed what was left of my hair under my hat and clamped it firmly on my head.

Out the door we went, Beau taking my arm and trying not to laugh at the expression on Henley's face. Instead of taking our horses, we climbed into a buggy, and Henley drove, not saying another word as we turned off Lakeshore Drive and into the streets of Chicago.

White's imposing brick mansion in Lincoln Park wasn't far. We hadn't notified anyone we were coming, but Henley handled that matter masterfully at the door, and we were escorted into a book-lined study by a rigid butler (who seemed to know Henley) and were told to wait. Beau and I sat on the sofa, and Henley stood by the fireplace, where a small fire had just been kindled. It was chilly in the room, and we hadn't been offered any refreshment. I was apprehensive but there was little I could do about that.

The door opened, and a tall man dressed in an immaculate business suit, his white hair carefully coiffed, stepped in. He stood over us briefly before taking a seat in the chair behind a massive, walnut desk, rather like a king on his throne.

"John Cornelius White. Who are you people, and what do you want?" His voice was commanding, but his face betrayed him. His eyes were bloodshot, and it looked as though he hadn't been sleeping well.

Not the greeting I'd hoped for but, given the paucity of information he'd been given, not unexpected. I cleared my throat.

"Mr. White, I'm Charlie Birdsong." I pitched my voice into the familiar lower tone. "This is Mr. Durant and Mr. Henley. We're very sorry for your loss. Mr. Durant and I were on the train with your daughter-in-law and disembarked to follow the outlaws that killed your son and abducted your granddaughter. We caught up to them north of Peoria, but one eluded us, taking your granddaughter with him. It was our understanding he was coming to you with a ransom demand."

The man's face paled, and he jerked upright, reaching for the bellpull. "Get out of my house."

Henley was very fast. He grabbed White's arm and gently forced him back into his chair. "Sir, I think you need to listen. Please. These two young gentlemen are guests of Mr. DeMonte, and, as you know, I am Mr. DeMonte's factor." White sat back, red spots of anger mottling his cheeks as he didn't really have a choice. He didn't look like a man who was used to not having a choice, and I don't think we were the first to put him in that position today. I looked at Beau in desperation.

He took over, his soft Southern drawl soothing. "Mr. White, I know this is difficult for you. We're just tryin' to help here, and whatever we can do, we will. We only want to help you and Amelia. I know you don't know anythin' about us, but you can trust us. Mr. Birdsong here has already been injured in the pursuit, but we persist—for the sake of your granddaughter and for your family."

White sat very still, thinking over what had been said. He briefly closed his eyes and then opened them, fixing us with a hawk-like stare. He reached for the bellpull once again, putting up a hand to forestall Henley.

The butler appeared in the doorway. "Yes, sir?"

"Please tell Laura to join us, will you, Grayson? And arrange for some coffee."

The butler nodded and turned away. We sat in silence for a few minutes, and the door opened once again. Laura White, the distraught woman from the train, entered the room. She

THE TRANSFORMATION OF CHASTITY JAMES

stopped in shock, staring at me and Beau, her hand at her throat, then rushed over to us.

"Oh, my God, it's you two. Have you seen Amelia? Do you know where she is?"

I stood up, taking her hand and gently pulling her down onto the sofa between us. "Yes, but the situation is more complicated, I'm afraid. We didn't have time to introduce ourselves properly," I said. "I'm Charlie Birdsong, and this is Beau Durant." She looked at me, puzzled, and I squeezed her hand. "I'll explain later," I whispered.

We'd already decided to leave out the part about killing Tom Ridley's brothers, saying that only Tom Ridley had ridden off with the girl. We'd told Henley and Mama Rosa, neither of whom seemed to be much bothered by the information, given the circumstances. I wasn't sure how long it would take the authorities to discover two bodies in the woods and figure out who they were, but I had a feeling it wouldn't take long, which could lead to complications we didn't need. Beau told them everything else, editing carefully. When he finished, both the Whites were pale, but the older man recovered quickly.

"Have you heard anything from Tom Ridley?" I said. "He didn't seem the sort to delay."

John White hesitated, and Henley stepped in smoothly. "Mr. White, I want to assure you Mr. DeMonte vouches completely for these young gentlemen, who have been caught up in this unfortunate situation simply out of a desire to help your family." He shot me a look. "Even though I myself feel they may be out of their depth here, as Mr. DeMonte's representative I take full responsibility for them and respect their ability to assist you, if we may do so."

White sighed heavily and leaned back in his chair. "Last night a message was delivered. We were warned not to tell anyone and especially not to contact the law or Amelia would be killed. He wants one hundred thousand dollars, which is ridiculous. Can you figure out how to manage that?"

Laura White gasped. "You didn't tell me, John. How could you keep this from me when you know I've been frantic with worry?"

"That's precisely why I haven't mentioned it, Laura," White snapped. "You being hysterical is of little help. I'm going to handle this. In fact, I think you should go upstairs and let us discuss this. Your nerves, you know."

Laura looked as though she'd been slapped, and my own temper flared. I stood up, putting my hand on her shoulder. Beau shook his head, but I was beyond caring. White seemed to care more about money than he did his granddaughter—and certainly more than he did his daughter-in-law.

"I insist Mrs. White not only stay but be informed of any developments, from now on, and I value her input on this whole affair," I said. "She knows more than any of us what's best for her daughter. Besides, she's been the one, besides me and Durant here, who's privy to what happened and the sort of person we're dealing with."

This time it was John White who looked as though he'd been slapped, but he held his hands out in surrender, scowling. I wondered how amenable he'd be if he knew I was a woman. Likely not at all, so that was best left until later, or maybe never.

The coffee arrived, along with sandwiches, and the maid put the tray down hastily on the desk, leaving without a word. It was good timing, helping to defuse any ill feelings. We served ourselves, even Laura White, who looked as though she hadn't eaten a bite for two days.

Henley sipped his coffee. "All right. What else did Ridley say? What's the next step, Mr. White?"

White eyed all three of us with some skepticism, but Laura stared intently at him, and he coughed. "He sent a street boy to tell me that he'd give me instructions on how to pay the

money and get my granddaughter in another message sometime today. George tried to grab him, but he got away."

"Have you told anyone else, the police or ...?"

"No." White shook his head. "I've been debating on that,
but no. No one but you." He stared at the wall behind us for a
few seconds. "To be honest, I've never had to deal with
anything like this, and I'm not sure what to do. What kind of
person would do the things he did?"

"An irredeemable piece of trash," Beau said. Everyone
looked at him as though a decision had been made, and I
guess it was. "We'll get Amelia back for you, Mr. White, but
you have to understand that what we plan to do and how we
do it is somethin' that never leaves this room. Do you agree?"

"Now wait a minute, young man," White said, frowning.
"This isn't the wild West, and I don't even know you people. I
can't condone something that's against the law."

"Damn you, John," Laura White said, standing up and
putting her hands on the desk. "That man killed Richard and
has my daughter, and you're sitting here like some scared little
boy whining about law? I wish you'd been on that train, then
you'd know." She turned to me and Beau. "These two were
the only ones with enough courage to do anything then, and,
if they're offering to help now, we're damn lucky."

John White looked at her as though she were a fluffy kitten
that had just scratched him for the first time.

"All right, all right, calm down, Laura," he said. "You're
right." He put his head down in his hands. "I've not been able
to think straight for the last two days."

This man, one of the lions of Chicago banking, was
clearly distraught and needed direction. He turned to me, for
some reason. "What do we do?"

I swallowed. My arm hurt like the devil, and maybe that
made me a little out of sorts, but we didn't have a lot of time
to waste.

"We wait for the next messenger, grab him, and see what

he knows. He had to come from somewhere. It's a big city, but we'll track him. If that doesn't work, we go to Plan B." I was making this up as I went.

White glared at me. "What's Plan B?"

"Take him the money, get your granddaughter, and then hold him for the police. Or kill him, which is frankly more likely, given the circumstances may be somewhat frantic, and I'm more concerned about Amelia and not at all about the fate of Mr. Ridley." I was sort of waiting for a collective gasp, but one never came. John White, however, did raise his eyebrows.

" 'Think therefore on revenge and cease to weep'," I said. "Don't you agree?"

For the first time, John White cracked a smile. "Oh, Mr. Birdsong. Who *are* you people?" He fixed me with a stare. " 'Cry havoc and let slip the dogs of war,' eh?" He stood up. "Fine, let's to it, then."

CHAPTER 22

We collectively decided to wait at White's house for the messenger to show, since we had no idea when that would be. I was fading a bit, so Laura led me to a bedroom upstairs, Beau following protectively, while Henley stayed with George and John White downstairs. I took off my hat and lay down gratefully on a down-filled counterpane, taking care to leave my boots pointing at the ceiling. Laura sat beside me.

"So, tell me why you're pretending to be a man. I don't understand any of this, but this particularly doesn't make sense."

"It's a long story, Mrs. White," I said. "All I can say right now is please trust us and go along with my little disguise. I think your father-in-law would be reluctant to allow a woman to go after Ridley if he knew." I smiled at her. "Nerves, you know."

She gave a stifled laugh. "I'll have to agree with your conclusion there. Thanks for standing up for me. He can be very intimidating and always gets his own way." She stood up. "Get some rest; you look like you need it." She left, closing the door softly.

"Well, this is a fine mess," Beau said, but he smiled, stroking my forehead, which was regrettably sweaty. "I told Henley to send for our rifles and saddlebags. There's no tellin' what could happen next."

"True," I mumbled. "I'd take that damn laudanum right now, but it's good we don't have any, 'case I have to shoot somebody."

"You know, Chas, I'm not a bad shot myself," Beau said. " 'Course I can't say I'm as good as you, so don't get your dander up, deadeye."

"What time's that doctor supposed to show up at Julius's?"

He shrugged. "This afternoon, so he said. 'Course, he's just coming to check on his patient, who's supposed to be resting in bed. Those stitches won't come out for at least a week. I guess he'll be disappointed."

"I guess he will," I said and fell asleep.

I dreamed. They weren't good dreams, but full of blood, gunshots, and remorse. I kept trying to justify the things I'd done, and, in the way of dreams, I did, although a cloudy feeling kept hovering and swirling around the phantas-magorical actions, as though I were a spirit that was keeping watch over myself. *Chastity James*, it said, *who have you become?* The answer was nebulous but not one that caused me to weep or change the outcomes each time the dreams recycled.

It was the yelling that woke me up, then the door slam-ming. It was dusk, by the look of the light coming into the bedroom. I swung my legs off the bed, dizzy for a minute but not as bad as this morning, and made my way to the stairs.

Henley and George were dragging a boy across the entry hall and into the study, a street urchin by the look of him, and he wasn't happy about it.

"Youse bastards, lemme go! I don't know nothin'!" he screeched, but nobody seemed to care.

By the time I navigated the stairs and made my way into

the study, they had ensconced him in a chair, still holding onto his arms. Beau stood over him.

"Calm down, son," he said. "We're not going to hurt you. Just tell us who gave you this message." He looked over at George. "This the same kid who brought the first one?"

George nodded, tightening his grip on the kid. "Looks like him to me."

The boy wriggled some more and spat in Beau's direction. "I ain't tellin' you shit."

Beau shrugged. "Yes, you are." He wiped the spit off his shirt. " 'Cause if you don't, we aren't gonna be so nice, comin' right up. Maybe you should think it over."

He couldn't have been over twelve. Dirty, his clothes ragged, and his boots held together with what looked like baling wire, his eyes were fierce and his jaw set. This wasn't going to go well.

"Hey," I said and stepped in beside Beau. "We need your help. Whoever gave you this message to bring isn't a person who cares about you or anybody else. How much did he pay you?"

"Five dollars. Like you care about anybody your own self," he snarled.

"Well. Five dollars is a lot," I said. "How do you feel about twenty dollars to tell us where he is?"

The kid quit struggling, and his eyes lit up, but his smirk was a dead giveaway. "Like you'd give me shit. And I just met him on the street, anyway. I don't know where he lives or nothin'."

I leaned down. "Oh, I think you do. What's your name?"

"Charlie."

I laughed. "Well, ain't that a coincidence. My name's Charlie, too. We got a lot in common, Charlie. You know, Charlie, I'm a nice guy, but my friends here"—I looked around—"they aren't. Maybe you and I can come to agreement before they lose their tempers."

He looked uncertain for the first time, his eyes darting to George and Henley and then Beau, none of whom looked friendly in the least.

I took a twenty-dollar gold piece out of my pocket and held it up. "What you think, Charlie?"

Charlie's eyes lit up. "Maybe I could remember somethin'."

"Like where you met this man?"

"Yeah." He looked at me. "You gonna let me go, if I tell you? With the money?"

"Yes," I lied. "So?"

"I think he was in one of the squats over south on Clark Street, behind McLain's Tavern, or at least he came from that direction."

"Really," Henley said. "He meet you there, or stays there?"

The kid shrugged. "How should I know, sport? He was there yesterday and today, too."

"If you're lying," Henley said, staring at him, "we'll find you. Believe it, you little gutter rat."

"I'm not, I swear," Charlie squealed. "I'm tellin' you true."

We all looked at one another and came to a joint decision. It was all we had.

"Tie him up," I said. "We can't afford to have him running around."

Charlie spat and howled, but nobody cared. Trussed in the chair like a feral cat with his tail belled, he soon quieted, shooting us hateful glares. I felt rather bad for him, but not enough to let him go and warn Ridley. We decided to move him into the kitchen, and Henley and George picked him up, chair and all.

The message read: "Bring the money, $100,000, or the girl dies. Tonight at ten o'clock. Behind McLain's Tavern. No police, no tricks. Come alone." The last was underlined.

I was surprised there were no misspelled words, but that

was the schoolteacher in me, I guess. Ridley had surprised me before, and it wouldn't happen again.

We sat down to dinner in the main dining room—even George, strictly against protocol for a butler, but White didn't seem to be holding to protocol and wisely so. In fact, I discovered that White, contrary to his earlier dismissal of Ridley's demands as ridiculous, had arranged to have the money delivered late that afternoon. I revised my earlier opinion of his parsimoniousness and concern for his granddaughter.

Personally, I had no intention of paying Ridley anything, so White needn't have any worries. Ridley wouldn't live to spend it anyway. I kept that to myself. Charlie Birdsong was a reasonable man, not some vengeful killer. Which was true, really. I didn't want to kill Ridley, necessarily, but I had become very pragmatic when it came to solving problems. Mercy had ceased to have a lot of meaning for me when it came to the Ridleys of this world, and, even though I realized this wasn't a trait that would serve me well for long, it seemed to be one that fit these particular circumstances quite well. I'd deal with the consequences of conscience later, if they became problematic. That may have been an issue for Chastity James some time ago, but I'd be willing to bet my life that matters of conscience didn't keep Wyatt Earp or Charlie Bassett from sleeping at night. Besides, I'd always been adaptable.

Our early dinner was a solemn affair, all of us apprehensive of the events to come later this evening. That in no way diminished the quality of the food nor the elegance of the table at which it was served.

White speared a bite of roast beef. "Gentlemen, I cannot begin to tell you how I appreciate your assistance. Just saying that is inadequate, but be assured you have my undying gratitude, and that comes with remuneration."

"Sir, we are happy to assist in this tragic situation," Henley said and took a sip from a very good Burgundy. "Mr. DeMonte would not think of doing anything less."

White smiled. "Ah, yes, Mr. DeMonte. I do appreciate his honorable presence in this city. He is a gentleman of taste and discernment." He glanced at Beau and me. "You are aware he's the Earl of Sandbrooke, are you not?"

Apparently White was ignorant of Julius's less than aristocratic theatrical bent, and I saw no point in enlightening him.

"Yes, sir," I said. "We have been apprised of that."

White nodded. "I assumed as much, Mr. Birdsong. What is your connection to Mr. DeMonte?"

Touchy, that. I thought fast. "We did some business in import goods, up from New Orleans," I said. "Mr. DeMonte has many ventures, as I'm sure you're aware." To cement that and stop further speculation, I added, "Also, we have a distant family connection."

That seemed to satisfy him, but then, Julius's business was not the main occupation of anyone's thoughts. Laura White sat at the other end of the table, taking desultory sips of soup and ignoring the rest of the courses as well as the conversation but shooting me glances now and then. Her face was white, and her hand shook when she lifted the spoon to her lips. She finally excused herself and left the table. I didn't blame her. If this were my child, perhaps I wouldn't want to hear any more either. Then again, if this were my child, I'd likely be the first one out there with a gun in my hand. Laura White and I were very different people, even if we'd been raised in similar circumstances.

We finished our meal in relative silence and returned to the study, just in case the servants might overhear us. This time, a hefty fire was burning, and we made our final preparations. The men had talked while I was sleeping and decided that John White would stay here, and George would act as his representative, even before the boy had shown up with the final ransom demand. Henley, Beau, and I would be backup and would stay out of sight, particularly Beau, since Ridley knew Beau on sight.

I toyed briefly with the idea of turning back into a woman for the evening's festivities, if only to confuse Ridley, but discarded it quickly. While Henley was well aware, letting that cat out of the bag to White could derail the entire venture. Best to wait.

Before dinner, Henley had reconnoitered the area around McLain's Tavern. Now he outlined the area on a piece of paper set on White's desk.

"Here," he said, pointing out a square he'd drawn on a road, with another bisecting it some distance away, "is the tavern itself." He sketched in smaller buildings behind it, drawing a lane beside them. "These are the squats the kid mentioned, likely where Ridley's hiding now. There's another bar on the east corner. Across the street is a store, closed at night, and a restaurant, although I don't know what time it shuts down."

His pen scribbled along the lane. "There's all kinds of debris and junk along there which could provide hiding places."

He looked up. "I think we should get there an hour early, stake out some places to hide, and have George and the bag show up at ten, as requested. When Ridley confronts George, we take him down. The girl is likely back in the place where he's hiding."

I was skeptical. "Since we don't know exactly where that is, how do we find Amelia? Suppose we take out Ridley before he tells us?"

Nobody answered, and the only sound in the study was the gentle hissing of the flames flickering in the fireplace.

"He's right," Beau said. "Ridley's a tricky bastard. I think we need to get over there right now and see where he's stayin'. Make sure the girl's with him." He looked at White. "I'm sorry, sir, but there's some chance she's not there at all."

White moaned softly and sat back heavily in his big chair behind the desk. "I know, I know," he said, rubbing his hands over his cheeks. "But, goddamnit, we can't think like that. I have to go on believing she's still alive and she'll be coming home ..."

I don't think he cried often, this scion of Chicago, but he did now, finally letting his defenses down. We waited, exchanging glances with each other. George finally patted his employer on the shoulder and offered a snowy white handkerchief. After a few minutes, John White composed himself.

"Let's get this bastard," he said, clenching his teeth.

My thoughts exactly. The clock chimed softly, signaling eight, and I stood up, settling the Colt on my hip.

"Let's go, gentlemen. Beau's right. We need more time to get the lay of the land and nose about before Ridley shows up. Now it's full dark; this is all the chance we're going to get."

Beau shot me an amused glance, not the first this day. I gave him a half smile back. *Chastity James, desperado,* I thought. It was a little scary how quickly I'd adapted into just that, but there it was. Beau wasn't overly surprised, having met Charlie Birdsong at a rather low point in his life, but I sometimes surprised myself.

We all solemnly shook John's hand, and George picked up the heavy bag containing the money. I'd been tempted to put just a few packets of real money on top and fill the rest with newspaper, but White didn't seem to care, and there was a certain amount of risk to that maneuver that I didn't want to be responsible for. We had risk enough.

We filed out the door and into the night, Henley in the lead, George behind him, while Beau and I brought up the rear.

"We're in for it now," I said. My arm hurt like the devil, but it wasn't my shooting one, so I'd be all right.

As we walked to the carriage, he pulled me close and kissed my temple. "I love you, Chastity James."

He hadn't said it before, and neither had I. Pleasure shot through me like an elixir, and I smiled in the darkness. I stopped suddenly and kissed him, my hands on both sides of his face. I pulled back and looked into his eyes, gleaming in the faint light from the gas streetlamps ahead.

"And I love you, Beauregard Durant."

He laughed softly, and it was the delighted laugh of a child relishing a secret. We walked on, our hands touching now and then. George and Henley had, fortunately, not even glanced back.

CHAPTER 23

It was over a mile to Clark Street, back in the mire of Chicago's streets. The nicer residential houses had been left behind, the commercial taking over. There were smaller buildings, one and two stories, between others that were higher, seeming to overtake Chicago's beginnings like a storm that chewed up the past and spewed it out into the big city it was fast becoming.

McLain's Tavern sat among those, on a corner that seemed to stretch between the two ideologies. It was a wooden building, light pouring out of the windows, raucous laughter and music spilling out into the street. A drunken man stumbled out the door and urinated in the street. The lane or alleyway beside it stretched into darkness, pinpoints of light here and there amidst the ramshackle structures beyond. Henley was right; there was debris aplenty but none I wished to hide in.

An occasional woman stood here and there, but the crowd was mostly men either accompanying the women or soliciting their company for the evening. The women were positioned against the front of McLain's as well as the bar across the alleyway, which looked even more disreputable, if that were possible. In the Western towns, authorities at least kept things somewhat civil, but here there was no such order and too many people who clearly did whatever they felt like doing with no threat of retribution from the law or anyone else.

We drove past and left the carriage with the money inside as well as White's coachman, Joseph, a burly man who looked like he could take care of himself, and George. They were stationed a block away and around a corner. Henley, Beau, and I positioned ourselves across the street from McLain's, in the doorway of a closed mercantile of some sort.

Henley turned to me. "Any thoughts, Mr. Birdsong?"

"Not off the top of my head," I snapped. "It's your town. Know the area?"

I could see his smirk in the lights from across the street. "Not really."

"Oh, Henley, I'm surprised," I said. "And here I took you for such a sophisticate." He'd annoyed me since this morning, and I knew my own apprehension was beginning to show itself.

Beau stepped in smoothly. "All we know is that Ridley said to meet him behind McLain's, and he hasn't ever seen you, Mr. Henley, so you are the logical choice to see if he's in McLain's. We'll scout a bit farther down the alley. That would make sense."

Henley peered at him in the dimness. "How will I know it's him, since I've never seen him?"

"I apologize," said Beau. "The man wears a patch over one eye. He's hard to miss. We'll meet back here in a few minutes."

Henley nodded and headed to the tavern. Beau and I headed into the dark alley behind McLain's—not my wish, but the only choice we had. A twelve-foot-wide space full of crates and a wagon, driverless, sat behind the tavern itself, and a man in an apron threw some empty boxes out a back door, quickly going back inside.

The alleyway itself was as bad as I'd feared, malodorous with garbage and God knows what else. A rat ran across my foot ten steps in, but I swallowed my shriek and followed Beau, his back a beacon of normality in this morass. My boots squelched in runnels of water, likely sewage, from the smell.

Christ Jesus, I thought. *People live in this swamp? Apparently.* I heard a child's cries, caught the smell of something frying, and heard a woman yelling that she wasn't going to take it anymore, and we went on. So far, I'd seen no trace of Ridley or Amelia, but the night was young and not inclined to give up its secrets so soon.

We crept on. A man shouldered his way out of a shack, a woman shrieking at him from within, but he kept going, uncaring. Another child whimpered behind a shuttered window, and I ignored it. We couldn't save the world. Not here, not now.

Some of the dwellings, if they could be called that, were dark, and I couldn't help but wonder who lived in them and what their lives could be like. Others were lit, but there was no conversation to be heard. Ridley and Amelia could be in one of those, but we had no way to tell.

"This is fruitless," I whispered to Beau. "They could be anywhere."

"No," he said. "They're here somewhere. I can almost smell it." He grabbed my hand and pulled me along. "We'll find them."

The alley ended abruptly in a brick wall, and I almost bumped into it, except for Beau's hand pulling me. The man had eyes like a cat. I certainly didn't.

"Back?" I whispered needlessly. There wasn't a lot of choice.

We turned around and walked slowly towards the street. Halfway down, a door swung open, and a man stepped out. We shrank back, pressing ourselves into the tar paper wall of the shack behind us. He walked with determination toward Clark Street, but his gait looked familiar.

"Is it Ridley?" I hissed.

"Might could be," Beau whispered in my ear. "Can't tell yet."

I noted the shack he'd come from, and we trod silently in his wake, staying a good thirty feet behind him. He entered the space behind McLain's and went through the back door before we could see his face.

"Let Henley take it from here," I said. "If it's Ridley, he'll know."

Beau shrugged, and we made our way across the street.

We waited. Beau had borrowed a pocket watch from Henley, and it read nine o'clock. We still had time to hide if we needed to, but we wanted to see if Henley had recognized the man we saw go into the tavern.

It was cold. I stamped my feet quietly, keeping my toes warm. After about twenty minutes, Henley emerged from the tavern. He looked around and quickly joined us in the dark enclave of the store's entrance.

"He's not in there," he said. "A lot of nasty characters, but nobody wearing an eyepatch or even anybody needing to do so." He lit a cheroot, blowing the smoke in a plume towards the street. "How'd you do?"

"We thought a man who came out of one of the shacks and went into McLain's could've been him," I said. "But if you never saw anyone like that, I guess not. Say, could I borrow those matches?"

Henley handed me the matchbox. "If it was him, he stayed in the back. No eyepatch." He threw the cheroot into the street. "Let's get George."

The carriage was right where we left it, Joseph perched like a motionless golem on the seat. George opened the door and stepped down. He was not liking this at all, I could tell.

He set down the bag with the money, and his hands were shaking. I didn't blame him; I didn't like it much either.

"We'll be back soon, Joseph," I said. "We will very likely be in a hurry, and don't be alarmed if you hear a shot or two."

The coachman grinned. "I won't, Mr. Birdsong. You gents do what you have to do; I'll take care of getting us home safe." He pulled back his coat, and I saw the gun on his hip. I grinned back.

The four of us returned to our store entrance, and we went over the plan again.

"George, wait another five minutes and then head to the back of McLain's. Keep on the lookout for any rough characters. We're going to be watching and back you up, but you won't see us," Beau said.

George swallowed audibly. "I understand."

"When Ridley shows up, don't give him the money before he tells you where to find Amelia. We'll be in hearing distance," I said. "He tries to run, don't stop him. We'll get him."

"If shootin' starts, drop to the ground," Beau said, patting George on the shoulder. "You'll be all right."

We filed across the street like shadows and proceeded down the alley. Henley took up a position behind some large boxes in back of McLain's while Beau and I went a bit farther down, blending into the shadows and the edges of the shacks. I hoped Ridley didn't emerge from one of them, but for some reason I was nearly certain the man we'd seen earlier was Ridley. Where he'd gone inside the tavern I didn't know, but I trusted Henley.

"I want to check on that squat the man came out of," I said and moved off down the alley. "Maybe Amelia's in there."

Beau grabbed my arm, the good one, or I would've let out a screech. "No, Chas. We don't have time."

"The hell we don't," I said and shook his arm off. "It'll

only take a minute. Stay here; I'll be back." I knew he wouldn't stop me.

I crept back down the alley towards the shack we'd seen the man emerge from before. When I got to the door, I leaned my ear against the boards, but I didn't hear anything. I drew my Colt and pulled back on the crude wooden handle. It was completely dark inside, but I took a tentative step into the interior.

"Hello? Amelia?" I whispered and took another step. It smelled like an outhouse, and my nose crinkled with distaste. A faint whimper came from somewhere in the right corner, and I kept going. My foot struck something and sent it scattering across the dirt floor. The whimper turned into a soft moan, and I followed the sound.

"Amelia?"

"Yes." Faintly. It was all I needed. I plunged ahead, taking out Henley's matches. "I'm here to help you. Can you come to me?"

"No, I'm tied."

Christ Jesus. I lit a match, and there she was, tied hand and foot to a wooden chair in the corner, her hair falling over her dirt-streaked face, clothes filthy as well. The match burned out as I reached her. I pulled out my knife and felt for the ropes. I cut the bottom ones and lit another match. Her frightened eyes stared up at me.

"Don't move. I'm going to cut the ropes on your hands, but I can't hold the match and the knife at the same time." She nodded. I blew out the match and knelt down, carefully positioning the knife so as not to cut her, too. The ropes fell, freeing her hands, and she clutched frantically at me. "You're safe."

She took a deep breath, and I could feel it. Then she started to cry. I shushed her before she could get hysterical. I couldn't blame her if she did, but we couldn't afford the noise. We had no idea where Ridley really was.

"Listen to me, Amelia," I said softly. "We're going to leave now, but we have to be very quiet. Do you know where the man has gone?"

"Nooo," she moaned. "He left awhile ago. He told me to be quiet, or he'd know and he'd kill me. He said that a lot."

Of course he did, the bastard, I thought. What I said was, "He's not coming back, Amelia, but we have to stay quiet so we can leave. All right?"

She nodded, her head rubbing against my chest. We stepped over to the door and made our way outside. I was holding her with my left arm, and it hurt fiercely, but I didn't want to put up my Colt just yet. We took a few steps down the alley, and a darker shape loomed in front of us.

"Jesus, Chas," Beau said. "You got her."

Amelia stiffened at the sound of another voice, her fingers tightening on my waist, but I reassured her. "He's a friend, sweetie. Stay still and let's go."

We walked cautiously towards the street, just as George came around to the back of McLain's. I was hoping he wouldn't come before we got Amelia to the carriage, but there he was.

"Damn," Beau said. "Now that we've got Amelia, we should get George and the money out of here before Ridley shows up."

"We may be out of time."

"I know."

Keeping to the shadows, Beau found Henley behind the boxes and told him we'd found Amelia. He nodded at me, and George's mouth flew open in surprise as I scurried with Amelia to the street and then down the block to the waiting coach. I put her inside and covered her with a robe. Joseph was standing guard, and I was confident no one would get past him while we dealt with Ridley. I tucked the robe around her.

"I have to go back," I said. "You'll be fine here with Joseph, and we'll return soon."

She clung to my arm. "Don't leave me. He'll get me."

I pried her fingers away. "No, he won't, Amelia. You have to be brave just a little longer. I'm going to make sure he never gets anyone again."

Before she could say another word, I shut the door. "Keep her safe."

Joseph nodded, and I sprinted down the street to McLain's. George met me halfway, still carrying the bag. "He's not shown up yet, Birdsong. Henley and Beau told me to get to the coach."

"Good. Help Joseph with Amelia. We'll be along shortly." George wasted no time, running down the block. I did the same—in the opposite direction. My mind was whirling. We got Amelia, and we still had the money. Now to deal with Ridley, wherever he was. I didn't have a watch, but I was pretty sure it wasn't yet ten o'clock. That didn't mean he hadn't seen us, however, and that worried me a lot.

I slowed to a walk, and, just as I entered the alley, Tom Ridley came out the back door of McLain's. He saw me at the same time I saw him, and he ducked back into the tavern, quick as a snake diving into a gopher hole.

Henley ran after him, and Beau joined me. "I'm going in the front in case he heads that way. You all right back here?"

"I'll be fine. Be careful; he's a tricky bastard." I said. But I wasn't fine. It was hard for me to stand straight, I was so tired. That doctor had likely been right, but I couldn't stand aside. Ridley was slippery, and he'd outsmarted us before. Where had he been hiding? I stood there for a few minutes, trying to think like him. First thing I'd do is check on the girl. I didn't have time to get to Beau, and I could be mistaken, so I started back down the alley towards the squat where I'd found Amelia.

It was unnerving and so dark. I pushed open the door and

lit a match. No one was there. I quickly blew out the match and spun around. I thought I'd heard a footstep behind me, but I couldn't see anyone, my eyes blinded from the match light. I don't know how he could've gotten past us, but he'd done it earlier, so he must have another way. When the arm came around my throat, I could smell him. Rank—stinking of sweat, whiskey, and rotten teeth.

"Gotcha, you little fucker. You must be Durant's little pal, and just as trigger-happy as he is. I don't know which one of you shot my brother, and I don't care. Before I break your neck, where's Durant? I owe him, too."

I couldn't breathe, his arm was so tight. I elbowed him in the ribs ineffectually, and he laughed. He took my Colt from its holster and tossed it. I heard the thud as it landed inside somewhere.

"Don't know how you hooked up with White, but it ain't gonna do you no good. I'm keepin' that money and my little treasure, too. We're good friends now, and she's a sweet piece."

At those words, something snapped. It was like Duane Olson's arm holding me, mouthing foul words that burned into my brain. I couldn't begin to think what hell Amelia had been through. Ridley was just another depraved specimen of a man who didn't deserve to live in the same world with decent people. I tried to draw a deep breath, and, even though I couldn't see anything in the darkness, red and yellow swirls of light exploded behind my eyes. I groaned, trying to relax my muscles, and the crushing weight on my throat lessened.

"Where is he?"

"Behind you," I croaked, and it was just enough. He turned slightly, his concentration broken, and I slid the Bowie knife from its scabbard. I stabbed backwards as hard as I could, and the knife went in to the hilt. Ridley grunted in surprise. His arm dropped from my neck, and I turned around and pulled the knife out, which was harder than thrusting it in. This time I aimed higher, and a high-pitched scream erupted from his throat. He fell over, pulling me down with him.

I scrambled up, stumbling against his legs in the dark, searching for my gun. This wasn't a man who was going down that easy. I scrabbled around desperately, and, just when my hand closed over the Colt, a darker shape appeared in the open doorway.

"Chas?"

"It's Ridley!" I yelled. I fished in my pocket and lit one of Henley's matches. "He's on the floor. Shoot him!"

The light flared, and, in its sudden glow, Tom Ridley reared up like some flesh-eating monster from a nightmare, blood streaming down his chest, aiming his gun at Beau. Beau was only three feet away, his gun in his hand, and he shot Ridley right between the eyes, the body thudding back onto the floor. The match died out, burning my fingers.

Gunsmoke filled the room. I lit another match. In the swirls of acrid smoke, Ridley lay on his back, his mouth open in surprise. Blood pooled beneath him, its copper tang melding with the gun smoke in its age-old aroma. I coughed, staggering towards Beau, who caught me in his arms.

"Jesus, Chas, you scared me. I got a bad feelin', and, when I came to find you, you were gone, and I knew he'd gotten around us somehow." He pulled me so close I could hear his heart skittering, and mine was doing the same. "If I'd lost you, I don't know how ..." His voice broke.

"I know," I murmured. "I know." I clung to him, relief and love flooding over me in equal measures.

Henley found us. He lit a match himself and took in Tom Ridley's body.

"We need to get out of here. Now."

We hurried back to the coach, climbing inside just as we saw a wagon bearing the insignia Chicago Police Department arriving. Apparently, even in this neighborhood, gunshots alerted the authorities. George and Henley sat opposite Beau, Amelia, and me. Amelia grabbed me the minute I sat down on the seat beside her, her thin body still shaking. I held her close, wrapping the robe around her, and discovered I was shaking, too. She needed me, and she needed time. We both did.

Joseph turned the coach around smoothly and we drove back to Lincoln Park. For all anyone knew, we were just some swells out on an evening ride, amused by the doings of the lower classes at their drunken pleasures. Sometimes things went awry in these revelries, but nobody would be terribly concerned by the discovery of a body in one of the squats. Just another disagreement between criminals. Perhaps they would never even know that the corpse was that of the notorious outlaw Tom Ridley. That was fine with me. Scum didn't deserve an epitaph, or even a mention.

CHAPTER 24

*A*ll the lights in White's house were blazing as we pulled up, and the front door was flung open by John White himself. We climbed out of the coach and into the now-familiar study, Joseph quickly driving the coach out to the stables behind the house, as though no one had ever been out this evening.

There was no conversation yet; all of us were just getting our bearings. Grayson decamped after a brief exchange with White, setting down the bag of money beside the desk before he left. Beau, Amelia, and I collapsed on the leather sofa by the fire. Henley stood beside us like a sentinel. We seemed to be a unit, Amelia still clutching onto me as though if she let me go for one second, she'd disappear or, even worse, find herself back with Ridley. I was no expert on shock, but if I'd ever seen it, this was it.

Laura White flew into the room, reaching out to hug her daughter, but Amelia shrank back, hiding her face in my shirt. Laura knelt on the floor beside us, tears sparkling on her cheeks, while John White looked on as he leaned on his desk, his face pale, his dark eyes intense.

"Darling, Mummy's here," Laura crooned. "We've been so worried. I'm so happy you're safe ... let me hold you ..."

Amelia wasn't having it, her fingers digging into my side so hard I nearly winced.

"No," she said clearly. "Only her."

White's eyebrows shot up. "Her?"

Well, that ruse was up. Laura turned to her father-in-law. "Yes, John, her. We'll talk about this later. Right now, we must tend to Amelia. She needs to be looked after, bathed, fed, and settled." She turned back to me. "Since she won't leave your side, perhaps we might accomplish this together?"

I nodded, standing up and pulling Amelia with me. Upstairs, in an elaborate bathroom, a tub of warm water was standing by. Laura left nothing to chance. The woman would have made a good majordomo of a castle. We both stripped off Amelia's ragged clothing and gently deposited her in the water. True to my word, I didn't move more than inches away from her in all the time it took to gently wash her hair and bruised body. During that time, no sound escaped the girl's lips, nor mine. Only Laura's soft moans broke the silence when I gently sponged the dried blood from Amelia's thin thighs. If I could have stabbed Tom Ridley again in that moment, I would gladly have done so.

We dried Amelia off with fluffy towels and pulled a soft, lawn nightgown over her head. I led her, still clutching my hand, to her bed and pulled a comforter over her. Her eyes were wide open. When Laura and I made to leave the room, Amelia sat up, reaching for me.

"Stay with me; stay with me," she murmured. "Stay with me." And so I did, lying down beside her, despite my damp, blood-crusted clothes. Laura sat on a chair beside the bed. Within minutes, Amelia's eyes closed, and her breathing became even.

Laura turned down the lamp until it was a soft glow. "It happened to you, didn't it?"

"Yes."

She nodded. "I don't even know your name. All I do know is that I'll be grateful to you for the rest of my life."

"My name is Chastity James," I said. I watched the emotions play over her face, first surprise and then acceptance. "Ah. Well, Chastity James, I instructed the maids to pour another bath in the guest room," she said. "Please. I'll be with her." Laura was clearly an astute woman.

"Thank you," I said and gently disentangled my hand from Amelia's.

I didn't care what was going on downstairs. I was sure Henley and Beau could handle the details for White. I sank into the warm water scented with gardenias and put my head down on the back of the tub, holding my bandaged arm above the water. I even managed to wash my hair, ridding it of the stench of blood and gun smoke. I noticed more of the brown dye coming out, tinting the water. I lay there until the water cooled, my aching muscles beginning to soothe, then dried off with more fluffy towels. Laura had thoughtfully laid out a fresh shirt and a skirt, as well as trousers. *In for a penny*, I thought, and put on the skirt. I made my way back downstairs and opened the study door.

"Join us," White said, holding up a glass of whiskey. "Amelia is asleep, then?"

I nodded, taking the whiskey from White's hand and downing it in one swallow.

I held it out. "Another, please."

He didn't even blink. I gave him credit for that, and he poured me another. I took it and sat down on the couch beside Beau. Henley was in a chair beside the fire, his legs crossed indolently, and White sat on another wing chair beside him.

"Your colleagues here have been filling me in on the events of the evening," he said. "As I said to them, and now particularly to you, I am deeply grateful for all that you have done for us."

I nodded and sipped my whiskey. Beau took my hand, and we sat in silence for a moment.

White cleared his throat. "Of course, there will be no repercussions from any actions taken; I can assure you of that. The police commissioner and I are close friends, should any questions arise." He took a drink himself.

Well, that's convenient, I thought, glancing at Beau. I watched a familiar smile playing on his lips. He stared briefly at White, then concentrated on his whiskey.

Henley stood up, depositing his empty glass on the table. "Sir, it has been a very long day, and everyone needs their rest. Perhaps it would be best to reconvene in the morning to go over any remaining details."

"Of course, of course," White said. "Gentlemen ... ah, and lady, again my most heartfelt gratitude. Until the morning, then."

The buggy we'd arrived in this morning was waiting for us in the drive out front. We climbed in, and Henley snapped the reins briskly.

"You trust him?" I said to Beau, the brisk night air welcome on my face.

"Hell, no," he said, holding me close. "Not for a minute. Then again, I don't trust hardly anybody anymore, 'cept you, Chas."

* * *

"Darlings."

I pried open one eye. Sunlight streamed through the thin gauze curtains. Julius, elegant as ever, sat on a chair beside the bed, a delightfully fragrant cup of coffee in his hand. *Christ Jesus.*

I nudged Beau, who grunted and rolled over, still deep asleep. I sat up, pulling the sheet over my breasts.

"Can I not have you out of my sight for even a few days?"

He sighed theatrically and sipped his coffee. "Trouble seems to follow you two. One cannot say I didn't make every effort."

"Oh please," I sighed. "Is there more of that coffee?"

"Of course there is. I'm not a barbarian. Tuck your sheet, my dear." He deposited a tray on my lap. A silver coffeepot, complete with a pitcher of cream, bowl of sugar, cinnamon toast, and a bowl of strawberries were arrayed on it. I blinked again.

"Allow me," Julius said. He poured a cup and handed it to me, saucer and all. Beau still slept on.

"What are you doing here?" I said— and too late realized how rude I was being. It had been a hard night.

Julius only laughed. "Sometimes I get a bad feeling. This time I was right. Henley has filled me in. Anything you want to add?" He eyed the bandage on my arm.

I sipped my coffee. "Well, we killed some people. Henley tell you that? Justified, but still."

"So I heard," Julius said as he picked up a piece of toast. "Sometimes that's unavoidable, but we have to make sure there are no consequences. Apparently White knows you're a woman, but he doesn't know *which* woman. How's the girl?"

I finished my coffee and poured another. "Not certain, truthfully. She was raped before we could rescue her. We tried, but …"

Julius grimaced. "I'm truly sorry, my dear. Considering your own history, that must be traumatic for you as well. But she's safe, at least. What do you think is best now?"

"Well, you know White better than I do," I said, and I took a bite of toast. It was delicious. Beau roused, peering at Julius. He didn't seem surprised in the least and seemed more interested in the coffee. Raising himself on an elbow, he poured a cup for himself.

"Good mornin', Julius," he said. "Thank you so much for the hospitality."

"God, I love Southerners," Julius said. "I think they'd say

thank you for the bullet that ended them. Such gentility from an American always delights me."

Beau snorted. "Maybe some of 'em, but not this one."

Julius laughed. "Touché, son." He stood up. "Enjoy. See you downstairs in the drawing room whenever you've collected yourselves. We've put out some clothes that may work for you." He put his cup down on the tray. "Don't take terribly long. We've a great deal to do."

Those admonitions energized us. We finished our coffee and dressed hastily. Julius's taste was impeccable. I wore a dark-blue suit with a lace blouse and Beau, a black suit similar to Henley's austere taste. Beau checked the bandages on my arm. The wound had bled through, but the doctor would be by eventually, so I shrugged off his ministrations, only allowing a fresh bandage.

"It'll be fine. We'll deal with it later," I said. Beau frowned but followed me downstairs without further protest.

Julius sat at an elegant French writing desk while Henley stood beside him. They looked up as we entered.

"So. We are gathered," Julius said. "I understand White is aware you're a woman, but does anyone else know who you are?"

"Laura," I said. "I told her. I mean, she already knew I was a woman, anyway."

All three of them scowled at me. "Shit, Chas," Beau said.

"Well, it just came up," I said. I was defensive, but, really, what difference did it make? White was going to find out soon, no matter what. Besides, I trusted Laura. Best to just get it out there. If I had to run, I would. I was getting pretty good at it.

"I sent a messenger around to White's," Julius said, brushing invisible lint from his trousers. He took a closer look at the two of us and smiled. "You two make a pretty pair. No one would suspect your darker sides. Then again, that's true of many of us, isn't it?"

I curtseyed, spreading my skirts, and now Julius outright

laughed. "The outfit precludes a holster, but I'd bet you've got that damn knife hidden somewhere."

I grinned and pulled up my skirt to give him a glimpse of the leather scabbard on my thigh. "No takers on that."

It was a short drive to White's house. We were welcomed once again into the study by Grayson, but this time John White himself came around the desk and warmly greeted Julius, taking his hand.

"So good to see you again, sir," he said. "It's an honor. I was not aware you were in residence until your message came this morning. Please." He gestured toward the seats around the fire, and we all settled in. "Your young friends have saved my granddaughter's life, and I cannot thank all of you enough."

"How is Amelia this morning?" I said.

"I've had the doctor in, and that didn't go especially well," White said. "Laura is with her, of course. Amelia's not speaking at the moment. She did ask for you, however." He stared at me, surprised, I think, at my attire, so different from the day before. "Before anything else, I want to express my utmost gratitude for the service you have done this family." His gaze took in Beau, Henley, and me. "If there is anything I can do, anything at all, I am at your disposal."

Julius gave a languid smile. "Well, as a matter of fact, there is one particular thing." Always the showman, he took my hand and drew me up. "I'd like to introduce you to a longtime friend of my family, Miss Chastity James."

I smiled sweetly and mischievously thought of that curtsey but controlled myself. White took my hand. "Delighted to meet you. I thought you were perhaps too pretty a young man." He laughed at his own joke, and then the smile died on his lips. I could almost see the wheels turning in comprehension in his mind. He dropped my hand.

"You're her," he stammered, "the 'savage schoolteacher.'

Oh, my God." His eyes were wide as he looked at Julius. "What in hell, DeMonte?"

"Be assured Miss James did not commit the crime she's accused of," Julius said smoothly. "She is the daughter of Leland James, the owner of Harrowhill. I myself have known Chastity since she was a child, and she's an outstanding young woman." He took White's elbow and guided him gently back into his chair. "I think it best if Miss James explained things for herself. If you allow it?" White nodded, waving his hand vaguely.

Even I was impressed with Julius's performance. I didn't dare look at Beau's face, because I knew that familiar little smile was likely to be lingering at the corner of his mouth, and this was no laughing matter, not really. I had a performance to give, and it had better be good, or I was likely to leave here in handcuffs. I cleared my throat.

"Mr. White," I said. "Last summer, I arrived in Dodge City to teach school at their new schoolhouse, and, from nearly the first week, things didn't go as they had promised." Here I paused, a tear rolling down my cheek. "My father was very opposed to the entire proposition but allowed me, as he put it, to spread my wings and learn more of the world while bringing my own idea of education to the children of the West. We agreed to a year, no more. Now I fear I may never see him again, and it breaks my heart." Another tear or two escaped.

White was listening intently, staring at my face. I told my tale, Duane Olson and all, the escape from Dodge City, rescuing Beau, meeting up with Julius, and the disastrous train robbery that had brought us to this very morning. I downplayed my affinity for knives and handiness with firearms and, of course, any prior knowledge of the Ridley brothers.

"So, you see, when Amelia was abducted, I had no choice but to try and help her, and Mr. Durant felt the same," I said. "We could not leave her to face the same fate that had befallen me." It was all certainly true, but White was no fool. "I wasn't looking for absolution or legal help, sir, but only to save her, something that I wish someone had tried to do for me." Here I dropped to my knees and grasped White's hands from his lap, bowing my head and gently pressing my forehead onto our joined hands. The tears were running so freely now, I surprised even myself.

"Darling girl," Julius murmured, helping me to a chair and handing me a snowy linen handkerchief. He was shaking his head in despair. "I can't bear to see you like this, reliving that horror."

White hadn't said a word. We'd taken a very risky gamble, and I was frankly terrified. While Julius held undeniable cachet in society as an eccentric English aristocrat, the real political and financial power in Chicago and beyond was John White. If he wanted to help me get out from under the murder charge, he could. And, just as certain, he could have me in chains before lunch, and nobody would be able to stop him.

John White leaned his head against the high leather chair back and stared at me. "Sometimes in life we are given an opportunity to right a great wrong, Miss James. I believe this is one of those times. Your actions were importunate, but in defense of your life, just as you have defended my grand-daughter's. Truthfully, I was somewhat perplexed that you and young Mr. Durant were so adamant about helping us, and I assumed incorrectly that you were simply taking advantage of a situation in hopes of a financial reward, which, of course, I am still prepared to deliver. Now, I understand."

He stood up, holding out his hand to Julius. "I appreciate you asking for my assistance, and I want to assure you"—he turned and looked at me—"and you, my dear, I will make this right. I am sorry for the hell you have endured." He then held out his hand to me as well and took mine in his. "You have a great friend and protector in Mr. DeMonte, Miss James. We should all be so fortunate."

"Thank you, Mr. White," I said. "How well I know." I kissed Julius's cheek and then, impulsively, John White's. He seemed a bit flustered but smiled. "Would you allow me to see Amelia?" I flashed a glance at Beau, who was sitting placidly in his chair, gazing at me with that look he had, as though he were looking on the best thing he'd ever seen. My God, I loved that boy.

"Of course," he said. "I think you are the only person she may open up to, and rightfully so." He opened the door for me. "We gentlemen will converse; take your time."

I stood outside the study door for a minute after it closed behind me, trying to process what had occurred in the last hour. My life had once again taken a turn I hadn't thought possible, providing White could deliver, and I had little doubt he could. My thoughts turned to Harrowhill, Leland, and Matthias, something I'd denied myself for too long out of the fear I'd never see them again. Most of those tears hadn't been false at all. I hugged the thought of seeing them again like a soft comforter that not only warmed but thrilled me at the same time.

I opened the bedroom door. "Amelia? I'm here."

CHAPTER 25

We spent the next weeks alternating between hope and fear, waiting to hear from John White about my legal issues. We'd had more than one sleepless night, but no news or inquiries had surfaced about a man found dead behind McLain's, or anyone anywhere else in Illinois. John White's influence reached much further than simply the city of Chicago, and it was considerable.

I had more than enough to occupy my time. My arm healed slowly, and there would always be a scar, but it was of little importance to me. Every morning I rode over to White's, spending time with Amelia; in the afternoons I walked on the lakeshore with Beau, or we rode up the coast, giving Rufus and Belle the runs they craved, when the weather permitted. When it didn't, Beau and I made good use of our lovely bedroom. Angel had her eye surgery, and I spent a great deal of time reading to her to help pass the tedium of not being able to see anything while her eyes were completely bandaged. She was quite amazing, that girl. I was becoming convinced she was Julius's daughter, but that was a secret he'd not divulged, and Mama Rosa was equally tightlipped. It didn't matter, and it was Julius's business, not mine.

Julius himself was a delight, and I'd come to adore him. I owed him more than I could ever repay. For Beau, Julius was like the father he'd lost, maybe even better. The two of them were inseparable: reading, talking, playing chess, even fencing, one of Julius's passions that quickly became one of Beau's. Many an evening, the two of them sat up discussing philosophy and God knows what else, until the wee hours.

It was a respite we both needed badly, and, for the rest of my life, I would thank Julius DeMonte for providing it—and so much more. He was truly extraordinary, this Englishman who'd lost much but given so much to others. To have met him was the education I'd been lucky enough to find, in place of the aborted effort I'd intended to give.

The first morning after we rescued her, Amelia was trembly, clinging to me as she had from the first. Gradually she came to life, telling me how it had been and what Ridley had done to her. I held her when she cried and told her some of my own ordeal, which seemed to reassure her, and she began to come back to life—at first, in small ways: eating, talking to Laura, listening to music, then taking an interest in her clothing, brushing her hair, and choosing ribbons or the shoes she would wear that day. Being able to talk about what had happened to her was like bursting open the boil of an abscess, excising the poison, and freeing her to live her life beyond that.

The day she took Beau's hand when we went for a walk, smiling up at him, this beautiful man, was the day I knew Amelia would recover. When we arrived home that afternoon, she hugged her grandfather without a qualm. John White had tears in his eyes as he mouthed "thank you" to me over her head, and that made everything we'd had to do worth it all.

An early spring came to Chicago, despite the wind off the lake. I found the wind stimulating, but Beau, with his Southern blood, wasn't so happy about it. One morning I came upon daffodils in Julius's garden, and I grabbed his hand.

"Look," I said. "Spring."

He turned up his collar but smiled down at me. "If you say so, Chas. The day comes when I can take off my shirt, well, then I'll believe it."

"Curmudgeon," I said and kissed him. "Next will be tulips."

That thought sent me into doldrums, and I turned away, wandering down the path, my daffodil enthusiasm forgotten. Spring at Harrowhill was magical. Those tulips would be coming, and I wouldn't be there to see it. Not only tulips, but the pale green leaves on the trees; the foals, legs trembling on their first step; the smell of moist earth; the wind off the ocean, not all that far away. I was so homesick I was miserable company for the rest of the day. Would I ever see it again? Suppose White couldn't help? Suppose I'd be on the run again? Where could I go? Canada?

Beau finally cornered me that evening before dinner.

"I know you're worried, Chas," he murmured, his lips on my hair. "I am, too. We've got to have a little faith, girl. If White can't get the job done, we get out of here and go where they can't touch us." He lifted my chin and gazed into my eyes. "You think for a damn minute that I'd let anythin' bad happen to you? We have to run, we run. We're partners. Now and forever."

I smiled, the tears close. "James Beauregard Durant, I love you."

" 'Course you do, Chastity James. I'm a lovable sort. 'Sides, you're stuck with me." He kissed me very softly. "We saved each other, and you're my home, don't matter where it is."

That helped. But, even more than just the worry and the homesickness, I had to search my conscience. I'd never set out to be a killer, but I'd become one. So had Beau, and I knew he hadn't set out that way either. Circumstance and injustice had led us to do the things we'd done, but people had died.

"You ever feel guilty about the lives we've taken?" I said.

He looked at me, clear eyed and guileless, as was his way. "Not for a minute. Nor should you. Way I figure it, we did a service to society."

I nodded. Good to know, because I felt exactly the same way. I'd do it all again in a heartbeat. I had no regrets. If that made us bad people, it was a badge of honor as far as I was concerned. Case closed.

* * *

THE NEXT MORNING I was having breakfast with Amelia. She was excited about going to the museum and was hardly able to finish her omelet, despite my urging. John White stepped into the dining room.

"Can I have a word with you, Miss James?"

"Of course," I said, putting down my napkin. "Eat your fruit, Amelia. I'll be right back."

John escorted me to the study and sat behind the desk, after waving me to a chair beside it.

"The charges against you in Kansas have been dropped, not guilty in self defense, in fact. The notice is out, the wanted posters taken down. There will be no further issues."

I felt as though an anvil had lifted from my shoulders. I took a deep breath.

"I dare to ask," I said, somewhat breathless, "how did you manage this?"

"Let's just say I was one of Governor Anthony's largest contributors, Miss James," White said, smiling tightly. "The Kansas cattle business is important to Chicago, as I'm sure you can imagine. It doesn't do to offend people who make a big difference to your supporters."

I knew how things worked. Leland himself had been no stranger to politics, even though I'd paid little attention, growing up. From now on, I certainly would.

"I don't know how to thank you," I said, and I meant it.

"Ah, Miss James. It is I who doesn't know how to properly thank you," he said. "To correct a legal wrong for you doesn't begin to repay you for the care you have given to my granddaughter, and the great gift you've given to me. Please, think no more about it. I only hope it goes some way to repairing the damage inflicted upon you."

I had hope, something I hadn't dared to have for months. The nightmare of being hung or incarcerated was finally gone. While it would have been even better to have been believed on the strength of my own truth, I was realistic enough to know that was not the world I, or any woman, lived in when we didn't even have the right to vote. That would change—but not tomorrow, and an entire culture would have to change as well. At least I was lucky enough to have men in my life who valued me and treated me as an equal.

When I rode home to Julius's house that day and turned onto Lakeshore Drive, I went for the sand and gave Rufus his head. We galloped along the shore, the horse and I, both happier than we'd been for weeks, the wind and spray in our faces and joy in our hearts.

* * *

DINNER THAT EVENING was a lavish affair, a celebration. Not only because of my news, but Angel's bandages had come off that morning, and the Swiss surgeon had declared the eye operation a complete success. Angel was ecstatic, more talkative than I'd ever heard her, her delicate features lit up and a lovely blush on her cheeks. Her beautiful blue eyes were clear, and she reminded me of a pretty bird, her head turning and taking in everything here and there. Julius watched her, the love he held for her obvious. Mama Rosa raised her glass.

"To Chastity and Beauregard, my young friends. You leave us soon to restart your lives with no retribution hanging over you. You will be very happy; I have seen this." I hoped she was as reliable on this as she was with weather.

We all drank, our glasses quickly refilled by the attentive servants. The Earl of Sandbrooke certainly knew how to staff a household. For a second there I thought I'd have to discuss this with Leland, but then I knew he could've cared less. We did have a wonderful cook, though.

"Thank you," I said. "If not for all of you, none of this would have happened for us. I toast you, Julius, along with Rosa, Henley, and dear Angel. You have taken in strangers and redeemed us." At this last part, everyone laughed, as I knew they would. "Well," I amended with a wink, "as much as can be expected." Beau nearly choked. Amid more laughter, we drank again.

Later, Beau and I sat with Julius, sipping brandy in the library, my favorite room in the house. Bookshelves lined the room, an iron spiral staircase allowing access to the top tiers, and the leather and gilt bindings of a thousand volumes gleamed in the flames from the fire, as though enticing a reader to pick one and get lost in its pages.

"I know I've said this before," Beau said, staring at Julius over the rim of his snifter, "but everythin' you've done for us just isn't somethin' anybody would do." Julius raised his hand to protest, but Beau waved it aside. "No, I mean it. I've never met anyone like you, and I likely never will. Everythin' you've done and everythin' you've taught me has been a gift I'll never forget."

"Agreed," I murmured. "With every word Beau said, and a hundred times more, Julius."

"My dears," Julius said, "it's just how things work out. I do what I can *because* I can, which is something the rest of my class hasn't learned yet, but perhaps they will." He stared at both of us in turn. "The thing is, I'm not a saint, so don't put me on a pedestal. I've done my share of nefarious things, and I fully intend to do many more. You see, I believe in evening the scales of Lady Justice, so I do good along with what some might say is bad. Also, I have impeccable taste, especially in people, and I detest waste as much as injustice."

"Ah, God, Julius, how I love you," I said and put my arms around him. He returned my hug.

"And I you, my dear."

I sat back down, and Beau took my hand, smiling at me in the firelight.

"My only admonition?" Julius said, the remaining brandy in his glass glowing like a jewel. "Don't waste it. Pass it on if you can."

Beau and I held up our glasses. "Count on it," Beau said.

* * *

WE DECIDED to take Rufus and Belle with us, for sentimental reasons as well as some slight reserve of fear, however tamped down that was. You never knew when you'd need a good horse. Life, as we'd learned, took many turns. They weren't exactly the thoroughbred breeding stock at Harrowhill, but they'd have a good life, and they'd done us well so far.

We boarded the train at Union Station, waving to Henley, who'd accompanied us despite our protests. We'd said our goodbyes to Julius and the others earlier that morning. This time, we had a sleeping car, a bit more elegant than the last train trip we'd undertaken together. As the train pulled out of the station, I turned to Beau.

"Think that's the last we'll see of the West?"

He smiled and put his arm around me. "As Julius says ..."

I kissed him, cutting him off. "I know full well what Julius says, Mr. Durant. Let's make our own history."

Beau shrugged. "You think Leland will like me?"

I laughed. "Of course he will. It's Matthias you'll have to look out for." I'd not mentioned a word of my uncle.

"Who's that?"

It was a long trip. I'd have plenty of time to tell him.

CHAPTER 26

*H*arrowhill

WE LEFT the train in Boston, changed our clothes, and saddled up Rufus and Belle. Once outside the cobbled streets of Boston, I pulled my old hat down on my forehead and galloped after Beau. It felt good to be back in a saddle, and Rufus responded like a young colt on his first ride outside the corral. We ran for a few miles, then stopped and gave the horses a rest, laughing like children let out of school. It felt even better to be back in Massachusetts.

It was late afternoon when we entered the gates of Harrowhill. I pulled Rufus to a stop and just gazed at the hills, green in the first beginnings of spring. I hadn't missed it after all; in fact, there was always a snowstorm or two after this false start. But it was an enchanted vista—the trees, the hills, the white fences, and the horses, dots here and there, running and standing in the distance. I breathed deeply of home. I looked over at Beau, who was watching me closely.

"You love it, don't you?"

"Oh, yes," I said. I loved Harrowhill and all it meant to me. Not just home, but security, safety, tradition, and love. "You will, too."

Beau smiled, his little sideways smile. We made our way down the drive toward the house. It was white, with green trim and shutters, and seemed to grow into the trees that surrounded it, its two stories canopied in their branches. Porches spread out from the double front doors, surrounding the house with chairs that seemed to be just waiting for someone to sit down, scattered here and there on the shining white boards.

Smoke came from the biggest chimney, and, as we dismounted and tied Rufus and Belle temporarily to the porch rail, I could hardly wait to go inside.

Before I could turn the polished brass doorknob, the door was flung open, and Leland caught me in a hug that lifted me off my feet. I thought he'd never let me go, and I was pretty happy with that, drinking in his familiar scent of bay rum, tobacco, and whiskey. He finally did, though, setting me back down.

"Christ Jesus, girl," he said, "you scared me damn near to death."

He couldn't stop staring at me, running his hands over my hair and face, pulling me inside. He finally noticed Beau, standing behind me. He dropped my arm and held out his hand.

"Leland James, son," he said. "You can only be Beauregard Durant."

"Yes, sir," said Beau. "That I am." He shook Leland's hand, which Leland didn't drop, pulling him inside as well.

"Glad to finally meet you; I've heard about you."

Hmm, I thought. *Not only had he gotten my letters, but I saw Julius's fair hand at communication at work as well.*

Leland, never one to stand on convention, ensconced us in the parlor and yelled for Lizzie and Hilda to come see who was here. He sat down close to me and kept touching me as if he were reassuring himself that I was really there.

"My God," he murmured. "I'd begun to think we'd never see you again." He was interrupted by a scream from Lizzie, followed by one from Hilda, who both hugged me in delight. Annie soon followed, drawn by the commotion. After a few moments, Leland shooed them out, and Hilda, wiping her eyes with her apron, promised tea would be arriving soon.

"Tea, phfft," Leland said and poured us whiskies. "Matthias is around somewhere, should be here soon. He's been doing his stoic Mohawk routine, but he's been more worried than I have, if that's possible."

I wandered around the room, touching the piano, books, a table, running my hand over all the familiar surfaces, as though I, too, needed reassurance that I was really here. Leland was gently interrogating Beau as I knew he would: where was he from, his family, what were his intentions. Oh, yes. I knew he wouldn't take long to get to that one. Beau indulged him, for the most part. Hilda arrived with the tea tray filled with sandwiches and cakes, patted me fondly on the cheek, winked in Beau's direction, and left. Another easy conquest for the Southern boy.

"*Kheién:'a.*" Matthias stood in the doorway. He opened his arms, and I ran to him, enfolded in the safest place I knew. The tears I'd managed to hold back so far burst out of me, and we stood there for some time, me soaking his soft leather jacket and him not caring at all.

I led him by the hand over to Leland and Beau. "Matthias, this is Beau," and Beau stood up and took Matthias's hand. "Beau, this is my uncle, Matthias."

"I'm happy to meet you, sir," Beau said in his soft drawl. "Chastity has told me so much about you and Leland and this place, and it's my pleasure to finally see you both in the flesh."

Matthias nodded and took a chair. Leland handed him a whiskey, too. "Well, now you've met both her fathers," he said to Beau, "the white and the red. I've never minded sharing, and it looks like it'll be a threesome, since I've seen the way she looks at you. Otherwise, she'd never have brought you here."

I laughed. "Christ Jesus, Leland, you never change. Just ignore the niceties and get right to it. On the other hand, you're absolutely right."

"Is that so, young man?" Leland said to Beau.

"I thought I might have some time to get to know you both a little better," Beau said, "but I think this may be just the right time, after all." He put down his whiskey glass and looked at Leland, and then Matthias. "Sirs, I would like to ask for Chastity's hand in marriage and would like your blessin' in this matter."

Well. I think I was just as shocked as the two of them. My Southern boy was a constant surprise, just when I'd thought I knew what he'd do next. Leland and Matthias exchanged a look and then gazed at Beau.

"Beauregard," Leland said. "In this family, as you have undoubtedly learned from my daughter, she is the one who decides how to live her life. I appreciate your request, and it demonstrates your good manners. You have our blessing, but it's not our decision."

"Thank you," Beau said smoothly as he knelt down beside me, taking my hand. "Chastity James, will you marry me?"

I stared into those eyes and that face I'd come to know and love so well. I didn't have the slightest doubt about him or my answer. "James Beauregard Durant, I most certainly will." I flung my arms around his neck. I'd never heard a rebel yell before, but I sure did then. Matthias and Leland laughed, but there were no Mohawk war cries, thank God.

It's not every day that a homecoming is also a marriage proposal. We finished off the bottle of whiskey, demolished Hilda's delicious roast beef and Yorkshire pudding, and managed to tell Leland and Matthias the truth of our time on the road, all before the clock struck midnight. I was fairly sure Julius already had told some of the tale, but there were a few details not even he knew, and we kept nothing back. Secrets are deadly between people who love each other.

"So that's what happened to your hair," Leland said, ruffling my short curls. "It reminds me of when you were six." He kissed the top of my head. "My God, I've missed you."

Matthias grinned. "He's been fairly intolerable, it's true. I've had to bribe Lizzie and Hilda. Cost me a fortune."

Leland snorted. "This is most you've talked since she left. Wooden Indian."

Beau smiled. "Are they always like this?" he whispered.

"Worse," I said. "We barely fit into the niche of polite company at the best of times. Wait until they start in on you. They're being very circumspect, but it won't last."

Beau rolled his eyes. "Well, I got in some good trainin' with Julius, at least."

Leland picked up on this. "And Julius," he said, opening another bottle. "I owe that rogue. I think I'll send him a horse."

"That's an excellent idea," I said, holding out my glass. "In fact, maybe he'll come to the wedding and pick one out for himself."

Leland nodded. "Perfect." He fell silent, as we all did after that, for a time. Matthias leaned forward, resting his elbows on his knees, and peered intently at me as well as Beau.

"Might as well get this out of the way since we've been tiptoeing around it for hours. Between the two of you, _kheién:'a_, you took the lives of four people. I do not judge either of you, and from what you say I believe those decisions were wise. Still, you are young, and, whether you realize it or not yet, that is a heavy burden to bear. Are your minds clear?"

Matthias was never one to mince words, and I knew he and Leland had discussed this thoroughly before today. They weren't the only ones. Beau and I had done the same. While we believed we had made decisions that saved not only our lives, but Amelia's and likely scores of other people—especially women that may have fallen prey to the Olsons and Ridleys of the world—we had indeed chosen to execute them for their behavior. True, every once in a while, the word "vengeance" floated through my mind, and I knew it always would. In the end, though, we deemed our actions justified. We slept well.

I said as much now to Leland and Matthias, and they listened intently.

Beau took up the narrative. "We never set out, either one of us, to kill anybody. We weren't raised that way. We both made choices that put us in harm's way, and perhaps those were foolish." He put his arm around me. "When bad things happen to people who don't deserve them, the rules change. Once that happens, people like me and Chastity have somethin' inside us that won't let evil rest. That somethin' gives us the courage and maybe the luck that we need. That same somethin' saves us from lettin' guilt eat at us when we put things right. That's it."

Leland looked at Matthias. "Satisfied?"

"Very."

"My dears, you've been through things no one should have to endure. When you left here, Chastity, I was not happy, but I knew you were confident, intelligent, and well-prepared. I must say, you were much more than that. You, Beau, have had tragedy and consequences in your life, and you've dealt with them fearlessly and with good judgment. I'm happier than I can say that you found each other. It was meant to be."

Matthias nodded. "*Riièn:'a*, welcome to our family."

It was very late as we all trudged upstairs to bed, but it was worth every minute we'd spent together tonight. Sometimes things must be settled before the future can be planned. I took Beau's hand, and we stopped by my bedroom door. Inside, I could see the firelight flickering over the snowy white counter-pane, and I couldn't wait to lay my head on those soft pillows.

"I had Annie take Beau's things to your room earlier," Leland said, grinning wickedly. "Moral indignation over bedrooms is pretty low on the list of things to worry about. Besides, we have a wedding to plan." He kissed both Beau and me on the cheek and went on down the hall, following Matthias to their respective suites at the end of the hall. We'd all slept in these same rooms forever.

Beau and I lay in bed, nestled against each other, too tired to even wash our faces.

"What's *rìièn:'a* mean?"

I smiled. "It means 'my son' in Mohawk. I think you passed a pretty big test pretty damn quick, Durant. But then, I never had a doubt."

We slept, at peace and in love. Home, and safe. All I ever wanted, and so much more.

$\mathcal{L}$ilacs could be nearly overpowering, but I loved them. Nothing said Maytime at Harrowhill like lilacs. I pirouetted, the white silk skirts flowing around me, and looked in the mirror. My hair was golden again, all the brown dye long gone. Annie had fashioned it into curls entwined with lilacs and pearls, and I loved it. There would be no veil, not for this wedding. No secrets, only love.

Annie had stood behind me, as pleased with her handiwork as I was. "Miss Chastity, you are so pretty and"—she blushed, her cheeks pink as roses—"Mr. Beau is like a fairy-tale prince come to life."

I hugged her. "Oh Annie, you are a delight. And Beau thinks so, too. Thank you so much." I didn't think her cheeks could get rosier, but they did. She left, shutting the door softly behind her. Hopefully she'd find her own prince someday, as I had. She deserved it.

"My God, you're beautiful," Leland said. He stood behind me, and I hadn't even heard him enter, I was so caught up in admiring myself. He put his arms around my waist, and we stood there, caught in the mirror's reflection.

"How your mother would have delighted in seeing you on this day. You look so much like her."

"I think, somehow, she does," I said, tears pricking behind my eyes. I blinked. No tears today. Only this. Leland released me and quietly stepped out of the room. Within seconds, Matthias entered in his place. I turned to him, and he gently clasped me in his arms. He turned me, and we looked into the mirror once again. He was tall, elegant in his black tuxedo as Leland had been, his hawk-like visage and dark eyes penetrating. Like Leland, his hair reached far past his collar. *What handsome men, my fathers.*

"Happy day, *kheién:'a.* You have found your soul mate, and my heart is full."

"As is mine."

I think Leland had invited half the county, but no one I really cared about. Only one guest and his retinue caught my eye. Julius, resplendent in a cream-colored waistcoat, stood at the bottom of the stairs, smiling up at me as though I were a goddess.

"Love you," I mouthed silently, and he grinned insouciantly. "Of course you do, my darling," he whispered as I paused on the bottom step.

Angel stood beside him, looking as angelic as her name, in a pale-yellow concoction, and Mama Rosa, who wouldn't have missed this occasion for anything, I knew, stood beside her, attired in an elegant gown of pale grey and smiling as I'd never seen her smile before. After the grand staircase entrance, Leland's idea, I waited for some time while the guests took their seats. My nerves were quivering.

I stepped into the parlor, where all the furniture had been removed and replaced with white folding chairs from what had to be every church in Lexington. A white cloth pathway stretched between them, lined with lilacs and roses and ivy on each aisle chair, a replica of the simple bouquet I carried.

Matthias and Leland each took an elbow and guided me

down the aisle to stand before Father Jensen in front of the
French doors. There were no bridesmaids, no groomsmen, no
flower girls, as we'd wanted none. There was only me, and
Beau, standing there waiting. My love, my life.

He was beautiful, this gentle, strong Southern man I'd
discovered I wanted to spend the rest of my life with. His
blond hair gleamed, longer now in the style of Leland and
Matthias, and his face glowed. His green eyes were focused
solely on me, as mine were on him. Leland and Matthias left
me there at the altar with a kiss on each cheek and took their
seats.

Even to this day, I find it difficult to remember anything
Father Jensen had to say, but I remember "I now pronounce
you man and wife" and the kiss that followed—a kiss that
symbolized everything we'd been through and the commit-
ment to cherish each other forever. Oh, that I will remember
until I die.

My husband took my arm, and we strode down the aisle.
The rebel yell was silent, but the way he was grinning, people
began to applaud. I looked at Beau, and we laughed with joy,
the wedding guests following in our wake outside to the
garden. It couldn't have been more perfect.

White tents were set up on the lawn, with white tables and
chairs. Hilda had outdone herself, insisting on preparing the
food, although Leland had hired three girls from town that
had come for the last two days to help cook and serve. I had
admonished her to not overdo and let the girls help her more,
but I knew she'd scarcely slept for two days. I'd come across
her in the kitchen yesterday morning, where mounds of
dough were resting on the wooden boards, and bowls were a-
brim with delectable things.

"Hilda, you let those girls help you more," I'd said, and
she'd shushed me like she had since I was a child. Hilda had
her own way, and nothing anyone had to say was going to
change that.

Tables were piled high with honey hams, roast beef, stuffed quail, fragrant loaves of bread, bowls and bowls of vegetables from new spring asparagus to sweet potatoes. A wedding cake with six tiers sat alone on another table, and the bar was already six people deep, two bartenders working as fast as they could.

"Reminds me of the barbecues back home," Beau said. "People'd come from all over the county, and it'd go on until the next mornin'."

"You miss it?"

"Some. But it'll never be like it was, Chas. Don't want to go back." He kissed me on the temple. "I've got used to snow. The stuff makes for a damn nice spring."

Leland swept him away to introduce him to more influential people. Since we'd been back, Leland had been dragging him around to meet bankers, buyers, horse people. The two of them were remarkably similar: handsome and charming. I don't think I could have found anyone more like him, odd geographical match that they were. Matthias preferred not to mingle that much and took care of security, real estate, and general operations, but they both shared the love and oversight of the horses. But where Beau really began to impress them both was his skill with the horses themselves. I'd seen it before. All he had to do was whisper in their ears, and horses not only listened, they were mad to please him. I teased him that it was that soft drawl of his, but it really was impressive. It was clear to everyone he was an extraordinary horseman. Even Julius had remarked on it the day before, when he'd chosen a beautiful bay mare, just as Leland had promised.

"The lad has a way about him," he'd said. "It's rare, that. You found yourself an interesting husband, Chastity."

"Oh, I know that," I'd said, but I was pleased he'd seen it, too. Of course, Julius didn't miss much.

"It's rather like he was meant to be at Harrowhill," Julius had said, and it was true. Life takes many turns. Mama Rosa's face skittered across my mind, her knowing eyes and uncanny ability to sense futures and dreams. I'd never doubt her.

The afternoon wore on, full of laughter, food, and drink. The string quartet Leland had hired transformed itself into more of a foot-stomping band with the addition of a drummer and a guitarist, and people danced around the lawns, enjoying themselves. I'd had to get used to being among this many people since my time fending for myself, and, truly, I'd never been much of a social butterfly. I'd chosen Vassar over a debut, and Leland hadn't argued. I think most of Lexington was surprised I'd found myself a husband, since I'd rejected all of the young men around who'd shown an interest, but here they were, happy to celebrate, and I was happy for Leland's sake as well as theirs.

Girls I'd gone to school with, dressed in their spring finery, had fluttered around me with congratulations and surreptitious glances at Beau, who'd captured all their attention, half of them clearly smitten.

"Oh, Chastity, he's so handsome," they'd said, "so just downright gorgeous, wherever did you find him?"

Under a tree, half dead, I wanted to say. You should've seen him then. Instead I said, "Thank you, Charlotte (or Mercy or Mary), you're so kind. He is lovely indeed."

When the cries of "cut the cake" came, I was more than ready. Beau and I put our hands on the silver, beribboned knife and did so, feeding each other a first piece to much applause and hooting. Then the village girls took over, cutting it up, and everyone took a piece, as the champagne flowed.

"Think it's time to get out of here?" Beau whispered in my ear. He had a piece of cake frosting on his upper lip, and I stood on my tiptoes to lick it off.

We escaped, nearly unnoticed, into the house to change our clothes. I draped my beautiful dress over a chair and changed into riding clothes. Beau went to the kitchen to help Hilda load food and supplies into our getaway carriage, and I took a last look around the room and ran down the stairs. As I passed Leland's study, I heard a muffled cry and peered around the door, which was slightly ajar. Benjamin Newhouse, an industrialist who'd bought horses from us for years, was holding Annie against Leland's desk.

"Quiet, girl. My own servants never make such a fuss," he said. "I won't have it from some country chit, and I know Leland won't mind." His face was red, and he was out of breath from the struggle.

I crept up behind him, grabbed a silver letter opener from the end of the desk, and held it to his hefty waist, jabbing just a bit. Startled, he turned around, letting his grip on Annie loosen. His eyes widened in shock, and I pushed a little harder.

"What do you think you're doing, Chastity?"

I smiled. "I think the question is, what do you think *you're* doing, Benjamin?" I looked at Annie.

"He was going through Mr. Leland's desk, Miss Chastity." Her voice shook.

"Thank you, Annie," I said, jerking my head towards the door. She pulled away from him and fled.

"She's a liar," Newhouse snarled.

"Get the hell of this house, Newhouse, and don't ever bother to come back. You'll never buy a Harrowhill horse again." I gestured towards the open door with the letter opener. "Now."

He sneered. "I think your father would have something to say about that. Besides, I heard all about you and your murderous ways, and I'll make sure everyone else knows, too."

"You go right ahead and do that," I said. "I'll be sure to tell them of your habits of snooping in people's houses and manhandling servants, so I think it's a draw. Right now, because it's my wedding day, I'm going to give you a gift and not stick this into you."

"Don't be so hasty, Chas," Beau drawled. "It's my weddin'

day, too, darlin', and I was lookin' forward to some pig on a spit."

Newhouse's face paled as his eyes went to my husband, who stood in the doorway. The smile on Beau's face was terrifying. Matthias stood beside Beau, and he didn't look very friendly either.

"This is just a misunderstanding," Newhouse stammered. "Let's just all calm down before this gets out of hand. I'll just be going."

"Yes, you will," Matthias said, taking his arm and shoving him into the hallway.

"And, as Chastity said, you won't be buying horses from Harrowhill again."

Newhouse stumbled down the hall and out the front door, gaining momentum as he went.

"Well. That was unfortunate," I said, and I set down the letter opener. Matthias sighed and shook his head, a small smile twitching at the corner of his mouth.

"I swear, Chas, you'd find trouble in heaven," Beau grinned. "Annie's fine. Let's get out of here before there's any more wrongs for you to right."

Matthias smiled. "I agree. Get yourselves into that carriage. I'll make sure Leland knows about this, but not until the party's over." He leaned down and kissed me, and then he shook Beau's hand.

We dashed out the front door and into the carriage. No one sensed anything amiss, but, by this time, everyone had discovered we were absent, and people were clustered on the driveway as we drove away amid well wishes. I waved to Leland, surrounded by wedding guests, enjoying himself immensely. He'd arranged for a cottage on the sea for us for a few days, and I couldn't wait to be alone with my newly minted husband. I wasn't going to let the Newhouses of the world taint this day or any other.

* * *

MAGICAL WAS the only word to describe the cottage on the beach. Built of stone and weathered timber, it looked as though it had stood there for a hundred years, and maybe it had. There were only two rooms, a kitchen/front room with a cozy fireplace and a large bedroom with a four-poster bed, hung with sheer white curtains that faced a large window looking onto the sea. Seagrass waved in the onshore breeze, and the sand dunes flowed down to the beach in gentle curves. The crisp, salty tang in the air revived us, and we quickly unpacked the food and supplies. Dear Hilda had given us provisions for days, even some wedding cake, all of which I stored in the pantry while Beau started a fire.

It was exceptionally warm for May and, just as the sun was setting, we raced down the sand to the water's edge, the air still warm. I carried some towels, and Beau held an open bottle of champagne.

"What you think, Chas? Risk it?" He gestured toward the water and set the bottle in a nest in the sand.

"We've got a fire, don't we?"

We both drank a few more swigs of champagne, threw off our clothes, and walked into the water, gasping at the cold but determined. It was a blessing of sorts, the salty water a purification and the tingle of our skins signifying the beginning of a new chapter. I felt more alive than I can ever remember feeling. Up to our necks, I nestled in Beau's arms, trying to ignore my chattering teeth.

"God, I love you, Durant," I managed.

"No more than I love you, Chas," he said. "Now let's get out of here before we can't move our legs and get washed out to sea."

Laughing, we scrambled up the beach, into the cottage with its roaring fire, and into that wonderful bed.

* * *

"SOMETIMES I THINK I don't really fit into polite society anymore," I said, licking pink cake frosting off Beau's chest. "I'm not sure what got into me, going after Newhouse with that letter opener."

My husband muttered something unintelligible and flipped us over, pinning my hands over my head. "No more frostin' and no more Newhouse, wife," he said. "We got other business to attend to."

And so we did, for a time. Of course, I brought it up again, because I was bothered by the incident, and Beau sighed, lighting a cheroot. I brought two glasses and the whiskey bottle to the bedroom, and we settled back into the comforters. The late afternoon sun was filtering through the curtains, drifting in the sea breeze. We'd been here four days, and I think we could have stayed forever, but for the sale. Harrowhill's annual horse fair started in a week, with buyers and breeders coming from all over the country and the world, and Leland needed both of us at home. It had always been a spectacular affair, and I was sure this year would be no exception.

"Chas, there will always be people in the world we don't like," Beau said. "Mostly they're not that bad, sometimes it takes a little educatin' or just lettin' 'em know what's acceptable and what's not." He handed me the cheroot. "Newhouse is an ass, but he likely fits into the first category, and we can forget about him."

I blew out some smoke. "Maybe. I guess it bothers me that I was so quick to pick up the letter opener. Is there something wrong with me? Am I just too angry? That's what worries me."

Beau shrugged. "I don't believe that, Chas. You're fine, just in a hurry to right wrongs and maybe too quick to find 'em. We both need to slow down a little and give things time.

We've been livin' rough, me longer than you, and run across some bad people. Comin' to trust people and give them a chance doesn't come easy after that. "

I handed him back the cheroot and put my arm over his chest. "True. Just don't expect me to ever wear ruffles again or gossip with the ladies after dinner with a glass of sherry."

Beau sighed. "It'll near break my heart, but I guess I'll learn to live with that, Calamity Jane."

"I'll make it up to you," I said, snuggling closer.

"Indeed you will, darlin'."

We left two days later, as dawn was breaking, promising the little cottage we'd come back. It was an enchanting place, and we loved it and the memories we'd always have. As we approached Harrowhill, I sensed something off about the six-foot, white sign that proudly proclaimed the place, and, as we got closer, I gasped. Across the length of the sign that said *Harrowhill, Established 1789* someone had written "Murderess" in red paint, so fresh it was still dripping like blood onto the green grass underneath.

"Christ Jesus," I breathed, shocked to my core. Beau grabbed my hand and snapped the reins, hurtling us down the drive to the house.

"Don't look back at it, Chas." His voice was angrier than I'd ever heard, his anger matching my thoughts as we pulled up in front of the door.

Apparently no one had seen it yet this morning, but within minutes Leland had dispatched a stable hand down the drive with a bucket of white paint and had sent for the sign painter in Lexington. We established ourselves in the dining room with coffee and breakfast like a council of war, but I could do no more than take sips of coffee, the way my stomach was churning.

"Has to be that goddamned Newhouse," Leland said, stabbing his fork into his eggs like they were trying to escape the plate. "Never liked that fat bastard. But what really makes me angry isn't his paint, but his intention to ruin your home-coming, not just the sale."

Nobody disagreed. It was highly likely he'd carried out his threat about me, and I'd been naïve to think he would do nothing.

"I'm so sorry," I said. "I've brought this on us, and I take full responsibility for Newhouse and everything that came before. If not for me, this wouldn't have happened."

"Stop it," Leland said, his voice rising. "That's nonsense. There've always been Newhouses out there, ready to go after my reputation. That's the horse business, and it's always been cutthroat. I just never thought anyone would have the coarse-ness to go after my daughter, and, by God, when I get my hands on him, he'll regret it, the sniveling bastard."

Lizzie came in and deposited another platter of bacon, looked around, and made a hasty retreat to the kitchen, the door swinging on its hinges.

"This is true, Chastity," Matthias said calmly. "We've plenty of friendly enemies, but this is no longer friendly." He looked at Beau. "Would you like to join me in an inquiry into this, *riièn:'a?*"

"Very much," my husband said. "Can't think of anythin' else I'd rather do today."

"Excellent," Matthias said, and, before Leland could even open his mouth, Matthias held up a hand. "You, Leland, are staying here with Chastity. She's clearly inherited the famous James temper from you, not my side of the family."

And that was that.

Leland and I busied ourselves with paperwork for the fair, trying not to discuss the obvious, and listening for the sound of hoofbeats that signified Matthias and Beau's return. I felt terrible, but Leland wouldn't listen to a word of my protests, instead patting my hand or kissing the top of my head every time he rounded the desk.

At sunset, they returned, and once again we all sat down, this time in the parlor with whiskey.

Matthias stood while the rest of us sat down, Beau beside me. He looked exhausted but not grim, deferring to Matthias to tell of their day.

"Well, get on with it," Leland said. "Christ Jesus, we've been waiting all day. I knew I should've gone with you."

"We went to the constable in Lexington and from there proceeded to Newhouse's office. He huffed and puffed, got red in the face, and would admit nothing except, finally, that some 'friends' of his, naming no names, had been incensed at the miscarriage of justice surrounding Chastity's crime and had taken steps to rectify this by painting our sign, although he was supposedly in shock to hear of this." Matthias took a sip of whiskey. "The constable was clearly skeptical of his explanation and warned him that if anything else of this nature ever occurred again, he would return and arrest him for defamation of property and mischief. We left with the constable."

"That's it?" roared Leland. "There are no consequences for this idiot? I knew I should've gone myself."

Beau looked at Matthias, who nodded. "Well, that's not quite it. We waited until Newhouse left his office, which wasn't very long, and invited him for another chat." He smiled that smile of his that wasn't a very nice one, and, for the first time, I noticed he was wearing his Colt. "This talk took place in the alley behind his building. I don't believe Mr. Newhouse will ever sully your name again, darlin'. Let us say he has seen the error of his ways."

"Still alive, is he?" Leland inquired nonchalantly and refilled his glass.

"Indeed he is," said Beau, "but I do believe his suit trousers are beyond redemption." He placed fifty dollars on the table. "He was happy to pay for the sign paintin', too."

Leland began to laugh, and it was so infectious I joined in

as well, as did Beau. Even Matthias chuckled a bit. Mr. Newhouse had definitely met his match.

Dinner was a much happier affair than breakfast had been, Hilda's roast chicken and chocolate cake a delight as always. Beau and I had talked some about a future before we returned to Harrowhill. Before, we'd been fugitives, and our choices centered around going further west, say Montana, or even Canada. It had been a nice respite to think we could return here and take up as though the last year had never happened, but we'd known that was not a choice we might have, much as we'd come to want it since we'd arrived. Given the day, I thought perhaps now was the time to be forthcoming, so, before brandy, I turned to Leland.

"I know things have been resolved, at least for now," I said. "But I don't think this will be the end of it." He began to protest, but I plunged on. "There will always be questions about Chastity James and her Kansas incident. Beau's past could also come back to haunt us, unlikely but possible. Newspapers are everywhere, obviously, and people talk. I don't ever want to be a detriment to Harrowhill. I love you and this place too much for that."

Leland began to splutter, as I knew he would. "Please, let me finish."

He nodded grudgingly, and I went on.

"We've thought before that establishing our own place might be best. I'm not sure where right now, whether nearby or farther west, but we'll work on that. I'd like to raise quarter-horses, like Rufus, not just thoroughbreds and Arabians, which have been the mainstay of Harrowhill."

Leland peered at me suspiciously over the rim of his brandy snifter, and I laughed. "I'm fully aware that you've been thinking along these lines as well, since I had an interesting conversation with Mr. Goodnight at the wedding. He brought you some horses."

Now Leland laughed. "I never could get anything past you, could I?"

"No," I said. "You never could. To add to that, Beau has a gift with horses, and his special training is something we can offer that no one else can."

Beau smiled at me and took up the narrative. "Mr. White has been generous to us for saving his granddaughter, and, with that seed money, I think we can get started."

It was silent, so silent I could hear the grandfather clock ticking in the hallway. My heart was near to breaking but we couldn't let them or Harrowhill carry our burdens. Then Matthias spoke.

"We have the land you need." He looked at Leland. "We've been buying land in upstate New York for years. Mohawk land, or what was Mohawk land, near Akwesasne. Now it's Mohawk land again, since I own it," he smiled, "along with Leland. Much of it borders on the St. Lawrence River, and there's a lot of it. Every time a parcel comes available, we purchase it. It's a legacy of sorts, to Fawn, and to you, Chastity."

I was stunned. So stunned, I couldn't speak. I looked at Leland, who smiled and touched my hand.

"It's true. Our way of trying to make things the way they should be. For your mother, for the Mohawk, for decency's sake." He shrugged. "We can't undo the damage for the tribe, but we own the land legally. If you want it, it's yours, my dear, as much as you need. Yours and Beau's. A wedding gift, if you like." He gazed at me. "The only proviso is, you must visit often and build a house big enough for guests, as we'll come often to visit you as well. Think you can manage that?"

I was stunned before, but now I was speechless. I threw my arms around him, overwhelmed. Beau seemed in shock, staring at Matthias, who, very unlike his stoic self, grinned and raised his glass.

The next hour passed in a blur. I had many questions, as

did Beau. They told us about the land, its geography and the nearest towns—not many, which was fine with us—and the river, which I remembered from visiting the Mohawk villages with Matthias as a child. I remembered also that it was beautiful and nearly empty of human encroachment, which suited me just fine. Beau was beaming from ear to ear throughout the conversation.

"Good thing old White gave you some money," Leland said, always practical. "I'm looking forward to a substantial house by Christmas. And stables, of course." He squinted at me. "I might be convinced to throw in a few horses to get you started."

For a day that had started so badly, it ended in the best way possible. I'd always been impulsive; I knew that. But this, happening so quickly, seemed to be destiny, and I embraced it with all my heart.

"Thank you, thank you," I said, hugging Leland and Matthias, as did Beau. "Are you certain?"

"Never been more certain," Leland said. "Glad you're up for it. At the rate you've been going, I was afraid you'd move to New York City and open some Vigilante Services Detective Agency."

I looked at Beau, who cocked his head and grinned. "Well, now that you mention it, that's not a half-bad idea. Maybe we could do both?"

"Christ Jesus," said Leland. "Matthias, can we put a caveat on that as well as the house?"

Matthias smiled. "We can, for all the good it'll do us. These two will always do whatever suits them, I guarantee that. Just the way you and I always did. We found our place, and they have, too, I think."

And he was right, as Matthias always was.

EPILOGUE

J stood on the bluff overlooking the river, gazing into the rolling hills of Canada on the far side. It was one of my favorite spots. There was always a breeze up here, sometimes more than a breeze, blowing my hair away from my face, the air scented with the smell of forest and earth.

"Mama!"

I turned. Two-year-old Amelia was riding on her father's shoulders, her blonde hair—just like his—streaming behind her, and the four-year-old twins were running, as usual, beside them. Devils they were, those boys, both dark haired and full of mischief, and I wouldn't have traded them for anything.

"The grandpas are coming, the grandpas are coming," Amelia chanted. "We came to get you."

I shaded my eyes and peered down the hill. From up here you could see for miles, and, sure enough, on the road leading into River Dell, two horses were approaching. Leland and Matthias were frequent visitors.

We headed back down the hill to the farmhouse, a white, rambling two-story building, banded in porches, set amid a grove of oaks, very like Harrowhill. On the east side, I'd planted gardens, now lush with flowers and vegetables. To the west, stables, corrals, and a training arena spread out, the white rail fences that bordered the entire property marching off across the hills, two hundred acres in all, dotted with the shapes of horses here and there. River Dell Farm, we'd named it, after Beau's old plantation in Louisiana.

We'd built a good life and started many others, from children to horses, and touched still more. It was home now, as Harrowhill still was, too. I had no regrets, only an occasional twinge of melancholy when childhood memories surfaced, as I know Beau also did when he thought of the original River Dell.

Over the years since, we'd still solved problems for people when they needed help. Sometimes it was a dispute over property, or trouble with the law, or, given where we were, an issue between white or Mohawk. Most important of all, for both of us, were the pleas for women who needed help for themselves or their children. We don't live in a fair and just world sometimes, as I had good cause to know.

Every once in a while, people would come to us, or send a letter through a trusted friend. We did what we could and were very careful. Old habits are hard to break, Beau said, and once you knew of injustice, it was impossible to ignore.

I think Leland and Matthias were fully aware, but they never mentioned a word about it. We raised horses and children, and that's who we really were, and all we wanted to be known for. We both knew they'd be there for us if we needed their help.

We reached the house at the same time the two riders did. They dismounted and were immediately assaulted by eager, loving children.

I held out my arms and embraced the two of them. In six years, they hadn't changed a whit—only a few silver threads here and there on both their handsome heads.

"Come on in," I said as we all trooped onto the porch. "I think we have some whiskey in here somewhere."

Leland laughed. "I'll bet you do, love. Christ Jesus, that was a long ride with Mr. Talkative here. I could use one."

Matthias raised an eyebrow and sighed.

Some things never change; they only get better. Although, as a very wise man I know once said, life takes many turns.

ABOUT THE AUTHOR

Kathleen Morris lives and writes in the desert Southwest. A history buff, she believes the key to writing good historical fiction is diligent research about the places and eras she writes about. A graduate of Prescott College in Arizona, she is the author of *The Lily of the West*, a novel of the life of "Big Nose Kate", and *The Wind at Her Back*. You may visit her website at www.kathleenmorrisauthor.com.

Made in the USA
Las Vegas, NV
26 October 2021

33135137R00173